GROUNDS FOR APPEAL

GROUNDS
FOR APPEAL

Bernard Knight

This first world edition published 2011
in Great Britain and in the USA by
SEVERN HOUSE PUBLISHERS LTD of
9–15 High Street, Sutton, Surrey, England, SM1 1DF.
Trade paperback edition first published
in Great Britain and the USA 2012 by
SEVERN HOUSE PUBLISHERS LTD .

British Library Cataloguing in Publication Data

Knight, Bernard.
  Grounds for appeal.
  1. Pryor, Richard (Fictitious character)–Fiction.
  2. Forensic pathologists–Fiction. 3. Wye, River, Valley
  (Wales and England)–Social conditions–20th century–
  Fiction. 4. Murder–Investigation–Wales–Borth–
  Fiction. 5. Detective and mystery stories.
  I. Title
  823.9´14-dc22

ISBN-13: 978-0-7278-8107-6 (cased)
ISBN-13: 978-1-84751-400-4 (trade paper)

All Severn House titles are printed on acid-free paper.

Typeset by Palimpsest Book Production Ltd.,
Falkirk, Stirlingshire, Scotland.
Printed and bound in Great Britain by
MPG Books Ltd., Bodmin, Cornwall.

ACKNOWLEDGEMENTS

The author would like to thank Yvonne Davies for valuable details of Borth in the 1950s and also Helen Palmer of Ceredigion CBC and Sian Collins of Dyfed-Powys Police for delving into their records of more than half a century ago.

ONE

November 1955

The bog was in its autumn colours, with reds, browns and yellows stretching across the billiard-table flatness that lay between the sea and the line of hills that bordered the mountainous heart of Wales. Today, the weather was being kind to the two figures squelching across the eastern fringe of the largest raised bogland in Britain. A Mecca for wetland naturalists, Borth Bog attracted a steady stream of biologists, many from the university in Aberystwyth, a few miles to the south. A pair of these had been working their way across the marsh for the past few days, following a line drawn on their large-scale map, lugging their equipment between points separated by hundred-yard intervals.

'Come on, Geraint, give those binoculars a rest and help me with the kit!'

Louise Palmer was a rather bossy young woman, concerned only with getting more data for her doctoral thesis. Her assistant, a first-year student, seemed more interested in watching the profuse bird-life around them. Sheepishly, Geraint Williams dragged his attention back to their work and unstrapped a bundle of tubes and various bits of metal and wood, while Louise once again groped amongst the contents of a large haversack. A roll of tinfoil, a spatula, glass jars, two notebooks, a bundle of labels and some indelible pencils were her passport to eventual academic promotion.

She was a clever, single-minded woman of twenty-four, rather plain with wiry brown hair and a figure that was ideal for tramping around swamps and mountains, though perhaps not for ballet dancing – especially in the heavy walking boots she wore over thick woollen socks. Dressed for business in a thick brown jumper and denim trousers, she looked very much the no-nonsense academic.

As they went through their much-practised routine at every hundred-yard site, Geraint looked at the area ahead that they had not yet covered.

'Another three cores and we'll be almost at the edge of the bog,' he observed, as he screwed together two sections of metal tube about the thickness of a walking stick.

Louise looked up and nodded. 'We'll pack it in then and after we've checked the results from this lot, see if the professor thinks that would be enough.'

They were engaged on a study designed to see how the bog's vegetation had changed over past centuries and relate this to its topography and the climatic variation. Taking samples of the underlying peat from different depths, an analysis of pollen grains and plant remnants should reveal the sequential history of Cors Fachno, the true Welsh name for Borth Bog. The samples were retrieved with the simple coring apparatus that they were now assembling.

'I'll soon be doing this in my sleep,' grumbled Geraint, a thin, tousle-headed youth, dressed in a tweed sports jacket with frayed cuffs, over a purple pullover and corduroy trousers.

He jammed the sharp bottom end of the long tube into the ground and pushed it down hard so that it stuck in securely without support. Reaching up, he screwed the central socket of a wooden cross-arm on to the top of the tube. As he pulled down again on this, his wellington boots sank a couple of inches into the waterlogged heather and spongy moss. The three-foot wooden bar, now making a spindly T-shape with the tube, came just within reach of Louise's hands and she reached up to grab one side, with Geraint on the other.

'Right, let's pull!' she commanded and they both added their weight to the contraption to drive it deep into the soft marsh. The object was to force a narrow cylinder of soil up the inside of the tube and, normally, they could get down to the full length of six feet with steady pressure. However, this time the tube went down as far as the joint at the three-foot level and stopped abruptly.

Louise muttered an unladylike curse. 'Bugger it! Another stone, I expect.'

Geraint gave a couple of futile wiggles to the upper part of the tube, but further pressure made no impression on the penetration.

'It's no good, we'll have to haul it out and try again a couple of feet away,' ordered his senior companion. The crossbar was now at waist height and the student hauled it upwards, then grasped the tube and pulled the rest of it out of the soggy ground.

'D'you want to keep the core that's in it?' he asked and got a scathing look in response.

'No, of course not! Every sample has to be from the same depth range. Push the damned thing out!'

With hands on hips, she watched as her slave laid the tube on the ground and, with a narrower tube with a blanked-off end, forced out a cylinder of black peat, which had the consistency of a Christmas pudding. Except that, unexpectedly, the bottom two inches of the core was almost white, instead of black.

'What the devil's that?' he asked, crouching down for a closer look.

Louise did the same, then reached to her side to take a small metal spatula from the haversack. Prodding the core with it, she separated the white material from the peat and rolled it on to the back of a notebook.

'This looks like some sort of animal material, not vegetation,' she announced.

'Maybe we've speared a dead sheep,' volunteered the student. 'There are plenty of those about here and some must die and end up in the bog.'

Louise peered more closely at the greyish-white cylinder, half the length of her little finger and about the same thickness. 'It seems to be some sort of fatty wax,' she declared.

Geraint shrugged and began to get to his feet.

'Some sort of long-dead animal,' he said dismissively. 'We'd better get on and finish these holes. I could do with my lunch.'

The woman ignored him and continued to prod at the lump of material. 'There seems to be a tough dark layer on top, almost like a skin.'

'Well, sheep have skin, don't they?'

Instead of answering, Louise took a pair of tweezers from her bag and picked something from the bottom end of the peat core, from where she had taken the white substance. She held it up towards her reluctant assistant.

'But sheep don't have bits of twine on them, do they!'

Geraint looked at her blankly. 'What are you trying to say?'

Louise took one of her small bottles from the haversack and carefully slid the white material inside, together with an inch of what appeared to be frayed cord.

'I think there may be a human body under there!'

The young man looked at her as if she had suddenly gone off her head. 'Why on earth d'you say that? Far more likely to be a sheep – if in fact it is animal tissue and not some fungus or something.'

'Nonsense! I've been reading about these bog bodies they've been finding in Denmark recently. This could be one of those.'

Geraint Williams showed that he was not so ignorant as he appeared.

'You mean like that Tollund Man they found a few years ago. But they were prehistoric, surely?'

'Well, Iron Age anyway,' she replied, excitement breaking through her usual cool nature. 'It would be great if this was another one! I'd get my doctorate just for being famous!'

'Much more likely to be a sheep,' muttered her student. 'Why should it be an ancient corpse?'

Louise held up her jar for a closer look. 'That skin has gone dark, just like the Danish people described. It's due to staining from the tannins in the peat.'

'And what about that bit of cord? What's that got to do with it?' persisted Geraint, a Jonah determined to bring her down to earth.

'That's what made me think of it,' she snapped. 'Some of these bog bodies were found with cords around their necks, probably ritual strangulation.'

Geraint's eyebrows rose at this. 'Strangulation! You're reading a hell of a lot into finding a bit of something half the size of a cocktail sausage!'

Louise rose to her feet and started to repack her haversack.

'Whatever it is, we'll have to tell someone about it straight away,' she said with typical decisiveness. 'I suppose it had better be the local police, not that they'll be all that interested in a two-thousand-year-old murder!'

*　　*　　*

The bog was bounded on the seaward side by the dead-straight railway and road that ran a stone's throw from the two miles of beach. At the southern end was the small town of Borth, a popular holiday resort. A one-street ribbon settlement, it suddenly rose at the end of the beach on to the hill of Upper Borth, from where the road carried on southwards to Aberystwyth. The two researchers had trudged across the marshland to reach the road and now walked downwards to the line of shops and boarding houses.

'I wonder where the police station is?' said Louise. 'I presume they've got coppers in a place like this.'

Geraint stopped a man coming towards them to ask directions, but he was obviously a late holidaymaker, as he replied in a strong Cockney accent that he hadn't the faintest idea.

'Better luck next time,' waspishly muttered Louise.

A little further on, they saw a young woman brushing the path in front of a three-storied house. A very pretty brunette, Letitia Matthews was a nurse, home on leave from her training in Cardiff. Trusting that she was a native and not another Londoner, Geraint spoke to her in Welsh and received a brilliant smile and exact directions in the same language. Smitten, as he often was by attractive girls, he would have lingered, but Louise prodded him in the back and, reluctantly, he began lugging his bundle of pipes further into the town.

'Well, did she tell you where The Law was to be found?' demanded his companion.

'In Upper Borth, apparently, so we'll have to walk on a fair way yet.'

Louise groaned. 'It's even difficult to report a murder in this place.'

Ten minutes later, after Geraint's longing glances into a fish-and-chip shop were ignored, they reached Borth's answer to Scotland Yard. This was a small annexe built on to the side of a police house, where a sergeant and a constable of the Cardiganshire Constabulary sat at a table behind a wooden counter.

Sergeant Edwards, a large man with a bushy moustache, left his cup of Nescafé and came to attend to them. Louise dumped her haversack on the counter and explained who she was, ignoring Geraint, who was content to sit on a hard chair near the door to listen to the rumbles of his empty stomach. After listening to the botanist's story about her unexpected find, the officer regarded her gravely. She seemed a sensible sort of young woman, he thought, not one given to making up fairy stories.

'Have you got this specimen with you, miss?'

Louise fished in the bag and took out the small bottle containing the lower part of the core.

'This is it. There's a piece of cord in there as well. I've read about a number of these bog bodies. They've been found mainly in Denmark and Germany in recent years, but there have been reports of them for centuries, some in Britain.'

The constable, a fresh-faced young man with big ears, ambled over to the counter to look at the sample. 'Yes, sarge, I've read about those. There was an article in *Reader's Digest* some time ago. Some horrible pictures of them, all shrivelled up and looking like leather.'

Sergeant Edwards ran his fingers across his moustache as an aid to thought. If even his constable had heard of this phenomenon, then he could hardly dismiss it out of hand.

'You found this just by drilling a hole in the ground?'

Louise Palmer nodded impatiently. 'We've taken about forty cores from the bog this last week. This was the only time we found anything unusual.'

'Can you find the spot again?' asked the constable.

Geraint answered this from his chair. 'Our coring plan tells us where it is to within a couple of feet – and I stuck a gorse branch in the hole to mark the exact place.'

Edwards pondered again and after Louise had again dismissed the obvious explanation that it might be a dead sheep, he turned the tube over his fingers and made his decision.

'I'll have to talk to my superiors in Aberystwyth, Miss Palmer. They may want to send this off to Cardiff to see if it really could be human.'

'That'll take ages, surely?' objected the young woman, who was anxious to claim the glory for finding a Welsh bog body.

The sergeant shrugged. 'If it's as you say and the body has been there for centuries, then a few days or even a week or two won't matter much, will it? If they decide it's worth investigating, we'll need you back up here to show us exactly where you found it.'

And with that, Louise had to be content, while Geraint was more concerned with calling at the fish-and-chip shop on their way back to the railway station.

TWO

Fortunately, Doctor Richard Pryor liked women and was very comfortable in their company. It was just as well, as there were already three attractive ladies in Garth House and a fourth was expected later that day. At the moment, he was hidden away in his study at the back of the detached Edwardian house, which sat on the western slope of the Wye Valley, with a great view across the river to the English side.

In the laboratory, which had been converted from the large dining room at the front, Priscilla Chambers sat at her bench facing a series of racks which held the day's quota of paternity tests. Across the room behind her, technician Sian Lloyd was handing some alcohol results to Moira Davison, their housekeeper-cum-secretary, for her to type in the adjacent office.

'It'll be great to have Doctor Bray back,' enthused Sian.

It was becoming difficult for her to know what titles to give the various members of the Garth House team, as when alone, the secretary and technician would refer to their two employers as 'Richard' and 'Angela', but to their faces called them 'doctor'. During the past few weeks, matters had become more complicated by the arrival of Priscilla, who although possessing a PhD like Angela Bray, insisted on being called by her Christian name.

'Angela was afraid she would be away for at least month,' agreed Moira, a neat dark-haired woman of about thirty. 'I'm so glad her mother's stroke wasn't as serious as they feared.'

'So am I, though it means I might be out of a job sooner than I thought!' contributed Priscilla from her workbench. When Angela Bray had hurried home to Berkshire to look after her stricken mother, she had agreed to stand in as a locum to cope with the forensic serology and biology that was Angela's preserve.

They had once been colleagues in the Metropolitan Police Laboratory in London, until Priscilla had emigrated to Australia several years earlier. This hadn't worked out and, since her return a few months earlier, she was existing on various locum jobs until something more permanent turned up.

Moira, though a good-natured woman who got on well with Priscilla, was secretly pleased that the very attractive redhead was not going to be a long-term fixture at Garth House. Though the young widow would hardly admit it even to herself, Moira was very much attracted to Richard Pryor and already had enough competition in the shapely form of Doctor Angela Bray, as well as the pretty and vivacious blonde technician, though realistically, Sian was too young to be a serious challenge.

Angela had left the 'Met Lab' earlier that year to go into partnership with Richard Pryor when they founded this private forensic consultancy. Moira, who lived alone in the next house down the valley, had impulsively taken on the job of part-time housekeeper and rapidly slid into being their typist as well, reviving her spirits from the loneliness that followed the death of her husband in an industrial accident.

'I'm sure they won't turf you out into the street tonight, Priscilla!' said Sian. 'Perhaps you can stay with us for good?'

Moira managed to suppress a frown as she went through to her office next door. Apart from the fact that there was not enough work for two biologists, the prospect of both Angela and Priscilla living in Garth House under the same roof as Richard was not one that appealed to her. She would have been reassured to hear the conversation that continued after she left the laboratory, for Priscilla, as she continued to pipette sera into her banks of little tubes, replied to the suggestion that she stayed on in the Wye Valley.

'It's great here, Sian, you've all been so kind to me. But I don't want to stay in forensic science permanently. I'd like to get back to my first love, anthropology. That's why I've been dithering around lately, waiting for a vacancy to turn up somewhere.'

The technician loved a good gossip and this was a chance to delve some more. 'I'm not quite clear what you did before this,' she asked.

Priscilla filled her last tube, then swung around on her swivel chair, her long auburn hair swirling above the collar of her white coat.

'I did a degree in physical anthropology in London, then my doctorate on blood types in different ethnic groups. After that, I went to the Natural History Museum in Kensington for a while, then moved to the police laboratory in New Scotland Yard, doing this sort of work.' She waved a manicured hand at the tubes and bottles on her bench top.

Sian listened avidly to this recital of achievement. 'And then to Australia and back!' she said enviously. 'You've never been married?'

Priscilla shook her head. 'Never seemed to have time – or stayed long enough in one place. Plenty of chaps, though!' she added with a smile.

'My life has been deadly dull compared with yours,' sighed Sian regretfully. 'I left school soon after the war to work in a hospital lab in Newport and stayed there until I had the chance to come here. I love this forensic work so much that I'm doing an external degree in biochemistry now.'

'What about chaps, though?' called Priscilla over her shoulder, as she swung back to get on with her work.

'Nothing serious yet, though there's a fellow on my day-release course that I get on with very well.'

Their tête-à-tête was interrupted by the door into the hall opening to admit Richard Glanville Pryor, the founder of the Garth House venture. Tall and wiry, he wore a rather crumpled suit of fawn linen, with button-down pockets and a half-belt at the back. It was one of those he had brought back from Singapore, which the ladies claimed made him look like a big-game hunter. Under a bush of brown hair, his lean face, which usually creased so easily into a grin, was looking serious for once.

'Just had a phone call from the police. Curious business! Sounds as if it might be right up your street, Priscilla.'

Moira came back in through the office door, clutching some unnecessary papers as an excuse to hear what was going on.

'Why me, Richard?' asked the glamorous serologist.

The doctor squatted on the corner of the big table that filled the large bay window. 'There's some suggestion that it might be a bog body, though I doubt it very much.'

Priscilla's hazel eyes lit up at the mention of these curiosities.

'A bog body! It would be a first in Wales, then. I've read a great deal about them. I even met Professor Glob once, at a congress.'

At Sian's insistence, she had to explain briefly about these ancient corpses, found mainly in Northern Europe, assumed to be sacrificial victims who were dumped in marshes, where their tissues were preserved for centuries by the tannins of the peat and the acid bog water. Professor Glob was the doyen on the subject, a Danish archaeologist who had studied a number found in his homeland.

'As I said, it sounds highly unlikely to me,' continued Richard. 'But the cops in Aberystwyth want an opinion. The forensic lab in Cardiff suggested me, as I'm now on their Home Office list.'

He told them the story, such as it was. 'So far, the only evidence is a bit of tissue accidentally recovered by a botanist. The police sent it to Cardiff, mainly to check whether it came from a dead sheep. But it seems that a precipitation test showed that it was human.'

'So what's going to happen next?' asked Moira, as intrigued as the rest of them with such an unusual story.

'I agreed that we'd do what we could for them, but we wanted to look at the sample ourselves first. The police are bringing it up from Cardiff in the morning. If it's definitely human, then I suspect they'll ask us to look at the body, if they can find it.'

'What do you want me to do?' asked Priscilla. 'Angela will be back at work tomorrow, so she may want to deal with it, especially as now I may soon be moving on.'

Richard laid a hand on her shoulder, raising another covert frown on Moira's face.

'She'll want a day or two to settle in, I expect. Then we'll decide how to play it. If our own tests on the sample show it to be a sheep or something, that's the end of it, but the Home Office lads in Cardiff are unlikely to have got it wrong.'

The matter was left in abeyance and was soon overshadowed by the sound of Angela's little Renault coming up the steep slope of the drive from the main road below. They all trooped down the corridor past the kitchen to the back door, to greet her as she stopped in the yard behind and then reversed into the open garages beneath the coach house.

She stepped out, as elegant as her friend Priscilla, both of whom were classy dressers. A few years older than Priscilla, Doctor Bray was tall, slim and had a mane of light brown hair in place of the striking auburn of her friend. Handsome rather than pretty, she had the features of what the somewhat socialistic Sian thought of as a typical English 'hunting, shooting and fishing' aristocrat. This didn't stop the technician impulsively running forward to give her boss a welcoming hug.

'Great to have you back, doctor! We've all missed you.'

Priscilla gave her a more restrained peck on the check, being careful of their make-up, and Moira went to squeeze her hand in both of hers and enquire after her mother.

Richard let the women do their thing, before going over and putting a welcoming arm around her shoulders.

'Time for a cup of tea before you get back to work, Angela!' he joked and steered her towards the back door. There was one more greeting to be offered en route, this time from the edge of the four acres that lay behind the house. Their handyman, gardener and occasional chauffeur was Jimmy Jenkins, a middle-aged scruff whom Richard had inherited along with the large house after the death of his aged aunt.

'Good to see you back, Doc,' he called, half a Woodbine bobbing on his lip as he spoke. 'Hope your mam is better! I'll bring your luggage in from the car.'

Angela smiled as she gave him a wave. She was glad to be back amongst her good friends, even though she loved the comforts of her family home, a large stud farm in Berkshire where her father was a successful breeder of racehorses. Their first stop was the big kitchen at the back of the house, where Moira bustled about making tea so that they could hear Angela's news and bring her up to date with events at Garth House.

Eventually, the three doctors adjourned to Angela's study-cum-sitting room, on the other side of the front hall from the laboratory. It had a matching bay window looking out over the valley, with the little-used front door between.

Priscilla came directly to the point. 'Now that you're back, I feel redundant,' she said. 'I'd better start making plans to move out.'

Richard Pryor shook his head. 'Angela and I discussed this on the phone the other night. We were fortunate in getting you to stand in when she had to go away, and we thought it would be for much longer than this. Thankfully, it wasn't, but we can't chuck you out so soon. Business is building up quite well, so will you stay for a bit longer? In fact, until you get fixed up with something else.'

Priscilla looked from one to the other. 'I'd love to – but I really think I should get back to London and keep looking for a job in archaeology. That's where most opportunities are likely to arise.'

She had been lodging in a bed and breakfast in the village half a mile away and, though it was quite comfortable, she missed the bustle of the metropolis, unlike Richard and Angela, who had settled happily into these beautiful rural surroundings.

Since they first moved in the previous May, they had lived together in the big house, no doubt giving ammunition for the village tongue-waggers in Tintern Parva, just down the valley. However, the arrangement had remained professional and platonic, though there had been a couple of occasions when the conventions had been a little strained.

Angela and Richard were equal partners in the venture, as when they had set up their partnership earlier that year, Richard contributed both his golden handshake from Singapore University, where he had been Professor of Forensic Medicine, as well as the house he had been left by his aunt. On her part, Angela had put the proceeds of the sale of her London flat into the pot and with the added help of a modest mortgage, they had raised the capital needed to make some alterations to the rooms and equip the laboratory.

'Then stay until the end of this month, at least,' suggested Angela and, without more persuasion, her friend agreed to remain for a couple more weeks.

When their business discussions were done, Richard told Angela of current cases and especially the odd request he had had from Cardiganshire about the alleged 'bog body'. Like Priscilla, his partner knew quite a lot about the finds reported in Denmark and elsewhere, which were obviously of considerable interest to all forensic biologists.

'Let's see tomorrow whether it's a sheep or King Arthur!' said Angela, happy to be back in harness herself.

The tests next day confirmed that it was not a sheep and, at a stretch, it could be King Arthur, for at least it was human.

At about ten o'clock next morning, a Triumph motorcycle roared up to the house and a helmeted police officer handed over a small package in return for a signature on his exhibit docket. Richard was due to go down to Chepstow to carry out a couple of routine post-mortems for the coroner at the public mortuary there, but he could not resist waiting to have a look at the specimen. The others crowded around, even Moira, who left her typewriter to have a look at such a curious sample.

Richard took the small glass bottle from the plywood box that protected it and found a sheet of paper wrapped around it. It was a note on Home Office letter-heading from Philip Rees, one of the forensic scientists at the Cardiff laboratory, whom they had met in a case a month or so earlier.

'It just says that they did a precipitin test and it was unequivocally human tissue,' he announced. 'He also says there's a small piece of cord as well, but they did nothing with that, as they were only asked to carry out a species identification.'

He peered into the bottle, then handed it to Angela, who diplomatically gave it to Priscilla to deal with. With the others watching, she carefully slid the contents out into a shallow glass dish. A greyish cylinder sat there, with a leathery cap. A short length of thin cord lay alongside it.

'Not very exciting, is it?' said Sian. 'Looks like a lump of dirty candle grease.'

Richard picked up the dish and held it to his nose. 'Adipocere, as I suspected from the story.'

He then had to explain to Sian and Moira. 'When body fat is left for a long time in moist surroundings, it's often converted into a kind of soap, which can persist for centuries. But bog bodies are usually around two thousand years since death and I just don't know if adipocere would last that long.'

'What about the scrap of string?' asked Priscilla.

Richard shrugged. 'I'll leave that to you clever ladies. If we confirm it is human – and I've no reason to doubt Cardiff – then there'll have to be an exhumation. Maybe then the reason for the string will become clear.'

'What about that dark bit on top of the fatty stuff?' asked Priscilla.

'Could be skin, I suppose. Can you snip a bit off one edge and give it to Sian to process for histology? We can have a look under the microscope then, see what the structure is like.'

He looked at his watch and hurriedly left for his post-mortem session. Angela, not wanting to appear as if she was supervising her friend, left to do her unpacking upstairs and Moira drifted back to the office before starting on lunch, as her duties included making a light meal for the doctors at midday and something more substantial in the evening. Cleaning, washing and bed-making were now the province of the appropriately-named Mrs Daley, from the village.

Sian began processing the skin fragment by dropping it into formalin, then had some spare time. She wandered over to Priscilla and watched her deft fingers manipulating small pipettes and a rack of narrow tubes. Sian marvelled at how she could keep her long red-varnished nails so perfect when handling glassware and chemicals.

'What exactly is this test?' she asked. 'I've heard of it, but I'm not quite sure how it works.'

'It's been around for ages,' answered the biologist, always happy to instruct. She pointed to a rack of labelled vials, taken from the refrigerator. 'These are made from the blood of rabbits immunized with sera from different animals, including humans. A small quantity is injected, which doesn't hurt the rabbit, but stimulates the production of antibodies specific for the proteins of that particular beast.'

Sian nodded, she knew about antigen-antibody reactions from her time in the hospital laboratory.

'How do you get a result, then?'

'Basically, an extract is made from the test sample and layered on top of each specific serum in a tube. If an antigen for a particular species is present, then a white line appears at the junction between the two fluids, due to protein being precipitated.'

She added small amounts of the fluids into a series of tubes as she talked. 'In this case, I'll have to get rid of all this fat first and get a clear solution. Let it incubate for a few hours and see what happens. Naturally, we have to set up controls and blanks to make sure the result is genuine.'

It was the afternoon before all this was done and Priscilla was able to confirm that the substance was definitely human in origin by the time they assembled for tea in the 'staff room', between the kitchen and the staircase that went up from the centre of the hall.

'I'd better confirm to the cops in Aberystwyth that they've probably got an unexplained body on their patch,' said Richard. 'They'll have to inform the coroner first of all.'

'Could it be an accident or a natural death?' asked Moira, pouring Brooke Bond into the cups from a large brown pot.

'Could be, I suppose. But when, that's the question? It was about three feet down and it takes a long time for that thickness of peat to accumulate if the deceased just fell on to the surface.'

'Someone would have seen him then,' objected the ever-practical Sian. 'Someone must have dug a hole to put him in.'

Priscilla looked doubtful. She had plenty of experience of holes in the ground from her work as an archaeologist.

'You can't be certain about that. Bogs change all the time and there may have been a pool there at the time he was dumped, which would have put him in deeper.'

'We're saying "he",' said Angela. 'It could be a woman.'

'True enough, replied Richard, taking one of Moira's Welsh cakes. 'But what about this bit of string, Priscilla?'

She had been cast as the expert on ancient bodies, with her qualifications as an anthropologist.

'Some of the other bog people were found either with their throats cut or with a ligature, presumably having been strangled,' she replied. 'But I think Richard's right, we won't know until it's dug up!

THREE

After he had the phone call from Garth House, Meirion Thomas knew he was in for a busy time. He was a detective inspector in Aberystwyth, the only one that the rural county police force possessed. It effectively made him the head of the CID, commanding a couple of sergeants and a few detective constables.

Though covering a large area, it was sparsely populated, except in the summer, when holidaymakers flocked to the beautiful coast and mountains. Meirion's usual diet of criminal investigations consisted of housebreaking, theft of outboard motors and sheep stealing. To have a buried corpse was indeed a novelty.

As Richard Pryor had anticipated, Meirion's first task was to notify the coroner, a local solicitor in the town. This gentleman was a little hesitant about taking official notice of the matter, as he felt that so far, the evidence of a corpse buried near Borth was a little flimsy. He recalled reading about a fellow coroner in London, who some years ago had declined to hold an inquest on a decayed foot found inside a shoe. It had been washed up on the banks of the Thames, but that coroner had decided that he had no proof that the owner of the foot was necessarily dead!

Cautiously, his Aberystwyth counterpart asked the detective to keep him informed of any developments and Meirion went off to arrange for the two young botanists from the university to revisit the scene next day.

Early in the afternoon, he picked them up from Penglais, the hill overlooking the town where many of the college buildings stood, and took Louise Palmer and her student away in a black Wolseley driven by his sergeant, Gwyn Parry. A small van followed them, containing a couple of uniformed constables and some scene equipment. They drove north up the main A487 road through Bow Street, then turned left on to a minor road that looped down towards Borth. After Louise's description of where in the bog they had made their discovery, the DI parked just beyond the hamlet of Llancynfelyn and they walked across sloping fields down to the level plain of the bog. Geraint Williams soon found the spot where his ragged piece of gorse was still sticking up from the bore hole.

'Here we are, the spot marked "X"!' he said with almost proprietorial satisfaction. 'The ground has dried out a bit since then.'

The detective inspector stared at the mottled browns and greens of the soggy marsh without enthusiasm. He was a stocky, red-faced man of about forty-five, looking more like a farmer than a police officer. This image was enhanced by the long, belted brown raincoat and the flat cap whose peak was pulled down over his forehead. He had a hunch that they were all wasting their time and that a dead sheep lay under the coarse grass and sphagnum moss at their feet. But his immediate superior, a superintendent who was also the Deputy Chief Constable, had said that both the forensic boys in Cardiff and this new Home Office chap in Tintern had declared the stuff that these students had found was human, so they had no choice but to investigate.

His detective sergeant, though younger and thinner, was another officer of agricultural appearance. Both of them were from farming families and spent a lot of time at night crouched under hedges or in the back of plain vans, waiting in a usually futile attempt to ambush the gangs of Midlands rustlers who invaded Mid-Wales in the small hours. Not unnaturally, sheep were very familiar to them and Gwyn Parry had similar thoughts as his DI about this patch of bog probably hiding a four-legged victim.

'What do you want to do about it, Meirion?' he asked in Welsh. The inspector pointed behind him to where two constables were approaching, carrying bundles of stakes and a coil of rope.

'Can't start any digging until the doctor comes tomorrow,' he replied, using English for Louise's benefit. 'We'll have to organize some muscle from the uniformed boys to do that. Just get our lads to put a cordon around this patch of ground. Though if this young lady is right and what's down there is a couple of thousand years old, I can't see that fencing it off for a night is going to matter much!'

Moira took the call from Aberystwyth later that afternoon and
went to find Richard, who was up with Jimmy Jenkins on the
sloping field behind the house. They were discussing the two
long rows of young vines that they had recently planted, the first
stage in Richard's almost obsessive desire to start a vineyard at
Garth House.

He came in to speak to Meirion Thomas, who confirmed the
arrangements for digging into the bog next day. Having already
discussed it with Priscilla, he suggested to the detective that it
would be wise to have someone else there who had experience
of archaeological excavations, either an academic or the county
archaeologist, if there was one. Confirming that they would be
at the police headquarters by eleven o'clock, Richard went off
to talk to the rest of the team.

'Who's coming with me tomorrow?' was his first question, as
he entered the laboratory. Angela pre-empted any discussion by
nominating Priscilla.

'She's the obvious person for this one, with her anthropology
and museum experience,' she declared. 'Anyway, someone has
to look after the shop and I'm still settling in after being away
for weeks.'

Richard suspected that she was being diplomatic in not wanting
her friend to feel as if she was being sidelined, now that she
herself was back in harness, but it did seem sensible to take
someone who had the most appropriate knowledge.

'An early start, then,' he said briskly. 'If it proves to be more
than a dead sheep, we may have to stay the night, so throw your
toothbrush into a case. It's at least three hours' drive from here
to Aber, so wagons roll soon after seven o'clock.'

Next day, the autumn dawn had grown into a red sky over the
eastern rim of the valley as the black Humber Hawk set off
northwards. Richard Pryor had bought it second-hand when he
came home from Singapore almost a year before and, like his
vines, it was his pride and joy. The car purred its way towards
Monmouth and he settled back for the long ride, feeling contented
at doing a job he relished, in spite of its often morbid and sometimes distasteful nature. He was glad to be back in his native
Wales after fourteen years in the Far East – and glad also to be

sitting alongside such an attractive and vivacious woman as Priscilla Chambers. Today she was dressed in gear suitable for digging corpses from a swamp, but still managed to look elegant. She wore a military-looking raincoat over a green roll-neck sweater and grey trousers. If necessary, her 'sensible' shoes could be replaced by a pair of wellingtons carried in the car boot.

Although Priscilla had been working at Garth House for the past three weeks, he had not learned much about her personal affairs, though he did not doubt that Sian and Moira had already extracted every detail of her life story. However, on the long journey across the centre of Wales, there was plenty of time to talk and Richard soon learned that Priscilla was born in Gibraltar of a military family, her father being a retired major in the Intelligence Corps. He was now teaching mathematics in an Oxford school, where her mother ran a small secretarial agency.

Priscilla had spent most of the war years in a boarding school in Gloucestershire, then in 1944 went to university on a scholarship. Some mental arithmetic told him that she must be just over thirty years of age, a decade younger than himself.

For her part, the drive gave Priscilla the chance to fill in the gaps in her knowledge of Richard. From laboratory gossip, she knew some of the facts, but by the time they reached Cardiganshire, she knew that he was the son of a retired family doctor in Merthyr Tydfil, where he had been brought up. Grammar school was followed by medical college in Cardiff before the war, then a couple of years' pathology training before being called up. He spent the war as an RAMC officer in military hospitals in Egypt and Ceylon before being finally posted to Singapore, when it was reclaimed from the Japanese. Taking local release with the rank of major there in 1946, he stayed on as a civilian pathologist in the General Hospital, doing coroner's and police work. This came with a part-time teaching post in the university and he ended his nine-year's service with a professorship in forensic medicine. A very generous redundancy payment had coincided with his aunt's bequest of Garth House and he had returned at the beginning of the year to set up his private forensic consultant practice with Angela. They had hatched his idea after meeting at a forensic congress the previous year. Angela was disillusioned with her job at the Metropolitan Police Laboratory, where there was little prospect of further promotion, so she threw in her lot with Richard and moved to the Wye Valley. That was six months ago and after a hesitant start, they were now becoming well established, gathering work from coroners, solicitors and the police, as well as Richard's part-time contract as a lecturer at the medical school in Bristol.

The roads were quiet and the journey passed pleasantly, Priscilla being enthralled by the lovely countryside and then the lonely hills beyond Rhyader. Like Angela, she was a Thames Valley girl and the Cambrian mountains were a surprise to her.

They rolled into Aberystwyth before eleven o'clock and found the police station on the elegant promenade, housed in a large granite building which used to be the Queen's Hotel. The detective inspector met them and took them to his tiny office in the Victorian building, where they were obliged to have a cup of police tea, almost strong enough to hold a spoon upright.

'My sergeant and few uniformed officers have gone up there already,' he explained. 'We've also asked a lady from the archaeology department of the college to attend, as she seemed very keen to be there.'

As they went down to the cars in the back yard, Priscilla thought that local archaeologists would be over the moon if an Iron Age bog body was found on their patch, but Richard still maintained that whatever it was, the presence of adipocere was probably too recent for that. They followed the police car in the Humber and, half an hour later, pulled up behind two vans and a pre-war Hillman Minx parked on the road between Llancynfelyn and Ynys Las, the nearest point to where a group of distant figures were congregated on the bog.

Taking Meirion Thomas's advice, the two from Tintern took their rubber boots from the back of the car and pulled them on, then followed him across the fields. Richard carried his square black 'murder bag' with his instruments, while Priscilla had a bag with a camera and specimen jars.

Gwyn Parry, the detective sergeant, introduced himself and Doctor Eva Boross, the archaeologist. She was a cheerful, rotund woman of about sixty, with wild grey hair and fingers stained brown from a lifetime of heavy smoking. Wearing a plaid lumberjacket and a pair of riding breeches, she was quite unlike Richard's mental image of a Hungarian, but her accent was still strong after twenty years in Britain. With their similar professional backgrounds, Priscilla took to her immediately.

'We started digging already,' announced Eva. 'The core sample was obtained from three feet down, so with care, nothing will be lost until we get near that depth.'

The posts and ropes had been moved further out and Doctor Boross had marked out a ten-foot square with pegs and white tape, centred on the borehole. Inside this, a couple of brawny policemen had dug out a deep hole four feet across. A portable pump, borrowed from the Fire Service, was chugging away nearby, discharging coffee-brown water from the hole into a pond fifty yards away. The diggers were putting the black peat into wheelbarrows, which another two constables were wheeling away to be placed carefully on a large tarpaulin laid well outside the working area.

'That's in case we need to go back to it and look through it in detail,' Eva Boross explained. 'Though trying to sieve this wet, fibrous stuff would be a nightmare!'

She retired to a safe distance to light a cigarette and meticulously dropped her ash back into the packet, though Richard thought this was a little overcautious. Even if the remains below were not all that ancient, he doubted whether a little fag ash on the surface would hinder any investigation.

'How far down have they got?' asked Richard, moving nearer the edge of the hole to take a look.

'Most of the way, but keeping the bottom in sight is the problem, with the water oozing in all the time,' said Gwyn Parry.

Shovelling more carefully now, the constables went down another six inches, then came up for a breather. Plastered up to their knees in black peat, they had a rest, then took over the wheelbarrows, while the other pair went down the hole.

For almost another hour, Priscilla and Richard waited patiently as relays of constables slid into the excavation, eventually using bricklayer's trowels rather than spades. The lady from the university used a long measuring stick at intervals, to check the distance from the surface to the bottom of the pit.

'Must be very near now,' she muttered. 'Those botany people were quite clear about the depth of their borehole.'

She had hardly spoken before one digger, almost doubled up in the hole, gave a muffled shout.

'I can feel something here! It's hard, like a stone.' His pal decided to clamber up to the surface, to give the other man more room. Everyone came nearer, craning their heads to see down the pit, but the policeman's large body and the muddy water defeated them.

'Be careful the pump doesn't suck anything out except water,' cautioned Richard, imagining vital trace evidence vanishing down the pipe.

'Easier said than done, sir! But I'll dig a sump well away to one side and put the nozzle in that.'

A few moments later, he reported that the suction was gaining on the seeping water table and that when he momentarily swept the water away with his hand, he could see a blackened mound alongside a hard whitish thing.

Doctor Boross looked at Richard.

'I think one of us should take over the digging now, doctor. Perhaps you should have a look first, to see what you can make of it?'

Thankfully, the constable climbed out of the excavation and Richard took his place. He wore a pair of old army jungle-green trousers inside his wellingtons and an even older leather jacket that he had had since his student days.

Immediately he was up to his ankles in water, but the powerful pump was more than holding its own, so that the level was slowly dropping back to the deep hole that the constable had dug in one corner. He could see a bulge in the bottom mud and pulled on a pair of thick rubber gloves that he had in his jacket pocket.

Feeling the lump, his fingers slid over a rounded mass and then, beneath the remaining water, encountered a hard structure, as unyielding as iron. Returning to the mound, he pressed into it and felt a slight indentation form under his fingers. More exploring under the surface gave him some idea of what was lurking beneath.

'It's a body alright,' he reported. 'I can feel bone – and from the shape, it's certainly no sheep!'

There was a buzz of excitement from the watchers gathered around the excavation. 'Is it human, d'you think?' asked Eva Boross.

'Can't tell yet. We need to get more water out and a lot more peat.'

Richard asked for a trowel and when one was handed down, he began carefully digging around the sides of the bulge, as the pump continued to gurgle the opaque water from the sump. After a few minutes, he managed to free both sides of the protrusion, before again feeling around whatever was being exposed.

'I'm sure this is a buttock!' he proclaimed. 'I can feel a small hole on top that I can get my finger into. It must be where their drill punched into it.'

'So what shape is the hard stuff?' demanded Priscilla, leaning over the edge of the cavity. Like the Hungarian lady, she was itching to get down there and use her archaeological talents.

Richard slid his hand lower, now getting the impression that the axis of the body was diagonally across the excavation. 'I can feel a thick shaft of bone – and, yes, that must be a femoral head!'

This was the large knob on the top of thigh bone, where it fits into the hip joint. He straightened up, his back aching. Waving the trowel at the detective inspector, he sounded almost exultant as he confirmed that now the police had something definite to report to the coroner.

'It's certainly a human corpse – though God knows how long it's been here!'

He clambered back out of the excavation, his old trousers plastered with black mud, for a discussion on how they should proceed.

'I suppose now it must be treated as a crime scene, doctor,' suggested Meirion Thomas. 'Just in case it's not a historical find.'

'And if it is ancient, it needs an equally meticulous procedure,' countered Doctor Boross firmly. 'Perhaps Doctor Chambers and I should take over from here; we know how it needs to be done.'

They compromised on a combined operation and while both a police officer and Priscilla took some photographs of the first appearance of the cadaver, the remorseless action of the pump took yet more water from the hole, so that the mound that Richard thought was someone's backside came more clearly into view.

It was now well past lunchtime and the DI called a halt, while a constable went back to the vans and returned with a large box of sandwiches, small pork pies and four Thermos flasks of tea.

'We're certainly not going to finish this tonight,' said Richard Pryor. 'We can't just drag this out of the ground piecemeal. It will have to be removed as intact as we can manage.'

Priscilla and her new-found friend Eva agreed. 'It will have to be moved on to some form of support. Perhaps a door or some planks would do,' suggested the older archaeologist.

'That means the hole will have to be enlarged to make more room,' said Priscilla. 'If it's human, we need well over six feet clearance.'

Sergeant Parry gave some instructions to a constable who was driving one of the vans and he hurried off, with instructions to return to Aberystwyth and come back with a couple more men and some equipment suitable for moving the body.

Then, eating and drinking finished, they went back to the excavation, where the pump had now almost dried out the area around the remains.

'We'll have a go at it for a bit,' declared Eva Boross and with Priscilla on the other side, they began carefully trowelling away peat into buckets, gradually exposing the corpse. Richard watched intently from above and saw the outline of a body slowly appear. It was obviously lying on its front, the buttocks and back exposed first.

When the slimy peat was wiped away with a hand, the wrinkled skin appeared almost black, though splits here and there allowed greyish adipocere to show through.

There was a circular hole in one buttock, where the botanist's coring tube had penetrated, before hitting the underlying bone of the pelvis.

'The legs are in a bad state, Richard!' Priscilla called up, after another hour's work. She was concentrating on the lower end of the body, while Doctor Boross was freeing the shoulders. 'They are fraying off below thigh level, just bones and some tendon.'

'Best leave them alone for now,' he advised, peering down at what she was doing. 'We'll have to leave them in a block of peat and slide the whole thing on to whatever they bring as a support.'

A couple of feet away, Eva Boross was also having problems. 'The skin is very friable, like wet paper,' she reported. 'The arms must be tucked under the body. And so far, I haven't located the head, though I've cleared the peat almost to the neck.'

The photographer was taking pictures every few minutes to record the progress of the exposure of the tattered corpse. The light was now fading as the afternoon wore on, so at intervals the scene was illuminated by the artificial lightning of a flashgun.

When the two women came up for a rest, two policemen enlarged the edges of the hole to make more room for removing the remains. The van came back with the top of a trestle table and some planks, together with a couple more muscular PCs.

When Doctor Boross went back down the hole after a quick smoke, she soon discovered two disturbing facts.

'Doctor Pryor, there's some thin rope here, coming round from the front, it seems. Very frayed, and seems fixed underneath.'

Richard looked down at a ragged end that she held up.

'There was a tiny strand of what could have come from that, caught up in the botanist's sample,' he said.

'Some of the foreign bog bodies were strangled with a cord ligature,' she said hopefully. 'I'll try to expose the neck area. I'm almost up to it.'

A few moments later, she made another more grisly discovery. 'There's no head here! I've probed up beyond the neck and there's nothing there except soft peat.'

Priscilla squelched up from her end and after feeling around, confirmed Eva's finding. 'Nothing there, Richard! Unless it's buried some distance away, it's certainly not attached to the body. I can feel the ends of the lower neck vertebrae with my fingers.'

With light rapidly fading under a leaden sky, it was obvious that they could do little more that day except secure the site, so after a discussion, they turned the pump off and laid planks across the hole, with the trestle holding down a large tarpaulin.

'I'll leave an officer on watch all night,' said Meirion Thomas. 'He can sit in a van up on the road and keep an eye out, just in case anyone comes nosing around.'

The sergeant and his constable from Borth had been around

all day, keeping a few curious spectators away from the operation. Now the local PC was deputed for the night watch while
the other uniformed men went back to Aberystwyth.

'We'll have to stay somewhere overnight, Inspector,' said
Richard. 'It's impossible to go back to Monmouthshire and then
return by morning.'

'I'd love to put you up myself,' said Eva Boross. 'But I've
only got a two-roomed flat near the university.'

'Don't worry, we can find you somewhere here in Borth,' said
the detective inspector. 'A lot of bed and breakfasts will be shut
in the off season, but I'm sure Sergeant Edwards here knows
someone who can put you up. I'll have to go back to Aber now
to report to the chief and notify the coroner.'

The sergeant, who knew every soul in the little seaside town, had
no difficulty in finding them lodgings and after dumping their
muddy boots into the back of the Humber, he drove back with
them to a line of tall boarding houses facing the sea across the
main road. Edwards went into one, part of a three-storey terrace,
and conferred with the lady who answered the door.

Within minutes, they were receiving a warm welcome from
Mrs Gwenllian Evans, a genial lady of ample proportions, who
showed them to a pair of rooms on the first floor, which had a
superb view of the twilit sea just across the road.

'I've only got a couple of commercial gentlemen staying
tonight,' she explained. 'So there'll be plenty of hot water for a
good bath – you look as if you could do with one, with all that
old peat on you!'

She was obviously bursting to know what was going on up on
Cors Fachno, the news of which was all over Borth within an
hour of the arrival of the police that morning. Taking pity on her,
after Priscilla had taken her small case into her room, Richard
gave Mrs Evans a short, discreet version, suggesting that it might
be a historical burial and that an archaeologist from the university
was there with them. He spoke to her in Welsh and was pleased
to discover that after years of disuse, he was still reasonably fluent.
Both his parents came from Lower Brynaman in Carmarthenshire
and at home in Merthyr he had spoken his native language until
he left for medical school.

After he had hauled a decent pair of trousers, pyjamas and dressing gown from his case in the room, he followed the landlady's instructions to one of the bathrooms down the corridor. Here he washed off the smears of Borth Bog and soaked away the slight aches from even his limited efforts of digging in a cramped hole in the ground.

He heard the door of Priscilla's room next door being closed after she returned from her own ablutions and, after a decent interval, went out and tapped on it.

It opened a short way and he got a glimpse of a silk petticoat and bare feet.

'Sorry, I thought you might be decent by now!'

She grinned at him. 'Don't worry, we're both doctors, of a sort!' she joked.

'I wondered if you fancied a walk along the prom and a drink at the nearest pub?' he offered. 'The landlady said that supper won't be until half-past seven.'

'Good idea! Give me ten minutes and I'll be with you.'

The walk along the prom turned out to be a trudge in the dark along the top of the two-mile embankment that kept the sea from inundating Borth. Richard entertained Priscilla with the ancient legend of Cantref Gwaelod, the sunken land directly out at sea, flooded when Seithenyn, the drunken custodian of the sluice gates, allowed the sea to inundate it. She listened intently and he realized that part of her undoubted attractiveness was the fact that she made everyone she met feel that they had her undivided attention.

After a quarter of a mile, they turned around and walked back to the town. Richard had an unerring instinct for good pubs and soon found a cosy snug in the Victoria Inn. In front of an open fire, Priscilla had a gin and tonic and Richard a pint of Felinfoel ale from the famous brewery in Llanelli, the first he had enjoyed for fifteen years.

She had changed into a different jumper and a flared green skirt, a camel-hair coat thrown over her shoulders. They sat in comfortable companionship, discussing first the events of the day and the prospects for tomorrow.

Richard felt utterly relaxed in the company of this stunning woman, though little niggles of guilt assailed him from time to time. By the middle of his second pint, he was feeling vaguely disloyal to Angela for being so contented, whilst she was sitting alone in an empty house a hundred miles away. The two women were totally different, he thought. Angela was very good-looking and exceptionally well dressed, but was a rather quiet, reserved woman. When Richard had first met her at that conference, he had thought her something of an ice maiden, though better acquaintance proved that she had considerable warmth under her protective aloofness.

In spite of living in such close proximity for months, their relationship had never strayed from the strictly platonic, though on a recent visit to London when they went up for a case, the glimmerings of romance had arisen, to be quickly suppressed for the sake of their professional relationship.

Priscilla, so very attractive in a more overt way, was a talkative, gregarious extrovert, spontaneous in the expression of her feelings. In Singapore, he had had several affairs with expatriates since his divorce, but that had all ended more than a year ago and being with Priscilla now revived feelings that had lain dormant all that time.

He thought ruefully that perhaps it was just as well that she was not a permanent fixture in Garth House – and that they were not living under the same roof, as he was with Angela. Reluctantly, he looked at his watch.

'Another quarter of an hour and we'd better get back to Mrs Evans,' he said. 'Mustn't miss her meat and two veg after all that digging we've done today.'

Priscilla used the time to discover more about his marital history. Though she had had an outline from Sian, she openly fished for more details and learned that he had met his former wife Miriam in the military hospital in Ceylon where he had been a medical officer during the war.

'She was a civilian radiographer and British girls were in short supply there,' he explained. 'We got married Army style, dress uniforms, arcade of swords, the whole works!'

Priscilla's big eyes gleamed at the thought of a tropical wedding with all the trimmings. 'But it didn't last?' she asked.

'It was fine for a few years. Then I was posted to Singapore and she came over when things settled down and I got a job in the teaching hospital. But we had no children and she got bored, I suppose. An expat society like that is not the best place for an attractive woman with too much time on her hands.'

Priscilla took his meaning and smiled sadly. Getting up, she shrugged her coat back over her shoulders and held out a hand to pull him from his chair.

'Come on, professor or major or whatever you are. Time for that meat and veg!'

As they walked back along the main street in the dark, she slipped her arm easily through his, as the waves hissed and sighed on the shingle beach nearby.

That night, as he lay on his bed, he was very conscious of the fact that Priscilla was lying only a couple of feet away on the other side of the wall.

FOUR

After a hearty Welsh breakfast at seven o'clock, they said goodbye to the amiable Mrs Evans, and in their working clothes once more, set off in the Humber, which had been parked all night in the road outside. When they reached the scene, all the players from the previous day were there, with the addition of the deputy chief constable, who in such a small police force as Cardiganshire, only held the rank of superintendent. David John Jones was a tall, dark man with the deep-set eyes of an Iberian Celt and though he was perfectly civil to them, Richard had the feeling that he was rather suspicious of outsiders from Monmouthshire on his patch. However, when the pathologist spoke to him in his native language, he loosened up and informed Richard that if this turned out to be a suspicious death, Scotland Yard may have to be called in, as their minuscule CID was not manned or equipped to run a murder investigation. This was a standing arrangement made by the Home Office to assist smaller constabularies.

They moved across to the excavation, where some officers had removed the coverings. Underneath, the hole was still partly full of water, though as the body had already been in a waterlogged swamp for an unknown number of years, another night's soaking should make no difference. The pump had been started and the level was dropping quickly. As they waited, Richard asked what facilities were available for him once they had got the body out of the marsh.

'There's a decent mortuary at Aberystwyth General Hospital,' replied Meirion Thomas. 'The whole place was rebuilt just before the outbreak of war. That's where the coroner's cases are sent.'

'You've told the coroner, Meirion?' demanded David Jones.

'Yes, sir, last night. He said to keep him informed about what we find today.'

Soon the pump had sucked the water down to the level of the sump and the remains were once again exposed. Richard courteously invited Eva Boross to be first in the hole, as she had the most experience of digging artefacts from the ground.

'Looks much the same as we left it, but some of the peat underneath has washed away while under the water,' she reported. 'Best plan is to clear all around now, then undercut the peat until we can slide the whole thing on to that door.'

It took an hour to carefully isolate the long rectangle of peat supporting the body, Priscilla and Richard taking turns to relieve Eva of the back-breaking task. Then a couple of PCs manoeuvred the door alongside and gently, the block of peat and its macabre cargo were slid across on to its firm support.

As the door was manhandled to the surface and laid on the large tarpaulin, the Deputy Chief stared at the body with a frown on his saturnine features. 'It's a very dark colour! D'you think he's black?'

'All those foreign bog bodies were like that,' said the archaeologist. 'It's the tannin in the peat that does it.'

The detective sergeant was whispering something to his inspector and Meirion turned around to look. Up on the road, there was now a small crowd of onlookers and he saw one with a camera.

'We've got an audience already! I'll bet the *Cambrian News* has got wind of it by now.'

The DCC scowled. 'Damned nuisance, they are! I'll bet if you found a body in the middle of the Sahara, there'd be people popping up from behind rocks inside half an hour.'

'I can't examine him properly here, especially with those folks watching, even though they're a good distance away,' said Richard Pryor. 'Better cover him up until we can move him.'

The edges of the tarpaulin were lifted up and folded over the remains, then secured with cord. Two brawny constables then carried it away like stretcher-bearers to the larger of the two police vans parked up on the road.

As soon as they had left, Richard stood with Priscilla and Eva Boross, looking down into the now-vacant hole in the peat.

'Definitely no head, unless it's still buried in the peat well away from the rest of the body,' he said.

The archaeologist agreed. 'To be on the safe side, I feel we should ask the police to clear the peat away for a few feet all around where the body was, even if it means making the hole a lot bigger. You never know what you might find.'

They collected their kit together and walked back to the cars, where, as David Jones had suspected, a young reporter from the local paper was with the dozen onlookers, ready with his camera and notebook. The detective inspector went over to him and had a few words, which seemed to satisfy him. Wellingtons came off again and Richard was glad that he had lined the floor of his car boot with old newspapers, which caught the worst of the mess.

They followed the police van back to Aberystwyth where its cargo was taken to the mortuary behind the hospital in North Road. The porter who acted as part-time mortuary assistant looked askance at the peat-stained bundle that was carried in to his clean post-mortem room, though at least it didn't smell, like some of the drowned bodies belatedly recovered from the sea or the river.

Sergeant Parry, with that facility that policemen have for cadging from local institutions, took the three scientists off to the doctor's dining room, where they were served with tea and sandwiches. Home-cured ham and fresh salmon were very welcome, especially at a time when the austerity of post-war rationing was only just disappearing.

By the time they got back to the mortuary, the porter and two policemen had unwrapped the body, and now the door lay on a slab, already shedding black peat on to the surrounding floor.

'Sorry about the mess,' apologized Richard, but the porter, a fat man with a shining bald head, had become philosophical about the debris. 'Don't worry, doctor, I'll hose it all down when you're finished.'

Richard took a long red-rubber apron from a hook on the wall and hung it from his neck by a chain, another chain hooking it around his waist. Priscilla gave him some rubber gloves from his case and stood by with their camera, to add their own record to those taken by the police photographer. Meirion Thomas, Gwyn Parry and Eva Boross formed the audience, plus a couple of policemen who stood with white enamel mugs at the back of the room, drinking tea made by the mortuary man.

'Right, let's get on with it,' said Richard, advancing on the body. He had a bucket of water and a sponge and began by gently cleaning the back surface of the trunk. Wrinkled and almost black, the skin was leathery down to the lower part of the buttocks, where it frayed off to expose the bones of the thighs. The lower parts of the legs and feet were still embedded in peat and when he removed it, they virtually fell apart into a collection of loose bones, ligaments and tendons, all stained brownish yellow. At the other end, removal of more peat revealed the bare end of the spine at mid-neck level, with two loose vertebrae not connected to anything.

While more photographs were being taken, Eva asked if he thought it was male or female.

'We keep calling it "him",' replied Richard. 'It's so distorted that it's hard to tell yet, until we can turn him – or her – over.'

The piece of cord was hanging loose and Priscilla used a pair of forceps to pick up the end for a closer look.

'That bit we had with the core sample must be a single strand of this – there are three, twisted in a loose spiral.' The DI, true to his farming origins, said that it looked like binder twine, a hemp or sisal cord used to tie up bales of hay.

The archaeologist's main concern was the date of the remains, though she had more or less given up hope of it being very ancient. 'Anything to suggest its age?' she asked hopefully.

Richard shook his head as he carried on digging away at surplus peat. 'Nothing yet, but the problem is I don't know how much being buried in an acidic bog full of tannin affects the rate of decay.'

'How long would a body last in ordinary soil?' asked Eva, who professionally had never had to deal with anything but ancient deaths.

'Depends on many factors, like the type of soil, especially acidity, wetness and temperature,' he replied, as he continued to ferret away at the encroaching peat. 'Left on the surface, there's often not much left after a year except bones, but animal predators like rats, foxes and insects are responsible for much of that. Buried, the corpse will last much longer, but again depending on whether or not it's in a sound coffin.'

'A couple of cases I saw when I was with the Met, still had cartilage on the joints and some tendons after a year,' offered Priscilla.

'Sure, but five years certainly sees off all the soft tissues, if they're not buried. Doctor Boross, do you know what the old bog bodies were like internally after all that time?'

The archaeologist, virtually a chain smoker, tapped the ash from her latest Gold Flake into the big porcelain sink.

'Quite good organ preservation in some, I recall. Even the stomach contents were identifiable, but some had very pliable bones, due to the acid water decalcifying them.'

Richard tapped the exposed thigh bone with a wide knife that he was using to dig out the peat. 'These are exceptionally hard, I must say! So again that's against our friend here being from the dawn of history.'

It was when he started sponging down the shoulders and upper arms that this speculation was abruptly confirmed. The arms were still tucked under the body, but on wiping the slimy coating from just below the right shoulder, Richard stopped and bent to peer more closely at the dark grey, wrinkled skin.

'What the hell's this? Priscilla, there's a torch in that case, can you bring it, please.'

They all clustered round as she aimed the beam at where his finger was pointing. Very faintly, there were darker marks under the surface and when he smoothed out the wrinkles between a finger and thumb, they saw the blurred outlines of a tattoo.

'I don't think Batman was around in the Iron Age!' he said, with a tinge of disappointment.

*   *   *

After their session in the mortuary, they adjourned to the DCC's office in the old police building on the promenade. It was now late afternoon and Richard and Priscilla had a long journey ahead of them back to the Wye Valley, but they needed to take stock of what they had learned so far.

David John Jones sat behind his DI's desk as they drank the inevitable cups of tea. The two from Tintern had been offered a meal in a local hotel, but as Richard decided that they would stop somewhere on the way home, they held their discussion straight away.

'So we've got a murder on our hands,' said the senior officer, with a sigh of resignation. 'We'll have to get the Yard in straight away. This is beyond us. I've only got one ranking CID officer for the whole of Cardiganshire – and we've already got a clutch of burglaries and two sheep-stealings to cope with.'

Richard nodded his understanding. 'We'll do all we can to help with the forensic pathology side, though of course, the Home Office lab in Cardiff must look at any physical evidence, like that cord that was used to strangle the fellow.'

The post-mortem had not been all that helpful, with such an incomplete and decayed body to work with, but there seemed little doubt that the ligature that had been wound twice around the neck was the cause of death. A length of similar cord had tied both wrists together in front of the body, even though the underlying skin and bones had disintegrated inside it.

'First thing is, we need to know who the bugger was!' said Meirion Thomas in his forthright manner. 'No fingerprints, as he had no fingers left. All we've got so far is a flaming tattoo!'

'What's this Batman business?' demanded the DCC, who was hardly up to date with modern trends.

'Apparently he's a character in Yankee comics and films, sir,' said Gwyn Parry.

'At least it can give us an earliest date for this chap,' declared Richard. 'Though how you discover when the Batman character was first published, I've no idea.'

Their earlier doubts of the sex of the body had been solved · by the pathologist's brief study of the pelvic bones, which were largely exposed in the collapsing corpse. The front of the cadaver was in a far worse state than the back, with hardly any skin left and all the organs degenerated, including the genitals. With no head, sexing it was down to an interpretation of the bones, but both Richard and Priscilla were in no doubt of its maleness – added to which was the fact that women rarely went in for tattoos.

'Have we any idea of his height, doctor?' asked the detective inspector.

'Looks about average from his bones, but Doctor Chambers here is the real expert. No doubt she'll need to take some accurate measurements of the leg bones when we get back to base.' Privately, he knew he could have done it equally well himself, but he wanted to give Priscilla as big a role as possible.

Superintendent David Jones looked quizzically at his two CID staff.

'Any outstanding missing persons in the last few years?' he demanded.

'Problem is, sir, we don't know how many years are involved,' replied Meirion. 'No one comes to mind from this part of the county, but I'll have to go through the records.'

'And you can't even hazard a guess as to the time this fellow died, doctor?' persisted the deputy chief.

Richard shook his head. 'I wouldn't want to mislead you by picking a figure out of the air. I'm sure he's been in that bog more than a few years – but it could be ten or even twenty, perhaps much more.'

He turned to Eva Boross, who had the inevitable cigarette in her fingers. 'Any possibility of the depth it was buried in the ground being helpful – or something to do with the vegetation at that depth?'

The Hungarian also shook her head despondently. 'I doubt it, but it might be worth me asking the botany people at the university. The body could never have sunk that deep from the surface in a few years, so it must have either been put into a hole dug in the peat – or there may have been a pool there then. The bog changes all the time, according to rainfall and changes in underground water.'

They talked around the apparently insoluble problems for a little longer, then the meeting broke up.

'I'll have to go and tell the Chief Constable what's happening,' muttered David Jones. 'I've no doubt he'll contact Scotland

Yard tomorrow. Meirion, you can let the coroner know what's going on.'

With mutual thanks and promises to keep closely in touch, Richard and Priscilla made their escape, saying goodbye to the archaeologist, with whom Priscilla already seemed to have made firm friends. It was beginning to get dusk as they drove up into the hills on their way home across Mid-Wales, with some of the unknown body's bones wrapped in newspaper in a margarine box in the boot.

'I don't know about you, but I'm starving,' complained Richard. 'Sandwiches and endless cups of police tea are fine in their way, but I could do with a square meal.'

They found a hotel in Builth Wells able to satisfy their pangs of hunger. It was an old-fashioned hostelry in the main street, a gloomy place with everything varnished a dark brown, but it had a dining room and quite an extensive menu. The food turned out to be surprisingly good, even though they seemed to be the only patrons that evening. Once again, Priscilla marvelled at the quality and choice on offer, considering that wartime food rationing had only ended the previous year. Over oxtail soup, roast beef and apple tart with fresh cream, they went over the events of the past thirty-six hours.

'I've really enjoyed it, Richard, thanks so much for letting me come,' enthused Priscilla. 'I thought mysterious strangled and beheaded bodies were only found in London and the big cities, not in a little place out in the sticks like Borth! What on earth can it be all about?'

Richard grinned at her. 'You English people, you think you have a monopoly on violent crime! There's as much intrigue and vendettas in rural areas as in any city, we're just better at concealing it.'

They went into the adjacent lounge for coffee and Richard ordered a couple of brandies to go with it.

'So what happens next?' asked the auburn-haired biologist. 'There seems little more we can do to help identify this fellow.'

'We urgently need the head, though God knows what state it would be in. At least we had a bit of bog tanning to preserve the trunk. We'd not have seen that tattoo but for that.'

'There's no doubt about him being strangled, I suppose?'

Richard warmed the brandy glass in his hand. 'There was that double ligature tied in a knot and what was left of the larynx had a crack through the cricoid cartilage. Of course, he might have been shot through the head as well, but as we haven't got it, we can't tell!'

'And the poor chap's hands were tied together,' said Priscilla, with a shudder. 'A nasty, sadistic sort of case.'

'More like some gangland killing,' agreed Richard. 'But there are not many gangsters in sleepy Cardiganshire.'

Eventually, they reluctantly dragged themselves away from the fire in the lounge and Richard went to find the landlord to settle the bill. Priscilla offered to pay her share, but Richard waved it aside.

'Like last night at Mrs Evans', we can legitimately charge it to the partnership as expenses. The police or the coroner will foot the bill eventually.'

Before they left, Richard used the coin telephone in the hotel corridor to ring Garth House. When he pressed Button A, he was strangely happy to hear Angela's calm tones, reassuring him that all was well and that she was looking forward to seeing them arrive home.

'It's not a bog body, but it's a murder, though heaven knows when it happened,' he told her. 'We'll tell you all about it in about an hour and a half.'

The rest of the journey seemed to take longer than that, as he peered down the tunnel cut by the headlights through the dark countryside. After her good meal and a brandy, Priscilla soon dozed off and only woke when the Humber revved up the driveway to the house. Angela had tea and biscuits ready for them and they sat in her lounge for a while, giving her a detailed account of their activities in Cardiganshire.

'So you've no idea who he was or when he was killed?' she asked at the end.

Priscilla raised her hands in mock despair. 'Not a clue, Angela! At least the only one is that he had this Batman tattoo. Have you any idea when that idiotic business began?'

The other woman shook her head. 'I've just about heard of it. Isn't it an American comic strip or something? Perhaps the dead man was a Yank?'

'Well, that's not our problem,' said Richard, yawning mightily. 'Let the police follow it up – probably your pals from Scotland Yard.'

He immediately felt that he might have said the wrong thing, for Angela was still bitter about the defection of her former fiancé in favour of another woman – and he was a detective superintendent from that same famous institution. However, she made no sign that it had registered, though he knew that Angela was adept at concealing her feelings.

'Time for bed, folks,' suggested Priscilla and soon Richard drove her the short distance to Tintern Parva, where she had comfortable lodgings in a bed and breakfast establishment used mostly by summer walkers and holidaymakers.

Angela waited up until he returned, then they both made for the stairs. 'Did you enjoy your night away with our glamour girl, Richard?' she said without a trace of sarcasm. 'I think Moira was afraid that you'd be led off the path of righteousness!'

He gave her one of his famous grins. 'Yes, we had a romantic drink in the local pub and then a passionate meat and two veg in Mrs Evans' den of sin!'

'No, somehow I don't see you as a lecherous seducer, Richard,' she said, as she left him at the upper landing.

As he went towards his own room, he wondered if he detected a hint of disappointment in her voice.

FIVE

Next day, they got down to the job of examining the material they had brought back from Aberystwyth.

The bones were laid out on a large sheet of brown paper on the big table in the laboratory and everyone, including Moira, was keen to see what could be discovered. They all stood around expectantly, the morning sun lighting the exhibits through the wide bay window.

'We've got a right femur, a tibia and half the pelvis,' pointed out Richard, who had put on a white coat and a pair of rubber gloves. 'And there are three vertebrae from the neck, as well as some soft tissues.'

Priscilla, similarly attired, had their osteometry board ready on the side of the table. This was a varnished board a couple of feet long with a long ruler screwed along one edge and a fixed ledge sticking up at the bottom.

'The police were keen to get his height, so shall I start with that?' she said. At Richard's nod, she put the long thigh bone, stained brown by the peat, on to the board, so that the knee end was against the ledge. Then she moved a sliding bar down from the top until it touched the upper knob of bone which would have fitted into the hip joint.

Adjusting the lie of the bone so that the maximum length was being measured, she read off the number of centimetres on the scale, which she wrote on a sheet of paper, then did the same for the tibia, the bone from the lower leg.

Turning to an open textbook and couple of loose dog-eared papers, she ran her finger down some columns of figures and scribbled some calculations on the sheet.

'According to Trotter and Gleser, he should be between five-foot eight and five-ten. Using the old Pearson formula, he's five-seven and five-nine.'

'How do you make that out?' demanded Sian, always thirsty for knowledge.

Priscilla laid a hand on the book and the reprints.

'Anatomists have published several surveys of bone length from bodies where they already knew the height. Pearson did that at the end of the last century, but Krogman wrote a guide for the FBI in 1939 and only a few years ago, Trotter and Gleser did another big survey on war casualties, including many from Korea.'

'So why do you get different answers?' persisted their technician, a valid query which Richard answered.

'These surveys were done on different populations, including different ethnic groups. And there's always an error zone of at least an inch and a half.'

Angela, her arms folded, looked down at the bones on the table. 'So the likelihood is that he was between five-feet eight and five-feet nine?'

'That's about the best we can do,' replied Priscilla. 'Certainly not very tall or very short. In fact, he was like most men in Britain, which doesn't help the police much!'

'Anything else you can tell us?' asked Richard hopefully. 'What about race, for instance?'

Their tame anthropologist picked up the thigh bone again and turned it over in her hands, sighting along the shaft.

'Nothing significant without a skull, but the only racial variation in leg bones is in the length of the femur in Negroid ethnic groups. This one's certainly not that.'

'What about the colour of that skin?' asked Sian, pointing to a glass pot in which a scrap of loose skin was immersed in fixing fluid. 'It's even darker than that little bit we got from the borehole.'

'Years of being soaked in black peat can account for that,' said Richard. 'But you'll have to process the bits for the microscope, just to check for melanin and exclude any racial marker.'

This was getting a little complicated for Moira who, with a sigh, went back to her office. She felt a little depressed that the other three women seemed so much at home with these technical matters and wished that she had better skills than just hitting typewriter keys.

However, Angela also felt she was contributing little to this latest case, as her expertise in serology seemed unlikely to assist in identifying 'Mr Bog', as Sian had started to call the victim.

'I suppose I had better do a blood group on the remains, though I can't see that an ABO and Rhesus are going to help much,' she said.

Richard immediately picked up on the fact that his partner was feeling left out of this investigation and hastened to draw her in.

'Of course you should; we must have as much information as we can, Angela. You never know, we might need to exclude someone the cops turn up, even if we can't get a positive match.'

Priscilla was carefully replacing the thigh bone back on the table, after finishing with the measuring device. As she did so, she weighed it up and down in her hand before laying it back on the brown paper.

'I know I'm more used to handling frail archaeological

skeletons, but don't you think these are unusually heavy?' she commented, looking at Richard with a slight frown.

'Yes, I noticed that in the mortuary yesterday,' he agreed, taking the bone from her and hefting it a few times himself. He looked across at Sian. 'Can you decalcify a piece, if I saw it out for you?'

Their technician nodded. 'But it'll take a week before I can cut sections,' she warned. To get a thin slice of bone suitable for looking at under the microscope required that the chalky calcium part must be dissolved out in weak acid.

Richard tapped the long bone against the edge of the table and felt it as unyielding as a rod of iron.

'I'd like to get this X-rayed, too,' he said. 'I'll take it up to Hereford Hospital; they'll do it for me. I've got a coroner's case there on Thursday, one of these operating theatre deaths.'

'What are you looking for, Richard?' asked Angela.

'I've got an idea brewing in the back of my mind – and an X-ray may also give some indication of the age of this chap. The internal structure alters with advancing age, though admittedly it's most useful when they are over fifty or sixty.'

He set about sawing a narrow slice from the shaft of the bone with a stainless-steel implement from his autopsy kit. Though the slice was only a quarter of an inch wide and went less than halfway through the bone, it took him five minutes and left him with an aching arm.

'My God, that's like flint!' he complained, as he handed over the sliver of bone to Sian to put in a pot of formalin.

'What else can we do?' asked Priscilla, waving a gloved hand at the debris on the table.

'This is where Angela comes in,' he replied, eager to involve her in the examination. 'I had a quick look at the vertebrae in the mortuary, but the light was not at all good in the late afternoon. See what you make of them, Angela.'

Though primarily a forensic biologist, the handsome brunette had had many years' general experience in the 'Met Lab', as everyone called it, and could turn her hand to most aspects of forensic science. She pulled on some gloves and carefully arranged the three spinal vertebrae so that they interlocked in the proper anatomical position.

'That's all there was left of the neck?'

He nodded. 'Just the lower three of the seven vertebrae. The upper ones must have gone with the head, as there was no sign of them anywhere in the adjacent peat.'

Angela picked up the top one, and looked at the central part with the hole for the spinal cord and the long spine at the back, between the two shorter wings that stuck out each side.

'It's had a bit of a bashing! Must have been chopped from the back.' She took a lens from the pocket of her white coat and studied the upper surface intently.

'There are deep cut marks, one almost going right through the left transverse process. And another that's split the back of the vertebral body.'

'Yes, I saw those. But what do you think caused them? A knife or something heavier?'

Angela took her time in replying, as she peered again through her lens. 'Heavier, definitely. The edges are crushed, rather than sliced. I would think something like a cleaver or one of those agricultural billhooks.'

'Not an axe?'

'It would have to be a very sharp one, if it was. I'd prefer something with a thinner blade.'

Sian was looking at the small bone with fascination, visions of Mary Queen of Scots with her head on the block filling her mind. 'But you're sure he had his head chopped off, then?'

Richard stepped in, afraid that the girl might have nightmares about this. 'Almost certainly after he was dead, Sian. He was strangled, remember?'

'Why would they do that, Doctor Pryor?' she asked, wide-eyed.

'Almost certainly to stop us identifying him – and they seem to have succeeded, so far!' he replied wryly.

'You think it was a "we", rather than a single killer?' asked Priscilla.

'Seems more likely, given he was tied up, throttled, beheaded and then buried out in a marsh,' replied Richard. 'Though it's always risky to be dogmatic in this business.'

'Nothing in the way of old injuries or scars, I suppose?' asked Angela.

'Unfortunately not. Almost the only surviving skin was on the back, so the abdominal area was missing, which might have had operation scars. All we have is that tattoo.'

'Well, let's hope the police have some luck with Batman!' said Angela, pulling off her gloves.

Two days later and a hundred miles away, they were not having much luck with anything. The police house in Upper Borth was far too small for an incident room, so one had been set up in a disused hut about half a mile from the place where the body was exhumed. An army camp had been built during the war for some undisclosed purpose on the sand dunes at Ynys Las, near the top end of Borth's great beach. Though it had been closed some years earlier, several of the long timber huts were still intact and with the power and phone reconnected, the police had installed the essentials they needed – trestle tables, chairs and the vital kettle and teapot.

As predicted, the chief constable had sought the help of the Metropolitan Police and late that afternoon, a detective super-intendent and a sergeant arrived from New Scotland Yard, after an arduous train journey to Aberystwyth via Shrewsbury. Meirion Thomas picked them up at the station and took them to the Headquarters on the seafront to meet the chief and his deputy.

'We've put you up in a hotel here in town for tonight, then comfortable digs in Borth from tomorrow,' explained the local DI.

In the chief constable's office, over coffee and biscuits, the London man, Paul Vickers and his assistant, DS Howard Squires, were given an account of the case, though so far, it was not very much. Paul Vickers listened impassively, leaving his questions until the end. He was not all that pleased at being sent down to a remote part of Wales at such short notice, especially as he had promised to take his fiancé to the opera at Covent Garden on Wednesday and had already bought expensive tickets. But his name was next on the rota of senior detectives to be farmed out to the provinces and having an eye on promotion to chief super-intendent, he could not afford to be difficult about it.

When Meirion Thomas had finished and the DCC had added a few more words, the London man laid his hand on the thin file that he had been given, which contained a summary of the investigation.

'So what have you managed to do so far?' he asked, trying to keep any condescension from his voice.

'All the usual preliminary stuff, without getting a whiff of a result,' replied the local CID man. 'House to house in Borth and the nearby villages, though without a photograph or any sort of physical description of the chap or even his clothing, it was a waste of time.'

'The only thing we have is that Batman tattoo,' added Gwyn Price. 'But it didn't ring a bell with anyone – though of course, being up near the shoulder, it would never have been visible unless he was stripped or in bathing trunks.'

'What about missing persons in the area?' ventured Squires. David Jones jumped back into the discussion, anxious to assert his rank.

'Trouble is, what area? And what time frame? We've got a few people reported missing in the county over the past ten years, but with a large summer tourist influx, the population is very fluid.'

Paul Vickers, a large, heavily handsome man of thirty-nine, with black hair and an expensive suit, pondered the answers.

'So what have you got on his body and time of death?' he demanded of Meirion.

'The pathologist says it's impossible to tell when he died to within a good many years, because of the preservative effect of the bog. But the tattoo must put some limit on it, when we can get some more information about this damned cartoon character.'

'What about physical description?'

'You'll see tomorrow that he was little more than bones and some skin, as well as being minus his head, so the pathologist can only estimate that he was around five-feet eight in height, give or take a couple of inches, which is not a lot of use. No other distinguishing marks, he said.'

'Who is this pathologist? Is he used to this sort of case?' asked the sergeant, in a tone that suggested that civilization petered out west of Reading.

Meirion Thomas jumped to defend Richard Pryor.

'He's a Home Office pathologist and, in fact, was a professor of forensic pathology. Not only that, but he had another lady scientist with him, who used to work in your laboratory in London.'

Vickers sat up in his chair and looked intently at the detective inspector. 'What was her name? Was it Doctor Bray?' His voice was suddenly tense, but Meirion shook his head. 'No, it was Chambers; she said she specialized in anthropology.' Sergeant Squires nodded. 'I saw her at a scene in Battersea once. A very attractive lady indeed!'

Vickers seemed to relax. 'The pathologist must have been Richard Pryor, the one that came back from Singapore. I met him briefly in a shooting near Gloucester some months ago.'

The social chat over, there was little else to be done except arrange for the two London men to be picked up at their hotel in the morning and taken to the incident room at Borth. The local DI and sergeant dropped them off at the Bellevue Hotel, just along the seafront from the police headquarters, then went to the nearest pub for a pint before going wearily to their own homes.

'That pair think we are still in the colonies,' grumbled Gwyn Parry. 'Condescending couple of bastards!'

Antipathy between county police and the Metropolitan Police was traditional. Some forces felt it was an admission of inferiority to have to 'call in the Yard', but Meirion Thomas took a more phlegmatic view of the situation.

'It's no good getting uptight about them, Gwyn. There's no way we can carry on with this on our own. This fellow could have been brought to Borth from anywhere and dumped in that bog. We can't go looking all over Great Britain for him!'

Next morning, while Vickers and his sergeant were travelling towards Borth in the back seat of a police car, Richard Pryor was sitting in his office in Garth House. He was holding up a large X-ray film to the window, so that Angela and Priscilla could see it against the daylight outside. They all looked intently at the dense white image of the thigh bone, which contrasted sharply with the black of the surrounding celluloid.

'What d'you make of that, ladies?' he asked chirpily. Angela could tell that he was pleased with what he had discovered, but she was not going to give in easily.

'I suppose the radiologist in Hereford told you what it was, clever-sticks!' she chided.

Richard pretended to be affronted. 'He only confirmed what I already suspected! Ever heard of Albers-Schonberg?'

'Sounds like an Austrian composer or a psychiatrist,' suggested Priscilla, facetiously. Richard grinned and waggled the film in his hand.

'No, he was a German radiologist, who described this disease in 1904. It's better known as "Marble Bone Disease", for obvious reasons.'

'It's not obvious to me,' said Angela, stoutly. 'Pris and I are proper doctors, not physicians!'

Richard became serious and pointed to the dense white shaft of the bone.

'We thought the femur was very heavy and with good reason. This is a quite rare genetic defect in which the bone becomes extraordinarily dense and thickened. Look, there's hardly any marrow cavity down the middle of the bone. It's all overgrown and as hard as a rock – in fact, the modern name for the disease is "osteopetrosis", meaning rock-like bones.'

'So what makes you so excited about this, apart from your academic interest?' asked Priscilla. Richard dropped the film on to his desk.

'Well, because it's so rare. Maybe there's a medical record somewhere of this chap, if he was ever seen in a hospital. Although the bone is so hard, it's brittle, so they get a lot of fractures. And it seriously affects the skull as well, so if they ever find a spare head somewhere, we could match it to this fellow.'

The two scientists were quite impressed after all.

'Quite a unique pair of identifying features, Richard,' said Angela. 'Albers-Schonberg disease and a Batman tattoo!'

'Better than nothing, which is what we had when we dug him up,' said Richard defensively. 'Something useful to tell the cops, anyway.'

Angela hauled herself off the corner of his desk, ready to go back to her work in the laboratory.

'You said something about possibly telling the age of the body from his bone X-rays . . . any joy there?

'Not really, according to the radiologist,' he replied.

'The presence of this great thickening obscures the details of the internal structure, especially as the marrow cavity is partly obliterated. Normally, the internal architecture of weight-bearing bones is modified as people get older. But he said there was no positive evidence of advanced age, for what that's worth.'

As the two women went out, he reached for the phone and dialled Aberystwyth, to leave a message for Meirion Thomas to contact him.

The investigators in Borth had just left the hut, to go over to the site of the excavation to show it to the London men. There was nothing really to see, apart from a hole in the ground surrounded by posts and tape, but Meirion Thomas felt that Vickers and his assistant should get a feel for the whole case. Howard Squires was very taken by the panoramic view, which included the huge bog, the sea and the surrounding hills, but his senior officer seemed distracted. He was thinking of a woman, in fact his former fiancée, Angela Bray. Engaged to her for over a year, he had suddenly become infatuated with a younger woman and broken it off. He was well aware how hard Angela had taken it and knew that it was a factor in her decision to leave London and team up with this Welsh pathologist, Richard Pryor. Some months earlier, he had been called to Gloucester to identify a murdered South London criminal, shot in a gang dispute. The pathologist was Richard Pryor and with him had been Angela Bray, which led to an embarrassing confrontation in the mortuary. Now history was in danger of repeating itself and he would have to be careful to avoid meeting her again, as 'hell hath no fury like a woman scorned'.

'Guv, have you seen enough here?' His sergeant's voice brought him back to earth.

'Er, yes, I think so.' With an effort, he focused his attention again and looked around. 'How would they have brought a body here? The same way as we came?' he asked the locals.

'Probably, it's only a few hundred yards from the road,' answered the DI. 'We assume that there were more than one and presumably they had some sort of transport. He was only of average height, but I doubt one person would have struggled here with the corpse.'

'Unless he was killed right here?' objected Squires.

Meirion gave a doubtful shrug. 'Possible, but it seems unlikely that they would cut off his head here and take it away.'

'The whole damned case seems unlikely!' muttered Vickers, as he took a last look around.

They went back to the police car and drove back to the headquarters in Aberystwyth, where an office had been put at the disposal of the Scotland Yard men. Vickers said that he would have to make a lot of telephone calls to get things moving, before going back to Borth after lunch.

In Meirion's own office, a message relayed from the incident room asked him to ring Doctor Richard Pryor and when he got through, the doctor told him of the confirmation of the rare bone disease discovered in the corpse. It took a few minutes for Richard to explain about Albers-Schonberg disease, but the detective quickly grasped its significance.

'So we've got to find a guy somewhere in Britain who had this disease – and find a skull somewhere which also suffered from it?'

'That's about it, Inspector! I'll see if I can find if there is any kind of central medical register of patients who have been diagnosed with marble bone disease. I doubt it, as it's so uncommon, but there may be some orthopaedic surgeons who have an interest in it.' He thought for a moment, then went on. 'It's a pity that I didn't find any old fractures in the skeleton. They are quite common in Albers-Schonberg, as the bones are brittle. They could have been matched with the X-rays of patients who had had multiple breaks, but we're out of luck on that score.'

'So we've got to find a head somewhere?' repeated the detective.

'That's about it – as well as someone with a Batman tattoo!' agreed Richard. 'Any progress on discovering when that character became popular?'

'The chaps from the Yard are looking into that. They're more likely to have people in London who would know.'

'Who have they sent down to you?'

When the DI gave the names, he heard a low whistle coming down the phone. 'Paul Vickers, eh? That's a coincidence, as I met him not long ago.'

He avoided mentioning that Doctor Bray knew him even better

and soon they finished their conversation and rang off. Richard pondered for a moment, then went in search of his business partner. He found her in her room on the other side of the hall, at her desk writing up some paternity results for Moira to type.

'Got a minute, Angela?'

She looked up and saw that he seemed to have lost some of his usual light-hearted manner.

'Why so serious? Have you just had our latest bank statement?'

He dropped on to the chair opposite her. 'Just a word of caution. The police in this bog case have had to call in the Yard to help – and the help they've been sent is Paul Vickers. It's none of my business, but after that incident in Gloucester, I thought I'd better tell you, so that it doesn't come as a surprise.'

She put down her pen and looked at him fondly.

'Thanks, Richard. You are a nice chap, aren't you? But it's OK, really, I'm rapidly putting all that behind me, thanks to Garth House and all this Wye Valley tranquillity.'

Relieved, his cheerful grin returned. 'Fine, but perhaps we'd better keep you away from Aberystwyth for the time being.'

Angela reached out a hand and laid it on his arm.

'Thanks again! But perhaps it would better to keep Priscilla away from him, rather than me. Attractive women act like a magnet on Paul Vickers!'

His duty done, Richard went back to the laboratory to see if Sian had started to decalcify the scrap of bone from the skeleton, so that he could confirm his diagnosis under the microscope, but he had time to hope that the Yard man would have no reason to come down to Garth House.

SIX

A week later, the only development that was made in the 'Mystery of Borth Bog', as the Press now called it, was some clarification about the Batman tattoo. Paul Vickers had phoned several of his colleagues in Scotland Yard and asked them to canvas any contacts they had in the newspaper and magazine business in London.

Several days later, he had a call from a detective sergeant who had been sent to lurk in the pubs around Fleet Street, an area which he knew well from other somewhat dubious assignments. He found it a salubrious assignment, as after a few pints of beer and the odd gin and tonic, he learned from men who worked in various publications that Batman was the creation of a couple of American cartoon writers in 1939, who had sold the idea tó *Detective Comics* and it had taken off from there in the United States.

'Very popular over there, sir, all through the war and now increasingly so. But virtually unknown here in Britain until recent years.'

Vickers had known that, according to the pathologist, it was unlikely that the body had been killed less than a decade ago, which took the murder back to at least the last year of the war.

'So do you think anyone over here, that long ago, would been keen enough on Batman to have it as a tattoo?' he asked, though he realized that the sergeant would have no better guess to make than himself.

'Well, he could have seen comic books about him brought over by Yank servicemen, I suppose. He could even have been a GI himself, comes to that. God knows there were enough of them knocking about here before D-Day.'

There was nothing else useful that he could tell him and they rang off. Vickers was becoming increasingly frustrated by being stuck in the back of beyond, as he thought of Cardiganshire. He had given up going to the incident room in Borth, as it seemed entirely futile. His sergeant, Howard Squires, stayed there for the sake of appearances, but absolutely no progress was being made. They could not even blame the lack of it on the 'local yokels', as Squires called them, as everything that could have been done, had been done. Nothing had come of extensive interviews with the community in Borth and a trawl of the hotels and boarding houses over the wider area had been equally unrewarding. Revisiting all the missing persons enquiries over the past few years again drew a blank. It was difficult to see how it could be otherwise, given that the dates were vague to within a number of years and they had no physical description of the deceased man.

Paul had spoken to his senior officer in London and told him that he felt they were wasting both their time and the Home Office's money, in keeping them down here.

'I feel sure this body was dumped a long way from where he was killed, sir,' he complained. 'That could have been anywhere in Britain and the investigation could just as well be run from London, as there's damn-all to be learned down here.'

The chief superintendent sounded sympathetic, but told Vickers to hang on for a few more days.

'But I've got to come back next week for a trial at the Old Bailey, sir,' protested Paul. 'I don't see much point in waiting. You could leave Squires here if you think it necessary.'

After getting a non-committal answer, Vickers went to find the local DI to tell him the little he had gained from London. Irritably, he repeated the sergeant's scanty information.

'He made the suggestion that perhaps the fellow was American, as this Batman was certainly not well known here in the time frame that we're thinking of. Were there any US army personnel in this area during the war?'

Meirion Thomas pensively rubbed the stubble on his chin.

'Yanks? I can't recall many, but I was a PC in Tregaron when the war ended. I'd just joined, having been on the farm before that, so I wouldn't have seen many strangers.'

'The incident room in Borth is in what used to be an army camp, I'm told. Were there any Americans there?'

Meirion Thomas shook his head slowly.

'Not that I know of. It was a purely British establishment, so I'm told. No one seemed to know what it was for. It was a bit hush-hush.'

Vickers gave up in disgust, as every lead seemed to peter out. He went back to his cubbyhole of an office and began making more phone calls to London, trying to keep in touch with other cases he had been forced to leave behind when he was sent into exile.

At Garth House, they settled back into their usual routine after the brief excitement of the headless corpse.

A police car had collected the bones he had brought back from Aberystwyth and returned them to the mortuary there, to be reunited with the rest of the mortal remains of the unknown victim. They would be kept in the refrigerator until the coroner decided what should be done with them. Richard explained to the mystified Moira that they could not be buried for a considerable time – and never cremated – in case someone was arrested and charged with murder, as the defence lawyers would then have the right to require an independent opinion from another pathologist. The coroner had decided to delay an inquest until, hopefully, some useful evidence was turned up, as there seemed little point in holding a useless enquiry.

It was now nearing the end of November and the days were becoming very short. The autumn colours had almost gone and even the Wye Valley looked sombre, as its trees became bare. Most days, Richard Pryor went off to local mortuaries to perform post-mortems on coroners' cases, which was the mainstay of his contribution to the partnership's budget.

He had been fortunate in that the coroner who served the area was an old classmate of his in the Welsh National School of Medicine, where they had qualified before the war. Brian Meredith had become a family doctor in Monmouth, but had also obtained the job of coroner for a wide area of the county. The old retired doctor who had previously provided him with a post-mortem service had died and Brian was happy to give his old friend a welcome start in his new venture as a freelance. So at the small public mortuaries at Chepstow and Monmouth, together with locums at the big hospital at Newport and sometimes Hereford, Richard had a few days' regular work each week. During the university terms, he gave lectures on forensic medicine to the undergraduates at the medical school in Bristol, travelling there across the Severn estuary on the ferry between Beachley and Aust. All this, together with occasional work for the police in his role as an accredited Home Office pathologist and some civil and defence work for lawyers over a wide area, allowed the Garth House consultancy to thrive. The rest of the income came from Angela's serology work, mostly blood-group testing in disputed paternity cases, and Sian's chemical analyses, mainly for alcohol in drunk-driving cases and a variety of drugs from coroners' post-mortems.

This peaceful routine was given an injection of new activity by a phone call taken by Moira Davison late one morning. Richard Pryor had just returned from Monmouth and was talking to Jimmy Jenkins in the backyard, inevitably about his precious vines, which appeared to have become leafless and possibly lifeless, as the winter approached.

'Should 'ave waited until the spring, doctor!' growled Jimmy.

'Or planted strawberries instead, like I told you.'

The neat brunette appeared at the back door to break up this oft-repeated argument.

'Doctor Pryor, there's a call for you in the office. A solicitor from Bristol.'

Leaving Jimmy to attach yet another Woodbine to his lower lip, Richard followed Moira back indoors and up the corridor to her office.

'I think he said it's about a murder Appeal,' she whispered excitedly, as she opened the door. She had recently sat in Gloucester Assize Court to listen to her boss giving evidence for the defence in the trial of a veterinary surgeon accused of poisoning his wife and ever since she had been hooked on reading about real-life crimes. As Richard took the receiver, she busied herself with papers at the other side of the room, but her ears were flapping as he spoke. What she heard was not very exciting, just a brief agreement to visit the lawyer in his office next day, but afterwards, Richard took pity on her.

'That was a solicitor from St Paul's in Bristol. He wants a conference with me about an Appeal that's coming up, for a woman who was convicted of murder a year ago.'

Moira looked at him with admiration in her eyes. She had more than a soft spot for her employer; it was verging on hero worship.

'St Paul's? That's a pretty run-down area of Bristol, isn't it? Not far from the city centre.'

Richard gave her one of his impish grins. 'So probably plenty of criminal work for lawyers there! Though for all I know, the appellant might live in a grand mansion on Clifton Down.'

Her brow furrowed in thought. 'Appellant? That's what they call the person who wants to appeal, is it?'

'Yes, though very few succeed. In most cases, the Appeal

is made on the grounds that there was some procedural fault in the original trial or investigation. It's rare for the actual evidence to be challenged at this late stage, but it must be something to do with that or they wouldn't be asking me to look at it.'

'Will the Appeal be in Bristol?' asked Moira hopefully, thinking of another chance to tag along to listen.

He shook his head. 'No, they're all heard in London, at the Court of Criminal Appeal. That's in the Royal Courts of Justice, in the Strand.'

As Richard left the room, she sighed wistfully, aware that there was no chance of going to London with him. That was something reserved for Angela Bray, who had recently accompanied him there in connection with a War Office case that they had been involved in. She went back to the kitchen to wash a salad for the doctors' lunch, feeling vaguely dissatisfied with the way her life was passing so quickly. Though she was eternally grateful for Garth House having lifted her from her chronic depression after the death of her husband, she felt that though having passed thirty, there was still plenty she could achieve – but she had no idea in what direction, though since coming here to work, her interest in the workings of the legal system had increased.

Meanwhile, Richard had gone off to look at the microscope slides made by Sian from the sliver of bone he had taken from the Borth Body. They had taken longer than usual to prepare, as his technician had reported that the 'marble bone' had been very reluctant to soften up sufficiently for it to be cut on her microtome, a device like a very accurate bacon-slicer that could deliver transparently-thin wafers of tissue.

A few glances at the pink slivers on glass slides, together with a quick check in a pathology manual, were enough to confirm that it was indeed Albers-Schonberg disease, with its dense overgrowth of calcium and alteration of the cells in the bone. He made a note about it in the file that they kept on every one of their cases, then leaned back in his chair and pondered what might be the reason for the lawyer from Middleton, Bailey and Bailey wanting to talk to him next day. Then his wandering thoughts drifted to the West Wales coast, as he wondered if any progress was being made with the murder investigation – and whether he would ever hear any more about it.

In Borth that day, the incident room was being closed down, as no one could find any more work for it to do.

In the two weeks since the body was discovered, virtually every house for five miles around had been visited by the police, a substantial task for so few officers. Absolutely nothing had come of these enquiries, which was hardly surprising given the years that had elapsed – especially as the actual number of those years was unknown, other than a vague guess by Richard Pryor that a decade might be a reasonable time-span. Added to this was the lack of any physical description, other than that the victim was of average height and had a tattoo on his right upper arm. Detective Superintendent Paul Vickers had already returned to 'The Smoke', rejoicing at his escape from deepest Cardiganshire and his sergeant was itching to follow him.

'It's a waste of time, I'm afraid,' he said to Meirion, as they gathered up the last of their notes and made for the Wolseley that would take them back to police HQ in Aberystwyth. 'There's nothing I can do here that you can't do better, with local knowledge. I agree with my guv'nor that the answer to this one is miles away from here – not that I think you're ever going to know after all this time.'

As they drove through the rain-soaked countryside, the local DI had to agree with him.

'My gut feeling is that this is a wartime job. All sorts of damn queer things went on then – and in the couple of years after it finished. Lots of blokes knocking about the country in the army, plenty of black-market fiddles and other rackets.'

Howard Squires, happy to be getting back to his home and family in Tooting, was inclined to agree. 'We'll keep in touch and if anything turns up at this end, we can come straight back. But I doubt you'll strike lucky having drawn a total blank so far.'

He was wrong, but it would be some time before this became apparent.

Richard did two post-mortems at the dingy mortuary in the council yard at Chepstow, before going on to Bristol.

One was a sudden death from coronary heart disease, the other more unusual, in that it was a fatal accident on a farm near Caldicot. Farms were dangerous places, mainly due to overturned tractors and falls from barns and hayricks, but this was unusual in that a worker had crawled into the outlet of a grain silo to clear a blockage, when tons of barley had suddenly fallen and suffocated him. Richard drove pensively the couple of miles to the ferry ramp at Beachley, thinking of how death could descend so abruptly even on a peaceful farm, just as harshly as on a battlefield. He never allowed such tragedies that he saw virtually every day to weigh too heavily on his mind, otherwise he would be unable to function. However, he tried to avoid the brashness of some of his colleagues who treated corpses with a boisterous nonchalance that he felt was an overreaction to a gruesome profession. Richard had noticed the same attitude in some mortuary attendants, policemen and even undertakers, who tended to refer to 'stiffs' and 'meat wagons', and talk and laugh with nervous exuberance to compensate for the macabre surroundings.

His pensive mood was lightened by the short voyage across the swirling stretch of the River Severn to Aust, the scenery bright in the mid-morning air, now that last night's rain had stopped. By contrast, as he drove the last few miles into Bristol, he saw again the rapid building activity that was both extending the city's limits and restoring the gaps left by the extensive wartime bomb damage. Some of the new structures were ugly, unimaginative boxes, thrown up quickly and cheaply from designs apparently created by architects who could only draw rectangles with their pencil and ruler.

Richard's destination was St Paul's, an old run-down residential area to the north of the city centre. Last evening's study of a map in his AA road atlas had given him a general idea of where he was headed and a final enquiry through his driver's window of a Jamaican lady pushing a pram, directed him to Grosvenor Road.

Cruising along a row of shops gave him the street numbers and he soon spotted the names of the solicitors in gold paint on the windows above a building-society office. Finding a parking space a few yards further on, he locked the Humber and walked back to a door alongside the shop, where a brass plate declared it to be Middleton, Bailey and Bailey.

The narrow stairs took him to a small reception office, where a cheerful middle-aged woman took him along a corridor to a door which predictably had 'D.G. Bailey LLB' written on it.

Douglas Bailey was unlike many of the rather desiccated, elderly lawyers that Richard had met in market towns in Wales and the West Country. He was what his father might have termed a 'city slicker', a slim man of about forty in a blue pinstripe suit which Richard suspected had shoulder pads. His dark hair was Brylcreemed flat on his head and he had a small Errol Flynn moustache.

However, in spite of this unpromising appearance, Bailey proved to be well spoken, well informed and very much 'on the ball'.

After the usual courtesies and a cup of tea provided by the matronly secretary, they sat each side of a cluttered desk and got down to business.

'I'll just give you an outline of the problem, Doctor Pryor, then let you take the file away to study at your convenience. If then you feel you can assist us, we'll meet again with Counsel to discuss the details.'

When Richard nodded his assent, Douglas Bailey leaned forward on his elbows to tell his tale.

'Our client is a woman, Millicent Wilson, though she went under the surname of her late partner, Arthur Shaw. I say "late", as he's the one who she was convicted of killing.'

'I presume when you say "partner", you mean it in the conjugal sense, rather than a business partner?' asked Richard, thinking of his own relationship with Angela Bray.

'Indeed I do. They lived here in St Paul's – just down the road, in fact – but were not married. She is twenty-seven; he was thirty-nine at the time of his death. They lived in an old terrace house which was divided into a number of flats, though that's a rather grand description for a scruffy collection of rented rooms and bedsits with a communal bathroom and kitchen.'

He gently diverged a finger and thumb across his moustache, as if encouraging it to grow a little more.

'Not to put too fine a point on it, this household was hardly genteel or sophisticated. A couple of the occupants, including Arthur Shaw, were well known to the police and some had done time in prison, mostly for theft, assault and general petty crime.'

'Did that apply to your client as well?' asked Richard.

'She certainly had no convictions, but she may have worked the streets at one time, though not recently. Anyway, this charming character Arthur Shaw used to knock her about regularly, usually when drunk, which again is not all that uncommon in this part of Bristol.'

He paused to drink down the rest of his cup of tea.

'As I said, I won't go into the details until you've read the papers, but in essence, Shaw had knocked her about a bit one evening, then she had gone with a friend to the cinema. He was at home, playing poker with some of the other men in the house. After she came home at about eleven thirty, sounds of a heated quarrel were heard from their rooms upstairs, but that was nothing unusual. She is seen to run out about midnight with a fresh black eye and cut lip, and goes to stay with her sister in the next street. In the morning, Arthur Shaw is found dead in their bedroom with a knife wound in his chest and a kitchen knife on the floor.'

Bailey handed the file across the desk to Richard Pryor.

'She denied killing him, but the prosecution medical evidence claimed that the time of death corresponded to her return to the house. The knife had her fingerprints on it, amongst others, though that meant very little as it was from the communal kitchen. But there were spots of his blood on her sleeve, though she maintained that it got there earlier when she had hit him on the nose with a milk bottle when he was assaulting her.'

Richard tucked the file into his briefcase alongside his chair. 'So she was convicted on mainly circumstantial evidence?'

'Yes, convicted of murder, though the defence tried getting a manslaughter verdict. Not that it's made that much difference, as the judge didn't hand down a death sentence, but commuted it to life imprisonment. I think that was mainly because of all this current political discussion about abolition, though the defence tried to claim that it was because of their mitigation plea of severe provocation by an abusive partner.'

Bailey sniffed to convey his opinion of the previous defence team.

'I have to say that their efforts were not all that energetic. That's why Millie Wilson changed solicitors for this Appeal. I hope we can do a better job for her, though trying to get the Court of Criminal Appeal to overrule one of their precious judges is an uphill struggle. Often, they even refuse to hear new evidence.'

Richard tapped the side of his briefcase containing the file. 'I gather the main issue as far as I'm concerned is the time of death?'

'Yes, she's got a cast-iron alibi when she was in the cinema and another when she got back to her sister's place. It's the half-hour interval in between that's the problem.'

He gave his moustache another few encouraging strokes.

'Also, if there's any mileage in disputing these blood stains, that would be useful.'

'My colleague is very experienced in that area,' Richard assured him. 'She was a senior biologist in the Metropolitan Police Laboratory, so if there's anything to be found, she's the one to find it.'

They spoke for a while longer, the solicitor telling him that the Appeal date had yet to be finalized but would probably be early in the New Year. Promising to send a preliminary report within a week, Richard took his leave and was back in Garth House a couple of hours later, having just missed a ferry at Aust.

Far too late for his lunch, Moira had kept it warm in the Aga and he sat in the kitchen in solitary state to eat his steak-and-kidney pie with mashed potato, followed by apple tart and custard. He had been abroad throughout all the difficult post-war years, so did not fully appreciate the recent improvement in living standards, following a decade of shortages that in some ways had been as severe as the war years themselves. He had missed most of the rationing, the spartan clothing bought on coupons with their E41 economy labels, unbranded 'Pool' petrol and books printed on thin, coarse paper.

As soon as he had finished, Angela, Priscilla and Sian came in to share the coffee that Moira was making and to hear what had happened in Bristol. He gave them a quick rundown of the case as he knew it so far, which was rather sketchy until he had read the case papers. 'So basically, it's an alibi problem. They say she did, she says she didn't!'

Sian, whose left-wing views ran in her family, was always a fiery advocate for the underdog, especially if they were female.

'Typical Establishment stitch-up!' she snapped. 'Some poor woman gets regularly beaten up by some drunken thug and when she cracks and sticks a knife in him, she gets life imprisonment and probably told she's lucky not to have been hanged!'

Richard smiled at her predictably feisty reaction. 'But she says she didn't do it, Sian,' he protested mildly. 'And we're being hired to see if we can prove she didn't.'

Moira put down her coffee percolator. 'I thought the prosecution had to prove guilt, not the defence prove innocence?' she objected.

Angela looked at Richard and both their eyebrows rose.

'We've got a budding lawyer in the house, folks! And you're absolutely right, Moira. But in practice, the two things are not all that distinct, especially in an Appeal. The appellant's lawyers try to torpedo the prosecution's case.'

Priscilla was listening with interest to this dialogue.

'I had a barrister boyfriend a couple of years ago and he used to say that evidence didn't matter much in the Appeal Courts – they were more interested in procedural errors. If the trial judge put a foot wrong, that offered a better chance of succeeding with the Appeal than picking holes in the factual evidence.'

Moira listened intently as the three doctors bandied experiences and hearsay about the rigid legal system. When there was a pause, she declared her fascination with the law. 'I used to be a typist in a solicitor's office, but it's only since I came to Garth House that it seemed to come alive for me. Thank goodness this poor woman in Bristol didn't hang, as she might well have done. I suppose it's all this fuss about Timothy Evans and John Christie that has made them reluctant to carry out the death penalty?'

'Evans came from my home town of Merthyr, poor chap,' said Richard, soberly. 'I see there's a strong movement again to get him a retrospective pardon this year.'

'And push forward the political campaign for abolition of hanging,' said Sian robustly. Timothy Evans had been hanged five years previously for murdering his wife and baby, but John Christie, the serial killer of Rillington Place in Notting Hill, had then confessed to the murders two years ago and caused a national furore about miscarriages of justice. Several major newspaper editors were trying to get the issue raised once again in Parliament, the campaign having been stimulated by the hanging of a woman, Ruth Ellis, earlier in the year.

Richard rose and started back to his office to read the file. 'Better start seeing if we can do anything to help this unfortunate lady – though of course, she might be guilty anyway. We mustn't prejudge these things.'

He winked at Sian as he left.

SEVEN

On the following Saturday afternoon, when Sian had gone home to Chepstow and Moira had returned to her house and little dog just down the road, the three doctors assembled in Angela's sitting room in the front of the house. It was a typical Welsh autumn day outside, a cold drizzle under grey skies, so Richard had no urge to go out and play with his embryonic vineyard on the hillside behind the house.

Instead, he sat with Angela and Priscilla on the old but comfortable three-piece suite that had been Aunt Gladys's pride and joy, to talk about the case that he had brought from Bristol. The main issue was medical, but there was the matter of the blood stains to consider and, in any case, he valued the general forensic acumen of the two women, who between them had a good many years' experience.

Though Priscilla said she would be leaving them at the end of the month to return to London and look for a job, she was happy to join in the discussion. Her digs in Tintern Parva were comfortable enough but she didn't particularly fancy spending a wet Saturday afternoon alone there. Richard had talked about getting a television set for Garth House, but so far nothing had materialized. They had agreed to go up to Monmouth that evening for a meal in one of the hotels, but for now, kicking around a forensic problem seemed the best option.

'I've read through all that file,' he said, pointing at the thick

cardboard folder that lay on the low table in front of them. 'Most
of it is circumstantial stuff and umpteen witness statements, all of
no real interest to us, apart from timings. You're welcome to
dredge though it, but the only two aspects that seem relevant to us
are the time of death and these blood spots on Millie's sleeve.'

'Were the convicted woman and the dead man of different
blood groups?' asked Angela.

'Yes, she was A-Rhesus positive, Shaw was O-positive, both
very common groups. The Home Office lab in Bristol did the
tests, so I doubt we can fault them.'

'How good is the prosecution medical evidence on the time
of death?' asked Priscilla, cutting to the core of the matter.

'In one word, lousy! It's the old story of doctors who think
they are Sherlock Holmes, instead of sticking to what can be
proven. Their pathologist gives the time of death to within limits
of one hour – which conveniently is the same hour in which
Millicent Shaw's alibi fails.'

'Who was he, this doctor?' queried Angela, snug on the settee
with her elegant legs curled under her.

'Anthony Claridge, a hospital pathologist from Gloucester. He
was standing in for the regular chap in Bristol, who was on
holiday.'

'Never heard of him,' said Angela. 'Do you know him,
Richard?'

'I've met him in passing at a meeting of the Forensic Medicine
Society. An old chap, must be about retiring age, I would think.
Seemed a bit full of his own importance.'

He opened the file and took out a couple of pages covered in
his own writing, notes he had made while reading through all
the evidence.

'Doctor Claridge wheels out all the old traditional stuff about
estimating the time since death, most of which is incapable of
proof. But with little better to put in its place, lawyers and judges
are happy to go along with what's in the old textbooks, most of
which just copy from other books and previous editions, without
any critical evaluation of its accuracy.'

Angela smiled at him, rather fondly.

'You always get hot under the collar over this, don't you,
Richard?' she teased. 'I've heard you thumping the table before.

Next, I suppose, you'll be blaming Spilsbury and the other old fossils in your profession!'

Her partner had the grace to look a little sheepish.

'Sorry, but it riles me to hear these chaps pontificate as if what they are claiming is the gospel truth, when it's really only speculation. My motto is, if you can't prove it, don't claim it, especially when someone's neck is at risk!'

'So what have we got as a baseline of fact?' asked Priscilla, still firmly identifying herself as a member of the team even though she was only with them for a short time. Richard tapped his papers with a forefinger.

'Millie Wilson had one of her frequent quarrels with Shaw in the early evening of a Saturday in June last year. Then she cleared off to the pictures with a woman friend at about seven o'clock. Plenty of other witnesses, as well as the friend, to prove where she was until ten thirty, when she arrived back home.'

'Presumably, Arthur Shaw was known to be alive during that time?' asked Angela.

'Absolutely! He was gambling in the kitchen all evening with three others who lived in the house. They all saw her come home at half-past ten. She came into the back room where they were playing poker and said something insulting to Shaw, about the bruising he had earlier caused to her face. They had a short slanging match and she went upstairs to their so-called flat.'

'What happened to the poor woman then?' demanded Priscilla, who, like Sian, was quick to sympathize with another female who was being ill-treated by some aggressive lout.

'Shaw, who had been drinking as usual, became angry and left the game to go upstairs, saying that she needed to be taught a lesson. There was a devil of a rumpus for a time, but as usual, the residents took little notice. Then Millicent came down with a swollen eye and a bleeding cut on her lip. She screamed some abuse back up the stairs and shouted that she was going to her sister's and was never coming back, then ran out of the house. This was at about eleven o'clock, give or take a few minutes, as the other occupants were also probably half-drunk and not too bothered about noticing the exact time.'

'And he was found dead in the morning?' concluded Angela.

'Yes, at seven thirty, by one of the other men in the house,

Don O'Leary. He and Arthur both worked in a car-breaker's yard a few streets away. When Shaw didn't appear at their usual time to go to work, O'Leary went up to wake him, as he knew that Millie wasn't there. He got no answer, but found the door unlocked and Arthur Shaw lying dead on the floor, with a knife wound in his chest. So the times are pretty well established to within minutes.'

'Are there any photographs?' said Priscilla.

Richard went to the back of the file and pulled out two police albums, containing half-plate black and white glossy prints stapled between cardboard covers.

'One is of the scene, the other the post-mortem. Not the greatest pictures, but they give the general idea.'

The two women took an album each, then swapped when they had looked at each photograph.

'Stabbed almost in the middle of the chest,' observed Angela. Richard nodded. 'Got him straight through the right ventricle of the heart.'

'Not much blood about,' said Priscilla, holding up a picture of the victim lying on the floor of an untidy living room.

'It's often the case with a single chest wound, especially if the body lies on its back afterwards. He bled internally, filling the bag around the heart so that it couldn't fill properly.'

'That's what you call a cardiac tamponade, isn't it?' said Angela, showing off some of the knowledge she'd accumulated from many years' experience in London.

'Yes, it wouldn't cause immediate death, but he would have been rapidly disabled and could die within a few minutes.'

'What about this blood on her sleeve?' asked Angela. 'Is this the picture?' She held up the last photograph in the scene album. It was of a pale bolero type jacket, laid out on a table.

'Yes, you can see a few small spots on the outside of the right sleeve, just above the cuff.

The two biologists looked at the photographs again, spending most time on the pictures of the scene, especially ones of the dead man lying on his back on the linoleum in the rather squalid living room, whose sagging furniture was decorated with empty beer bottles and overflowing ashtrays.

'Any blood elsewhere in the flat?' queried Angela.

'Nothing mentioned in the statements. It looks as if he was stabbed at or near the point where he fell. The only other room is the adjacent bedroom and there was nothing of interest found in there. The police searched the rest of the house, but again nothing significant turned up.'

'So how did the pathologist arrive at such a tight estimate of the time of death?' demanded Priscilla.

Richard shrugged. 'Using the old routine – temperature of the body, rigor mortis, post-mortem lividity, amount and state of the stomach contents . . . the same old mumbo-jumbo. Pick some figures from the air, then take away the number you first thought of!'

Angela smiled to herself at his forceful tone. She had heard this particular tirade several times, as time of death was one of Richard's hobby horses.

'So you think you can challenge that for the Appeal?' asked Priscilla.

'Damn right I can – and I will, given the chance!'

The Borth Bog investigation had run completely out of steam by the middle of the following week. There were only a few days left before the December page appeared on Detective Inspector Meirion Thomas's calender, a rather racy one from a local garage, depicting a fluffy blonde wearing more eyeshadow than clothes, sitting provocatively on the bonnet of the new Ford Zephyr Zodiac.

He looked at the dates glumly, thinking that his only murder investigation for the last five years had run into the sand and that its pathetically thin file would soon end up at the back of the bottom drawer of his filing cabinet.

Though he knew it was traditional in detective novels for senior officers and the Chief Constable to come breathing fire down the neck of the failing investigating officer, he had to admit that the two men above him in their small police force had accepted the dead-end philosophically. They had seemed relieved that the two rather supercilious men from Scotland Yard had gone home and that the Press, after a brief frenzy, seemed to have forgotten all about the case. But being a conscientious man, Meirion would have liked to have nailed someone for such a nasty crime. Failing that, it would have at least been satisfying to have identified the body.

With a sigh, he pulled a wad of papers towards him and settled down to devising night-observation rotas for the painfully few men he had available. Sheep rustling had become fashionable again and several irate farmers near Tregaron were demanding some action from the police, backed up by their insurance companies. This issue was of far greater concern to the inhabitants of Cardiganshire than one solitary, if bizarre death that probably occurred long ago.

Yet as he pulled out his Parker 51 pen, the previous year's Christmas present from his wife, the strange force of serendipity was working on someone he knew well, a hundred miles away in Birmingham.

'Not a bad pint, this!' said Gwyn Parry, studying the amber liquid in his glass, pulled from a barrel of Atkinson's Bitter. He was sitting in the snug of the Red Lion in Moseley, a southern suburb of Birmingham. He had been taken there for a pre-lunch drink by his wife's brother-in-law, Tony Cooper. The detective sergeant from Aberystwyth was spending two days' leave in the Midlands, bringing his wife to stay with her sister, who had just come out of hospital after an operation on some obscure part of her female anatomy. He was leaving Bethan there for a couple of weeks to help look after her, as Tony had to work shifts, being a sergeant in the Birmingham City Police. He was not in the CID like Gwyn, but was a custody officer in one of the central police stations.

Their talk was the usual mix of topics always voiced by off-duty policemen – complaints about pay, pensions and conditions of service, mixed with anecdotes of unusual cases they had encountered. They had been joined in the pub by an elderly friend of Tony's who lived nearby, a chain-smoking man in his late sixties with horn-rimmed glasses with lenses like bottle bottoms. Oscar Stanton was a retired journalist from a city newspaper and had a large fund of stories, ranging from the hilarious to the horrific.

Gwyn looked at the bar clock and reckoned that they had time for another round before going back home, where Bethan was making a meal. After that, he was driving back to Wales, to join in the fight against the sheep rustlers. When the drinks were in, their conversation continued and the detective got around to telling them of the curious case of the body in the bog, which seemed to have come to a dead end.

'So we haven't a clue who the fellow is,' he concluded. 'All we've got is a tattoo and a vague guess that he died sometime around ten years ago.'

'Strangled and his head taken off?' said his brother-in-law, shaking his head in disbelief. 'So certainly not some domestic squabble. It sounds like some gangster execution, but you couldn't get one of those in peaceful West Wales, surely!'

Oscar Stanton was looking thoughtful, slowly rubbing his bristly chin. 'Rings a bell, this does,' he said ruminatively. 'I've got this dim recollection of some rumour going around amongst the lads on the paper, way back around the time the war ended.'

The two policemen stared at him. 'What rumour?' asked Tony.

'I can't remember any details. It was a long time ago. But one of the older reporters who covered crime in those days had this yarn about a pub somewhere, where the landlord claimed to have a pickled head in his beer cellar.'

Gwyn Parry looked dubious. 'It could be a wind-up – or maybe some practical joke. I remember hearing about a shrivelled hand being found on the upper deck of a Cardiff bus. Turned out that a medical student had taken it from the college dissecting room.'

Tony was not so sceptical. Maybe after twenty years of policing a big, bad city, he was ready to believe anything. 'Have you any idea if the chap who was telling the story is still around, Oscar?'

'He died a couple of years ago, I'm afraid. But I still have a drink now and then with some of my old mates from the paper. I could ask around and see if anyone remembers the story.'

The Aberystwyth sergeant nodded his thanks. 'We've got damn all to go on at present, so any lead is better than none. Could you let Tony here know if you dig up anything?'

With this appropriate plea, they moved on to Aston Villa's chances at the coming weekend.

*   *   *

Richard Pryor, after a few hours poring over his collection of textbooks and journals, had written a considered appreciation of the possible forensic medical avenues that might assist Millie Wilson's lawyers. He was used to calling them 'the defence', but this was not strictly accurate in this instance, as she was 'the appellant'. The time for defending her was in the past, at the trial held at Bristol Assizes more than a year ago.

His report was carefully typed by Moira Anderson and sent off to the suave Mr Bailey. A couple of days later, he had a phone call asking him to attend a preliminary conference with their junior counsel, Miss Penelope Forbes, in Bristol on the last day of November.

'I think you should come with me, Angela,' he said to his partner. 'These blood spots on the coat are more in your territory than mine.'

This was only partly true, as the interpretation of blood splashes had always been the province of a pathologist, but latterly, the rapid advance of forensic science was burrowing ever more deeply into what formerly had been medical territory. Earlier in the century, there was no separate forensic science worth mentioning, but it rapidly grew away from the grip of the medical men until the tail was wagging the dog.

The thirtieth of November was a Thursday and it saw the black Humber again crossing the river from Beachley aboard the *Severn Queen*, with Angela Bray in the front passenger seat. She had never made this journey before, always travelling eastwards on the A48 through Gloucester to reach her parent's home in Berkshire. She found the short voyage across the dangerously turbulent currents of the estuary fascinating and Richard promised to take her up river one day, to see the famous Severn Bore when there was a high spring tide.

After bumping off the ramp at Aust on the southern bank, they set off for Bristol in the unseasonable November sunshine. Angela was dressed in what she called her 'Old Bailey outfit', a smart, rather severe grey suit with a fashionably long skirt and waist-nipping jacket over a white blouse. Richard, who had only a vague notion about A-lines and H-lines, thought she looked remarkably attractive, with her thick hair marshalled under a small saucer-shaped hat.

As he drove towards the city, his mind idly compared the four women in Garth House. There was Sian, the lively young blonde, full of bustle and energy, quite a contrast to the quiet neatness of Moira Anderson, to whom he often applied the old adage 'still waters run deep'.

Then there was Priscilla, who was undoubtedly gorgeous in a more flamboyant way, with a racier line in clothes and make-up, compared to the restrained elegance of Angela.

He sighed to himself, feeling a little like a boy in a sweet shop without a penny in his pocket. It was just not prudent to start any romantic or ardent relationship within their little forensic family, but it was a long time since he had had any romantic or amorous outlet – in fact, none since leaving Singapore a year earlier. Though his divorce was finalized not all that long before he left, he had been separated from his wayward wife for some time and had not wanted for female company amongst the expatriate community in the Colony.

Before his wandering thoughts developed into fantasies, he found that they were already in the suburbs of Bristol and had to concentrate on navigating through the big city to reach the centre. Most barristers had their chambers in or around Short Street, an aptly named lane in the oldest part of the city, near the remnants of the medieval town wall. The Assize Courts were halfway along the street, providing lawyers with the minimum of exercise to get to their trials. Richard had no chance of parking in Short Street, but eventually found a space not too far away.

'Traffic is becoming impossible in this country,' he grumbled, as he manoeuvred the bulky car into a narrow space. 'I can't imagine what it will be like in fifty years' time!'

'I read that Winston Churchill wanted to pave over Horse Guards Parade and The Mall for parking places,' said Angela, as they got of the car. 'But there is some scheme to fit coin-operated parking clocks in London in the next couple of years.'

They followed the directions given by Douglas Bailey and found the chambers in a narrow alley alongside the court buildings. In the rather dingy entrance, a long hand-painted plaque on the wall gave the names of the resident barristers in pecking order of seniority. A third of the way up, they saw the name of Miss Penelope Forbes, the only woman on the list.

Inside, a stoop-shouldered clerk took them upstairs and along a corridor to a small room, where Miss Forbes had her office. She rose to meet them from behind a paper-strewn desk which filled almost half the room. Douglas Bailey was already there and he pulled forward two hard chairs for them. After introductions and hand shakes, they all sat down, giving Richard time to look at the barrister who would appear for Millie when she assisted her leader, a Queen's Counsel.

Penelope Forbes was a tall, thin woman of about forty-five, with rimless spectacles and prematurely greying hair pulled back into a severe bun on the back of her head. Angela thought she looked very tired, but had a pleasant smile and a pair of sharp blue eyes. She began by thanking Richard for his report, of which she had a copy in front of her, as did the solicitor.

'I've discussed it over the phone to Paul Marchmont, our leading counsel, who said it sounded promising. We'll have to have another conference soon with Paul, of course, but I thought I'd just go through the main points with you today.'

Before they began, Richard explained Angela's presence, as a senior forensic biologist with years of experience at the Metropolitan Police Laboratory.

'Doctor Bray feels that the claim that the blood present on the sleeve came from the stabbing can also be contested.'

The barrister smiled at Angela. 'I look forward to hearing your opinion, Doctor Bray. Before that, perhaps you, Doctor Pryor, could run through a summary of what you feel about the vital time-of-death issue.'

Richard ran his finger through his hair, in a rather nervous gesture that was unusual for him. Angela suspected that he was not used to displaying his professional expertise to a woman, even though he already had a virtual harem back at Garth House.

He was given a respite by the appearance of a secretary bearing a tray of coffee in a motley collection of cups and saucers. While they drank the rather insipid brew, the conversation became more general.

'It's the old story of doctors sticking rigidly to the rules of thumb that they have been taught since they were students,' began Richard. 'I'm not blaming them for having poor methods to work with, for I'm in the same boat. But the problem lies in the dogmatism and stubbornness which many doctors have. I've got no better methods myself, but at least I am always willing to qualify the results with an acknowledgement that they are very approximate and prone to large errors.'

Penelope Forbes smiled again, a habit which seemed to come easily to her.

'Do I detect an allusion to the great Sir Bernard Spilsbury there? But I agree, I often come across such witnesses. Do you feel it's a fault especially with the older experts? The one in this case is certainly getting on in years.'

Richard agreed, with reservations. 'It's not just because they're old, in the sense of being doddery old fools. I think it's more because with years of practice behind them, they feel too sure of themselves – the "I've seen it all before" syndrome.'

Angela joined in the discussion for the first time. 'Doctor Pryor is right, I've seen experts steamrolling their way through their evidence, stubbornly refusing to accept any sensible contrary opinion.'

Richard hid a grin, as he detected a trace of bitterness in his partner's voice. He felt that in the past, she must have had a couple of frustrating contests with other experts.

'Yes, the harder they are challenged, the harder they dig their heels in and refuse to admit that they could be wrong,' he confirmed. 'It's often a matter of professional pride, and I'm afraid forensic medicine tends to attract the prima donnas of the profession, those who like to see their names in the newspapers.'

Having finished his rather insipid cup of Maxwell House, Richard got back to business.

'With the time-of-death issue, there are four aspects to consider – and, indeed, challenge. The first is rigor mortis, so beloved of crime novelists. Then there's post-mortem lividity, the discoloration of the skin after death. The next is stomach contents and the last, the only one with any hope of giving a decent estimate, is the body temperature.'

The solicitor asked the first question. 'How many of those can you challenge, doctor?'

'All of them, I hope. At least, what I can challenge is Doctor Claridge's interpretation of them. His confidence in his accuracy is completely unfounded and I suspect it was coloured by what the police told him of the circumstances.'

He began going through the items, one by one, keeping the explanation rather superficial, as he knew he would have to do it all again in more detail when they met the 'silk' – a lawyer's name for a Queen's Counsel, because of the gown he wore.

'The easiest one to contradict is post-mortem lividity, or "death staining" as it used to be called. In fact, the modern name is hypostasis, not that a new name makes it any more useful.'

'I see Claridge doesn't actually claim that this lividity points to the one-hour time window that's relevant?' Miss Forbes pointed out.

'No, he just says it's consistent with that time of death. What he doesn't say – and the defence didn't ask him – was that it would also be consistent with death far outside that time bracket. And that's the situation with the other criteria. They could all be correct, but they could also be hopelessly wrong.'

Miss Forbes seemed intent on being a devil's advocate, as well as one for Millie Wilson – which was quite right, as the opposition would be asking the same questions of Doctor Pryor.

'But Doctor Claridge said in his evidence that he took all those criteria into account together, in coming to his conclusion as to the time of death.'

Richard's laugh was a sardonic bark. 'Adding four lousy methods together still makes one lousy conclusion,' he replied. 'The answer doesn't get better by its multiplicity.'

'So that applies to rigor mortis as well, I presume?' asked the solicitor.

'Rigor is marginally better than lividity, but that's not saying much. Claridge saw the body in the mortuary; he wasn't even called to the scene. It had been dead since sometime the previous night when he examined it at two o'clock in the afternoon. There's no chance of pinning the time of death to within an hour after that delay.'

'You said that temperature is the best means of timing the death, doctor,' said Penelope Forbes. 'The pathologist here seemed to rely most heavily on that.'

Richard Pryor shrugged in dismissal. 'It could have helped a lot more, but the whole examination was poorly carried out. No one thought of taking the temperature at the scene, when the body was found. It was almost another seven hours before the temperature of the body was measured. The body was never weighed in the mortuary, so we don't know what his body mass was, which affects the cooling rate.'

Angela smiled at her partner, who was getting more voluble as he argued his case, gesturing with his hands, his unruly brown hair tossing about.

'So you've rubbished three of his criteria! What about the state of his stomach contents?'

Richard subsided a little, but shook his head dismissively. 'Another fairy tale, if you're looking for accuracy. There are so many variables, there's not a chance of settling on the true time many hours later. When I was in Singapore, I did a little research on this, in cases where it was known what time the dead person last ate. Comparing that time with what was in the stomach was too random to be of any use in evidence – and certainly not beyond reasonable doubt!'

For another half-hour they bandied the matter around, Richard giving his reasons why he felt it impossible to restrict the time of death to the time when Millie was back in the house in St Paul's.

'Of course she could have killed him in that half-hour, there's no denying that,' he said in conclusion. 'But equally, he could have died in the many hours after she left the house – and this medical evidence is so nebulous that it can't exclude that possibility.'

The junior counsel nodded her understanding of his argument and repeated what Moira had said back in Tintern.

'Of course, it's not up to the defence to prove that a person didn't commit an offence. The onus is on the prosecution to prove they did!' She sighed. 'But often it doesn't seem to work that way with juries. Especially when there's such a poor defence effort – they didn't even call any medical witness to try to challenge what Doctor Claridge was saying. I think they felt this was such an obvious case that it wasn't worth putting themselves to much trouble.'

Miss Forbes turned over a few pages in her file.

'It's fortunate that the plea in mitigation impressed the judge, over the assaults which Millie suffered from Arthur Shaw, especially during that fateful hour – otherwise she would have been hanged by now, instead of getting life imprisonment.'

She turned to Angela. 'Now, Doctor Bray, tell me about these bloodstains.'

EIGHT

O scar Stanton turned into the Crown Hotel, on the corner of Station Street in central Birmingham. It was near New Street Station and was convenient for those of his friends who travelled in from the suburbs for their regular dose of nostalgia. About eight retired reporters met for a few pints on the last Friday of the month, chewing over old times and reporting who amongst the newspaper fraternity of the city was sick or dead since the last session. They used an alcove off the main lounge, where a large table was covered in their glasses, half-eaten ham rolls, overflowing ashtrays and packets of crisps. Around their fourth pint or double Scotch, Oscar turned his pebble lenses on to the man sitting next to him.

'Brian, I was talking to a chap the other day, he's a CID man from Wales. He was telling me about some old corpse they'd dug up there recently, one without a head. It reminded me of that yarn that Piggy Donovan used to trot out years ago, about some pub that was alleged to have a bloke's head hidden in a pot.'

The old reporter, ten years senior to Oscar, took a long swallow from his tankard before answering.

'I vaguely remember something about it, soon after the war. But Piggy was such a lush, you couldn't depend on half he said – or what he wrote in his copy!'

'He's been dead these past five years, has Piggy,' said Oscar. 'Anybody else who might recall anything about it?'

Brian used a slight lull in the conversation around the big table to call across to a member on the other side.

'Duncan, you're the last one here to cover crime on the *Post*.

Ever hear a yarn about some preserved head kept in one of the pubs?'

Duncan MacKenzie was a few years younger and only recently retired from the *Birmingham Post*, the city's major newspaper. A thin man with an aristocratic goatee sticking out from his chin like a spike, he was a hard drinker, his lined face displaying many prominent veins, even more marked on his nose. He considered the question carefully, before replying.

'That story was going the rounds many years ago, I remember. Some connection with the gangs up in Winson Green. The coppers looked into it, but nothing more came of it.'

Another man, well into his seventies, spoke up from Oscar's left. 'I remember that, too. Piggy Donovan was carrying on about it. He said he was going to write a piece as a feature, then he suddenly went quiet. I think he'd been got at by someone.'

'You reckon it was up in Winson Green?' asked Oscar, hopefully. To his surprise, the old man nodded.

'Yes, he reckoned it was in the cellar of the Barley Mow, near Black Patch Park. A tough area, especially in those days.'

'It's pretty tough still,' said Duncan MacKenzie. 'But the Barley Mow has long gone. They demolished that part a few years back – and not before time.'

Oscar felt let down, as it had looked hopeful when some of the others had confirmed the rumour. 'Any idea what it was all about? Did anyone you know actually see this thing?'

There were grimaces and shaking of heads, but no hard information.

'Something to do with the gangs in that area,' ventured MacKenzie. 'During the war, there was all sorts of graft going on there, apart from the usual robbery and violence. Black-market dealing, mainly, on a wholesale basis. And plenty of bribery and corruption – the police and the council were accused of it every now and then.'

It was soon obvious that no one had any better information about a shrivelled head. It was just part of the city's underworld lore that came the way of newspaper men.

That evening, when he got home to Moseley, Oscar phoned his friend Tony Cooper and told him the little he had learned about the fabled head.

'The only possible lead was that the Barley Mow in Winson Green seems to be the place where the story originated. But that pub's been demolished long since.'

Sergeant Cooper was more impressed than Oscar had expected.

'Winson Green! That's the sort of place you might expect something like this. I'll mention it to our CID boys, but they might need an armoured car to go asking questions up there!'

There were a number of very tough places in and around the great city of Birmingham, but Winson Green was up there near the top of the list and had been even worse ten years earlier, at the end of the war. Birmingham's huge prison was in Winson Green and it was a stock joke that it was built there so that all the local villains did not have so far to travel when they were banged up.

After Oscar had rung off, Tony decided that before making enquiries through his own Force contacts, he had better speak to Gwyn Parry. He was due to come up for a day at the end of the week to collect his wife, Bethan, who had done a splendid job in getting his own wife back on her feet. However, he decided to give him a ring and a few moments later was put through to Gwyn at his home at Temple Bar, just outside Aberystwyth.

Bethan came in at the same time and he surrendered the phone to her for a few minutes. When she had finished her anxious enquiries about the children, who were enjoying themselves at their grandmother's house, Tony gave Gwyn the few scraps of information he had picked up that day from his newspaper cronies.

'There seems to be some substance in that rumour about a head,' he told him. 'Even down to where it was supposed to be kept, though the place has since been pulled down. Though why it should be linked in any way to your headless corpse, I can't imagine!'

He could almost hear Gwyn's brain working at the other end of the line. 'You say your pals suggested this might be linked to possible gang squabbles up there?'

'That area is one of the places where there used to be a lot of that sort of trouble. Still is, comes to that.'

'I'm not surprised,' retorted Gwyn with feeling. 'These bloody sheep rustlers and a lot of organized country-house burglaries are down to your Midland villains.'

'Do you want me to have a word with our CID, to see if they can make a few enquiries?' asked Tony.

Gwyn chewed it over in his mind for a moment. 'I'd better talk to my DI first and see whether he thinks it's worth bothering your lot with it. We've still got the Yard involved, though they got fed up and buggered off back to London. I'll let you know when I come to fetch Bethan on Saturday.'

As December had arrived, Priscilla's time was up as Angela's locum and she was leaving on Sunday to go back to London to look for a job. Richard Pryor would have liked to have kept her on at Garth House, but they both knew that there was not sufficient work there for two biologists. She was going back to stay with a friend again until something turned up.

'Farewell party on Saturday evening, then!' Richard had declared. He treated them all, including Moira and Jimmy Jenkins, to a meal at the large hotel in Tintern Parva, opposite the ruins of the huge Cistercian abbey. Afterwards they came back to the house and sat until midnight in the staff room, with the table well supplied with Lutomer Riesling, Mateus Rose, whisky, gin, beer and cider for Jimmy.

Well fed and relaxed, the conversation roamed over a variety of topics from growing vines to headless corpses.

The Borth Body was naturally prominent in their gossip, especially as it was the one case where Priscilla had been so useful in confirming the physical dimensions from the bones.

'The investigation seems to have come to a dead end,' said Richard. 'I had a call from the DI this week, saying that unless something turns up, the coroner wants to hold an inquest to get the paperwork tidied up.'

'I hear the Yard have gone back to the big city,' added Angela, with a tinge of relief in her voice. Richard guessed she was afraid that Paul Vickers might have shown his face here if the investigation had proceeded any further.

'A pity we'll never know how it got there,' said Priscilla

pensively. 'I wonder how many bodies there are knocking about the countryside which will never be found?'

'You archaeologists dig up far more than we pathologists ever see,' chided Richard. 'Are you still keen on going back to your digging, rather than forensic work?'

The glamorous redhead nodded. 'I had enough of that in Australia. Those couple of short digs I went on before I came here made me realize that was what I really wanted to do.' She looked despondent. 'But when – or even whether – I'll get the chance again, I just don't know.'

'Something will turn up!' said Angela reassuringly. 'You're too good a scientist to go to waste.'

Moira, who had had three glasses of wine, had shed some of her usual reserve. 'You're bound to be fine, Doctor Chambers! A couple of college degrees and bags of experience. I only wish I had had the chance to go to university, instead of just a secretarial college!'

'It's never too late, Moira,' said Angela encouragingly. 'These days there are part-time courses and grants for mature students.'

'Hey, hang on!' called Richard, in mock outrage. 'That's our wonderful secretary and chef you're trying to get rid of!'

Moira smiled a little sadly. 'Just a pipe dream, Doctor Pryor.'

He shook his head vehemently. 'Nonsense! We'll make some enquiries next week and see what part-time courses are around. You could have day release in the week like Sian here, then maybe later you'll want to go full-time.'

Jimmy stepped in to lighten the mood. Though he still wore his old poke cap, tonight he was wearing a baggy tweed jacket and a stringy tie for the occasion.

'I ain't going to no college, doctor!' he said stoutly. 'I already done fifty years in the university of life! And learned a lot about growing strawberries, not them old grapes!'

Richard was the constant butt of good-natured teasing about his desire for a vineyard on the acres behind Garth House. Though Jimmy, an inveterate cynic, was always scornful of the project, he had still worked hard to get the vines planted and now seemed resigned to 'the doctor' making a success of it.

'You wants some proper advice about it, doctor,' he proclaimed, over his third pint of local cider. 'Otherwise you'll fall flat on your face.'

And where am I going to get that, Jimmy?' enquired his boss. 'I've read umpteen books on viniculture, what more do I need?'

'You can read a dozen books on riding a bicycle, but that don't help you when you first gets on one!' retorted the grizzled old gardener. 'A pal o' mine down in Cowbridge does some hedgin' and ditchin' for a fellow nearby who has got about five acres of vines and has been making booze there for a couple of years. I reckon he'd let you go down there and have a look round and a chat if you got in touch.'

'Don't encourage him, Jimmy!' complained Angela. 'Or he'll end up closing our forensic business and going bankrupt trying to market Chateau Merthyr Tydfil or something!'

Her partner made a face at her and went into a huddle with Jimmy to get more details of this alcoholic Garden of Eden down in the Vale of Glamorgan. The time went on and eventually the party broke up, Richard taking the Humber down the valley to drop off Moira at her house and Priscilla at her lodgings, before taking Sian the five miles down to Chepstow, as the last bus had long gone.

When he got back, Angela had just finished washing up glasses in the kitchen and was on her way to bed.

'Thanks for the celebration, Richard,' she said warmly, as they walked up the corridor. 'It was good of you to give Priscilla a nice send-off. I know she's worried about her job prospects. She says she's got some savings tucked away, but they won't last long in London.'

'Perhaps she ought to look for a temporary place in one of the forensic departments there, even though she says she wants to go back to digging holes in the ground. I could have a word with someone in Guy's, or St George's or The London Hospital.'

Angela smiled affectionately at him as she moved to the foot of the stairs.

'You're a real Good Samaritan, aren't you? You've fixed up Sian to become a biochemist, you're encouraging Moira to become a lawyer and now you're going to get a job for Priscilla! What are you going to do for me, eh?'

She gave him a quick peck on the cheek and hurried up the stairs, leaving him thoughtfully touching his face as he contemplated the possible answers to her question.

NINE

Gwyn Parry sat in his detective inspector's office upstairs in the police headquarters on the promenade in Aberystwyth. Though a small room, its one window had a striking view across the beach and Cardigan Bay, from which sometimes Gwyn imagined he could see the Wicklow Mountains across the Irish Sea.

He was waiting for Meirion Thomas to finish his phone call, which he had made after the sergeant had told him what he had heard from Birmingham. The DI seemed more impressed with the rumour than he had expected, but being a cautious man, he kept to the old police principle of keeping his backside covered in case it was kicked by his senior officers. He had phoned the Deputy Chief and was speaking to him now.

From the rapid-fire conversation in Welsh, Gwyn gathered that the DCC was in favour of pursuing the matter and this was confirmed when Meirion put the phone down and picked up his 1953 Coronation mug of strong tea.

'Davy John says to go ahead with it, at least as far as asking the Birmingham City Police to see if there is any substance in this yarn. He suggests going through your brother-in-law to find out who is the best person to approach, then if it firms up, we'll have to make an official request for help.'

The detective sergeant nodded as he cradled his own dose of Typhoo Tips, in a cup inscribed 'A Present from Tenby'.

'Do you think there could be a connection?' he grunted. 'It sounds damned far-fetched to me. It's a hundred miles between Borth and Birmingham – and the trail would have been cold for at least ten years.'

Meirion shrugged as he looked out of the window at a lobster boat half a mile out at sea.

'We've got nothing else, boy! If B'rum will have a sniff around for us, we've got nothing to lose.'

'What about those two clever dicks from the Met?' muttered Gwyn. 'Will they have to come back in on the act?'

'Now fair play, Gwyn!' replied the DI placatingly. 'They did what they could, even if it was damn-all. Let's just wait and see if anything turns up, shall we?'

On Monday, Tony Cooper was on an early shift at the police station in Steelhouse Lane in the central part of the city, near the courts and hospitals. His wife's brother-in-law had come up over the weekend and told him of the blessing that the Cardiganshire Force had given to a discreet snoop around to see if there was any credibility in the legend of the mysterious head.

When his next refreshment break came, he went up to the canteen and, after a plate of bacon, egg and baked beans, took his tea over to another table where a detective sergeant he had known for years was sitting. He told him the story and asked him if he had any ideas about how to take this forward.

'If there's even a sniff of truth in this, then it'll become official,' he explained. 'But the Welsh chaps don't want to raise a fuss if there's nothing in it.'

His colleague had never heard anything of a trophy head, but offered to enquire amongst other CID men, once again lengthening the chain of investigation.

'I've always been either in the city or out east,' he admitted. 'But someone up in the Winson Green or Handsworth Manors might know something.'

He was as good as his word and next day, several plain-clothes officers in the older suburbs to the north-west of the city centre were asking questions of both their older colleagues and some members of the public. They were not going far from their normal routine to do this, but a natural curiosity, plus the not-unwelcome task of going into a few more pubs than usual, helped to spread the word quite effectively.

One of the older constables in Handsworth claimed that he had heard the same rumour many years before, probably soon after VE Day in 1945, but could recall none of the details nor whether it had ever been followed up. A day later, the best information came through a detective sergeant in the same area, who had occasion to meet one of his grasses, a local petty thief who in return for a few pounds and a relaxed attitude to some minor offences supplied him with snippets of news about local burglaries and the activities of worse villains than himself.

They met in a greasy spoon café at the end of one of the long streets of terraced houses, some of which still carried gaps like missing teeth, where Luftwaffe bomb damage had yet to be repaired. After the furtive-looking man in a stained war-surplus greatcoat had passed on this week's trivial criminal intelligence, the DS casually broached the subject of pickled heads.

'Ever heard of anything like that, Sweeny?' he asked innocently. The unshaven man opposite looked at him suspiciously, as he took a bent cigarette from a battered tin.

'What you wanna' know that fer? Going back donkey's years, that is!'

'Just some rumour going round the station that one of the old fellers claimed he'd heard. Said it was supposed to be in some pub around here.'

Sweeny, whose nickname inevitably came from his surname of Todd, looked uneasily around the single room of the café, empty but for the fat woman dozing behind the counter.

'Any money in it for the info?' he muttered.

'Ach, come on, man!' retorted the detective. 'This is a bit of local history, not jail bait.'

Sweeny pushed aside a dribbling bottle of HP sauce and leaned across the oilcloth on the table.

'I never saw it meself, but there's no doubt there were one in the Barley Mow, down Winson way. Years ago, that was, when Olly Franklin were the landlord.'

'If you never saw it, how d'you know it was there?' objected the detective.

'Anybody who knocked about with the gangs knew that!' replied Sweeny, scornfully. 'That's why the bloody thing was kept, wann' it?'

'I don't follow you,' said the sergeant. 'Are you having me on?'

The sallow face looked at him pityingly. 'It was a frightener, wann' it? I wasn't long out of the army then, but I soon learned that there were different gangs around here, real nasty bastards they were, too. I dunno who this bloke was, but he musta' done something that really pissed off Mickey Doyle, 'cause he had him wasted and then kept his head as a warning to others.'

Sweeny suddenly seemed to realize that he had said too much and stood up abruptly.

'You didn't hear nothing of this from me, mind!' he warned. 'I don't want to get mixed up with Doyle and end up with my own head in a bloody bucket!'

With that, he slouched off to the door and vanished into the street.

When Sweeny's information went back along the chain of police officers to reach Aberystwyth, David John Jones had no hesitation in rapidly turning it around again.

He phoned the Assistant Chief Constable (Crime) in Birmingham and explained the situation, being careful to take responsibility for initiating the informal snooping, to avoid making problems for the Birmingham officers.

'I thought the whole scenario was so unlikely that I didn't want to waste your time with a lot of nonsense,' he said with all the cunning of a Cardiganshire man. 'But now that we have heard several different mentions of this damned head, I thought we might put it on an official footing.'

He went on to tell his opposite number that the Yard were also involved and got the usual reaction.

'Let's make some more enquiries up here before we wheel them back in,' suggested the ACC. 'This man you mentioned, Micky Doyle, is well known to us. A villain of the first water, though he somehow manages to keep out of jail.'

'What could possibly be the connection between a body hidden down here and the rest of him being up there with you?' asked Davy John. 'Is this suggested gang connection feasible?'

'I came down here from Manchester, so I'll believe anything about gang warfare,' said the Birmingham officer. 'Anyway, I'll get some men on to it and get back to you.'

With a promise to mail the whole file on the 'Body in the

Bog' to him, David Jones rang off and sat back to ponder on when – or even, whether – to tell New Scotland Yard about this potential new development.

TEN

G
arth House seemed emptier without the colourful and vivacious figure of Priscilla Chambers decorating it. Even Moira, who originally viewed her arrival with more than a tinge of jealousy, missed her attractive personality and cheerful manner.

'Let's hope Priscilla gets a job she likes pretty soon,' she said to Sian, as the technician brought in some results for typing. 'She seemed so keen on going back to her old bones.'

'I thought that perhaps she and Richard might have got something going between them,' said the ever-romantic Sian. 'Especially as nothing of the sort seems to be developing elsewhere!'

She said the last part in a stage whisper, though Richard was at Hereford mortuary and Angela was in her front sitting-room, reading a newly arrived copy of the Journal of Forensic Sciences from America.

Moira failed to respond to Sian's comment, as although she knew it was a ridiculous fantasy, she had her own dreams about Richard Glanville Pryor. To change the subject, she told Sian about a phone message she had just received.

'They want another conference in Bristol over this Appeal,' she announced. 'The QC is coming down from London for it, so Richard and Angela will have to make another trip across the river.' She sighed heavily. 'I wish I knew more about the law. The more I see of it here, the more I want to learn. It seems far more interesting from this angle than all that dull stuff about probate and conveyancing that I used to type when I worked in a solicitor's office.'

Sian was upbeat about Moira's ambition. 'I'm sure Richard will help you. He promised he would and he never breaks his word. In fact, I heard him telling Angela only yesterday that he would have a word with his friend the Monmouth coroner, as his brother is a barrister.'

Encouraged by this, Moira began banging her typewriter with new enthusiasm, contented that her hero was still thinking of her well-being.

Christmas was now only a few weeks away and Angela was planning to have a few days at home over the holiday. She was still concerned about her mother, though she was recovering well from her slight stroke. Angela drove back to see her at their stud farm every weekend, just as Richard went quite often to visit his parents in Merthyr Tydfil. He could rely on being well fed there, instead of staying in lonely isolation at Garth House. Moira always made lunch for him on Saturdays, but Sunday was down to his own efforts, unless he went out somewhere to eat.

The message about the case conference with leading counsel also carried the news that the Appeal had been listed for early January, so Richard had resolved to go soon to the libraries of the medical schools in Bristol and Cardiff . He wanted to check that he had read everything available about the estimation of the time of death, so that he could not be wrong-footed if it came to a contest in court. He had just read an important article that had been published earlier in the year, originating from Ceylon, but wanted to make sure that nothing even more recent had slipped past his notice. Richard knew that Doctor Angus Mackintyre was one of the dogmatic old school of 'It is so, because I say so' philosophy, but he did not want the opposition to find even one chink in his own argument. Even if not relevant to the issue, he knew that once an expert witness is shown to have a weakness, it can be used to denigrate the rest of his evidence.

. However, he was distracted a little when, the next day, he was waylaid by Jimmy in the backyard, who told him that his crony who sometimes worked in the Glamorgan vineyard had spoken to his boss there about Richard's interest in establishing a similar project. The owner, Mr Louis Dumas, said that he would be happy to show Doctor Pryor around his estate and Jimmy had brought a crumpled piece of paper with a telephone number and an invitation to arrange a meeting. Richard was delighted, as his volatile imagination saw him soon being admitted into the arcane brotherhood of vintners. He phoned that evening and made an appointment to go down to visit Monsieur Dumas on Saturday of the following week – he already mentally applied the French title to him, after hearing the slight but definite Gallic accent over the telephone. When he told Angela later, she could not resist teasing him in her quiet way.

'Monsieur Dumas, no less! I suppose we'll end up having to call you the Count of Monte Cristo!'

She was not to know that this new contact was to lead to something more complicated than just growing grapes.

After the ACC in Birmingham had spoken to David Jones and agreed to launch an investigation into the missing head, he discussed it with his Head of CID, a chief superintendent, who next day called the DCI for the Division in which Winson Green and Handsworth were situated. The order trickled down this chain of command until it reached those officers who would actually have to do the work.

A copy of the slim file on the headless body arrived from Aberystwyth and eventually landed on the desk of a harassed inspector at the police station in Foundry Road.

Trevor Hartnell was an experienced detective, but had only been in this division for about three years and had never heard of this elusive head. However, the name Micky Doyle was well known to him as one of the local gangsters who was slippery enough never to have been successfully prosecuted.

Hartnell called his sergeant and four detective constables into his cubicle in the dreary CID room and explained the situation to them.

'The brass in headquarters want us either to find this bloody cranium or prove it's all a fairy story. The best lead we've got is what this snout in Handsworth said, about it being in the old Barley Mow.'

His sergeant, a burly bruiser named Tom Rickman, stroked the jowls under his chin.

'That's long gone, for a start. The Co-op have built a shop on it now.'

'Have you ever heard of this yarn, Tom?' asked the DI.

Rickman was dismissive. 'Yeah, but it's just a bit of the daft gossip that gets dredged up now and then, when folks have a few too many pints.'

One of the younger DCs had been scanning a copy of the file, updated with local information. 'That grass over in Handsworth mentioned the landlord of that pub, guv'nor. That seems fairly definite, doesn't it?'

The inspector nodded.

'That's what you lot have got to follow up. Find this landlord, if he's still around. Ask anyone you can think of, if they've any knowledge of this whole business. The chief super is keen to get this sorted, as he says he's got the ACC on his back.'

After a few more minutes discussing shift rotas and other bits of housekeeping, the team broke up and went their various ways, Tom Rickman heading straight for the place where the demolished pub had once stood.

His tall, broad figure strode along the depressing streets of the area, where rows of shabby red-brick houses were interspersed with small workshops and warehouses. Many of the faces he passed were West Indian, who were coming in increasing numbers to work in the factories.

A few Asians were beginning to appear as well and Rickman, born and bred in Birmingham, wondered what it would be like here in thirty years' time.

He strode on, his creased fawn raincoat belted tightly around his beer belly, a brown trilby pulled down to his prominent ears. On a corner just ahead, he saw the magic word 'Co-op' in large letters above the door of a shop. On each side, running up for fifty yards into each side street, were some new utilitarian maisonettes, the whole development built on ground once occupied by the old public house.

The detective sergeant stood on the opposite corner for a few moments, looking across as if he was looking into the past when the Barley Mow was still there. He remembered it as it was five years earlier, though by then it was well past its prime. He recalled its windows being boarded up before the bulldozers came to flatten it, together with an acre of adjacent terraced houses, making way for this cheap and nasty new development. No doubt a few brown envelopes had changed hands to ease planning permission, he thought cynically.

Crossing the road, narrowly being missed by an almost silent electric milk-float that came around the corner, he went into the shop, which was one of the new breed of self-service places that were springing up. A Caribbean girl was stacking bottles of Camp Coffee on a shelf and he asked her where he could find the manager. She pointed to a raised cubicle with glass windows looking down on the single till, where another girl was checking items produced from a wire basket by a customer.

Rickman went up a couple of steps and after tapping perfunctorily on the door he went in to find a middle-aged man in a brown warehouse coat peering suspiciously down at the transaction at the till down below.

'Got to keep an eye on them,' he muttered obscurely, as he turned to meet the visitor. The sergeant identified himself, but made no effort to show his warrant card, his usual practice unless challenged.

'Have you been here since this place opened, sir?' he asked. Like many people questioned by a policeman, the manager looked anxious, wondering which of his minor indiscretions was being probed. However, after he had admitted to being there since the place opened two years earlier, he was relieved to hear that the sergeant's interest was in the previous building.

'I remember the Barley Mow well,' he admitted. 'A damned rough place. I never drank there, even though I've lived within half a mile of it all my life. What's all this about, Officer?'

'Just routine enquiries, sir. Tell me, what happened to the cellars of the old pub? Are they still under the shop?'

The man shook his bald head. 'No, they filled them in with all the rubble they had from knocking it down. This is the only floor we've got, as there's a new storeroom built on behind.'

That's one line of enquiry knocked on the head, thought Rickman, recalling the mention of the elusive head being kept in the cellar. 'What about the last landlord, is he still around – or even still alive?' he asked.

This time, the manager's head wagged up and down.

'Olly Franklin? The brewery gave him another tenancy when he lost this one. I don't know where he went. It's a wonder he got another pub, though.'

'Why d'you say that?'

The man shrugged and made a face. 'It was such a dodgy place, the Mow! Some right nasty bastards used to drink there. Everyone knew they were fencing stolen goods – and in the war, a lot of black-market stuff used to be handled there. I don't remember that far back, I only got demobbed in 'forty-seven. But Olly had a bad reputation, as he was hand in glove with the gangs.'

The detective pondered this. If the pub had had such a bad reputation, it must have been well known to the police at that time. There should be records of what went on there, but Rickman was cautious, as if there was any signs of 'the blind-eye act' being operated by the police, he didn't want to be the one to open that particular can of worms.

He left the Co-op and went about his other business for the day, as there was plenty of crime to occupy him. At the end of his shift, he went to the DI's cubbyhole and found him still there, wading through the inevitable paperwork.

'Nothing at all left of the pub, guv'nor. The cellars are filled in, so there'll be no head to find, unless it's buried. And you'll have to demolish the Co-op for that!'

Trevor Hartnell sighed; he had enough work on his plate already.

'This landlord, Olly Franklin. Nothing known about his where-abouts, is there?'

The grizzled sergeant turned up his palms. 'Nothing, but I suppose a search of the electoral roll or the licensing authority might flush him out.'

He hesitated, but then took the plunge. 'What about our own records from a few years ago? I got the impression that the Barley Mow was a hang-out for real villains, so surely this station must have some dealings with it?'

Trevor Hartnell thought he caught a wink from Rickman's eye and he knew what was being suggested. Both of them were in other Divisions until a few years ago and were clear of any dubious goings-on before then.

'I'll get someone to go through Records to see if the place crops up. I doubt any pocketbooks will have survived from the end of the war, but you never know.'

Two days later, the DI held another morning briefing with his men. The youngest – and brightest – detective constable had been to police headquarters and trawled through the records for their Division for the latter years of the war and the first few after VE Day.

'Nothing very serious involving the Barley Mow, sir,' he reported. 'Quite a few attendances for drunk and disorderly conduct and a couple for riotous behaviour in the pub. A few people were nicked for possessing stolen property and some black-market prosecutions as well – but they weren't actually offences in the Barley Mow, they were folk who claimed that they had bought the stuff there, but no evidence brought to substantiate it.'

'Any sign of the ex-landlord, this Olly Franklin?' asked the inspector.

Another constable put his hand up. 'I found an address, sir. I checked with the licensing people first. Franklin went from the Barley Mow to the White Rose in Smethwick for a bit, but it looks as if the brewery that owned them gave him marching orders about two years ago.'

'So where is he now?

'He's not listed as a licensee any more. I went to the electoral roll and the Rating Authority and found he's registered as residing at 186 Markby Road.'

'That's right in Winson Green,' said Rickman. 'D'you want me to pay him a call, guv?'

'I think we'd both better go, Tom,' replied the DI.

ELEVEN

The weather had turned very cold by the time Richard Pryor and Angela were due to go to Bristol for another conference about Millicent Wilson. As they drove down the lower part of the deep Wye Valley to Chepstow, the leafless trees looked black, except for a rime of frost on the upper branches. Richard was glad of an efficient heater in the Humber, which was still a novelty for him, as his Austin A70 in Singapore would have needed a heater like the proverbial hole in the head.

Under a grey sky which threatened snow, they made the now familiar ferry crossing over the Severn on a choppy tide the colour of lead, then across a frozen countryside towards Bristol. This was the first really cold weather Richard had experienced since returning from the Far East, and he was glad that the women in his life had recently persuaded him to buy an overcoat. He had returned from Singapore with a selection of locally-made linen suits, which Angela, Sian and Moira had privately decided made him look like Stewart Granger in one of his safari films. They had browbeaten him into getting a couple of more sober suits, better adapted to the British climate, for which he was now grateful.

This morning, Angela was even better equipped for the frost, as over her slimline business suit she wore a dark beaver lamb coat, with a matching fur hat. As she sat snugly in the passenger seat beside him, Richard thought she looked cuddly, an image which sustained him for the rest of the drive into St Paul's.

When they arrived at the unprepossessing offices of Middleton, Bailey and Bailey, they found Penelope Forbes and Douglas Bailey already there, together with their 'silk', Paul Marchmont. He was younger than Richard had expected, probably just a couple of years older than himself. Instead of the portly, silver-haired orator that was the stage concept of a QC, Marchmont was tall and wiry, with an unruly mane of black hair which he kept flinging aside with a hand in an almost theatrical gesture. Richard guessed that he was bit of a showman, like many successful barristers.

After introductions were made, Marchmont got down to essentials, as his time was money – lots of it!

'Miss Forbes, Mr Bailey and myself have spent an hour going over the legal aspects of the case and reviewing the circumstantial evidence,' he began. 'This Appeal stands or falls upon a defence of alibi, which is really the only issue we can use, so the medical contribution is vital.'

He turned a ten-kilowatt smile on Angela, making her decide that he could either be a charming advocate or a deadly adversary.

'That includes you of course, Doctor Bray. Your opinion about the blood stains is very important. Perhaps we could lead off with that aspect first.'

Angela, a battle-hardened expert witness, had no hesitation in launching into a clear and succinct account of the significance of the blood found on the sleeve of Millie Wilson's coat. She had her sketches and an album of police photographs on her lap as she spoke.

'There seems no dispute that Millie hit Shaw twice on the nose with a pint milk bottle in retaliation for his assault on her late that evening. The post-mortem recorded a bruised and broken nose which accords with several heavy blows. Neither is there any doubt about the blood on her coat having coming from Shaw, as the forensic lab in Bristol clearly showed that it is of a group and subgroups consistent with him and quite unlike Millie's own blood.'

Paul Marchmont listened intently, then nodded and, having brushed back his hair, came to the heart of the matter.

'The Crown claims that it came from the fatal wound in the chest. You can dispute that?'

'Yes, and I fail to see why it wasn't challenged at the trial. The transcript of evidence shows that their pathologist agreed that it was "entirely possible" when it was put to him, but he wasn't pressed about it. There was no contrary evidence led by the defence on that point.'

'And you have some?' queried the Queen's Counsel.

'Part of this is more in Doctor Pryor's province, and I'm sure he can answer for himself. But from the forensic biology point of view, these blood "stains" are really blood "spots", having travelled through the air and landed on the sleeve of the coat, rather than being smears. I also found, from trawling through all the evidence, that she was left-handed and this was the left sleeve. That point was never raised at the trial.'

'But why could not the same spots have come from the chest wound?' demanded Marchmont. 'Her hand, whether left or right, would be virtually touching the chest if she stuck the knife in it.'

Angela shook her head and proffered the photograph album, opened at a page showing a close-up of the woman's jacket sleeve.

'These are a shower of tiny spots, quite well spaced. They are not contact smears; they are from a fine spray striking the cuff area.' She held out her left arm and indicated the outside of her own sleeve, just above the wrist.

'I think Doctor Pryor will bear me out in my opinion that a single stab wound through clothing in the chest, which did not penetrate any substantial arterial blood-vessels, would not produce any spray, as virtually all of the fatal bleeding was internal, within the chest organs.'

Though she needed little support, Richard came in here to confirm what she was saying.

'You can see from the photographs of the body at the scene that there was hardly any bleeding externally. He was wearing a vest, shirt and waistcoat and all that is visible is a stain soaked into the cloth around the narrow slit where the knife went in.'

'Could this spray not have come off the knife when it was pulled out?' asked Douglas Bailey. 'I've been involved in cases where there's blood all over the room – even on the ceiling – from spatter off a weapon.'

'Sure, that happens, usually with blunt instruments or things like axes. But almost always, the weapon has been applied to surfaces that are already bloody from previous blows. Usually, a single blow causes a momentary contraction of blood vessels and it's a few seconds before enough blood flows for the second or third blow to pick enough liquid to throw around the place.'

'And Millie hit him at least twice on the nose with her bottle,' concluded Angela. 'So she could have caused a splash with her second impact, throwing a local spray back on to her sleeve.'

'The other thing is that when the knife was found on the floor, only a close inspection could tell it had been used,' said Richard, with a quickening fluency of which his grandfather, a Welsh Methodist preacher, would have approved. 'There were some faint dried blood smears on the blade, but it took proper examination in the laboratory to confirm it. So there was very little blood on it, certainly not enough to cause a shower of spots. When a knife is pulled out cleanly from a wound, the muscle contraction can close the edges tightly against the blade and wipe it. And then of course there were three layers of clothing to give it an additional wipe.'

The QC nodded. 'You've convinced me, doctors, but we have to convince three sceptical Lords of Appeal. Now what about the time of death? That's where we will win or lose.'

Coffee appeared, giving Richard time mentally to gird his loins before setting off on a much more detailed argument.

'Let me make it clear, Mr Marchmont,' he began after they had settled down again. 'I cannot deny that Arthur Shaw might well have died at around eleven or twelve o'clock that night, as the prosecution claimed. But what I can do is show that, because of the uncertainty of the methods their pathologist relied on, he could have died several hours either side of that claim. Obviously, that could not have been on the earlier side, as a number of the people in the house saw him alive until he went upstairs to assault Millie. But the hours after that time are certainly in contention.'

'This is where we need a detailed argument, Doctor Pryor,' said Paul Marchmont. 'You are directly at odds with their expert on this.'

'Right, let's take the easy ones first,' said Richard. 'Their Doctor Mackintyre said that he relied on a concurrence of post-mortem lividity, rigor mortis, stomach contents and temperature to arrive at his conclusion that death had occurred between eleven and twelve o'clock. That is utter nonsense, as any medical man who, from an imperfect examination fourteen hours later, puts a time of death within a one-hour bracket is either ignorant or foolish!'

'Strong words, doctor!' said the QC.

'If he had said "consistent with those times", I would agree with him, but that then fails to destroy Millie's alibi, as someone else could have done the deed outside the very short time bracket.'

Marchmont once again tossed his hair back. 'Carry on, please, doctor.'

'First, lividity, or "livor mortis" as it was probably called in Doctor Mackintyre's day. Completely useless as a timer of death. It can even occur in deep coma, such as barbiturate overdose. But the time it takes to appear due to gravitational settling of the red blood cells is extremely variable. To use that to pin down a time to an hour, when seen half a day later, is little short of ludicrous.'

Penelope Forbes, who had been very quiet in the presence of her leader, came in with a query that showed that she had researched the case in depth.

'Haven't I read that this lividity becomes fixed after a certain number of hours, which can be used in timing?'

'That is certainly in all the textbooks, but in practice it is very variable and often doesn't occur at all,' was the firm reply. 'I've experimented myself and found it to be totally unreliable.'

Douglas Bailey was getting out of his depth here. 'Can you explain that, Doctor Pryor?'

'When the blood cells settle, they are still inside the veins under the skin, so that the dark reddish-purple colour is visible. The delay for this to happen is very variable – in fact, in some old or anaemic people, it is never visible. Now if the body is moved after death, such as being turned over, the blood may or may not reposition itself towards the new lowest areas. Sometimes it does, sometimes it doesn't. For years, pathologists and police surgeons have tried to put a timeline on when it stops moving and becomes fixed. But even when fixation does occur, it's so random in its timing as to be useless. I've copied out the opinions given for this and for timing rigor mortis from almost a dozen textbooks of forensic medicine and you will see that the range of disagreement runs to many hours, so it's of virtually no value!'

He passed around a few carbon copies of Moira's typing and waited until the three lawyers had scanned them.

'So what about rigor mortis? That's always held up in detective novels to be the bee's knees for timing death,' said Paul Marchmont.

'Much the same criticism as with hypostasis,' replied Richard. 'There are generalizations, which are not at all accurate – and so many exceptions to the generalizations that no useful rules remain.'

'Can you expand on that a little, doctor? asked Penelope Forbes. Angela watched her partner and recognized him getting into lecture mode. She knew he was good at it and wondered if his students in Bristol University appreciated him.

'Rigor is stiffening of all the muscles of the body after death, due to a chemical reaction affecting their proteins. The problem is that there are a number of factors which affect the speed and intensity of this stiffening. For example, strenuous activity shortly before death hastens it appreciably, which is why battle casualties often have a rapid onset of rigor. The same happens after electric shock. Then temperature also accelerates it and cold delays it. I've seen a body dead in the snow for some days with no rigor, but as soon as it was brought into the mortuary, it stiffened up.'

'It was a very hot period when Arthur Shaw died in June last year,' interjected the solicitor. 'It was virtually a heatwave.'

'I realized that, Mr Bailey, which was why I phoned the weather people at Bristol Airport the other day. Their records showed that the temperature, even at midnight, was much higher than usual for that date, so there's another factor to use in the argument.'

'What effect would that have had?' asked the QC.

'Rigor could have come on faster, giving the impression that death had occurred earlier than it really did. The trouble with that argument is that the accuracy of back-calculating is so poor that trying to adjust for temperature is not much use.'

'So the old formulae given in the books I've seen for calculating from rigor is just not correct?' persisted Miss Forbes.

Richard shook his head. 'It's the old story of the bell-shaped curve, which pervades much of biology. There's a high point on the graph where most of the cases lie where, say, rigor comes on in three to six hours or so. But on each side of the peak, there's a slope where the other cases lie, either earlier or later. If the bell is high and narrow, then accuracy is better, but if, as with rigor, the bell is low and flat, then there's no chance of accuracy.'

He cleared his throat. 'And that's just for the onset of rigor. It increases in strength, then eventually passes off, called resolution, but the time when that happens is even more unpredictable. Unfortunately, many of the textbooks stick to the myth of a reliable timescale and copy it from edition to edition, because there's nothing better to replace it with.'

'You sound a bit of cynic, doctor,' observed Paul Marchmont with a smile.

'I prefer to think of myself as a realist,' replied Richard. 'The younger generation of pathologists are hopefully more critical of these sacred ideas of the older, dogmatic school. I met a German pathologist at a meeting last year, who is combing all the medical literature for over a century to list the variations in opinions about hypostasis and rigor.'

'We've got stomach contents next; are you just as pessimistic about those?' asked the senior barrister.

Richard rolled his eyes towards the ceiling. 'Even worse! The old legend about stomach contents emptying in about two and half hours is again the top of the biological bell, but there are even more variable factors. The type of food, amount of liquid in it, amount of starch, personal variation and even variations in the same person. You can measure the speed of emptying in Bill Smith one day, then give him the same food another day and get a different answer! Fear, injury, coma, pain and emotional upset all modify the speed of digestion and emptying. To use it to calculate a time of death to within an hour is frankly ridiculous!'

'Is examining the stomach contents of no use whatsoever, then?' asked Douglas Bailey.

'Only in the very broadest terms, insufficient to use as probative evidence. It might tell you what the last meal was and therefore you'd know that death occurred after the time it was eaten. For instance, if a man ate a curry one evening and was found dead two days later with a stomach full of curry, you'd know he hadn't lived long enough to have his usual ham and eggs for breakfast next day.'

Angela came back here, as this was partly her province.

'Even that's not easy, unless digestion had not proceeded very far. We can often identify certain foods under the microscope, like meat fibres and some vegetables – but we're not like the sleuths in crime novels, who can discover that the deceased had consumed a salmon sandwich and a cup of Earl Grey tea three hours before death!'

Marchmont held up his hands in mock surrender. 'I get the point. Now what about temperature, which you said was the best method?'

'Well, I said the least inaccurate,' amended Richard. 'Doctors have been trying since about 1840 to devise a formula to calculate time of death from the obvious drop in temperature after death – unless, of course, you happen to die in some parts of the tropics, where the post-mortem temperature actually increases!'

'I don't think Bristol comes into that category,' said Douglas Bailey wryly.

'No, but the temperature at the scene is very important, and we know that Shaw was killed during a Bristol heatwave,' countered the pathologist. 'The problem is that the investigation was poorly carried out, as no one took the room temperature nor the body temperature when the scene was visited. Doctor Mackintyre didn't attend the scene and didn't even see the body until the afternoon, over six hours after it was found, when he eventually put a thermometer in the rectum.'

'And that matters in calculating the interval?' asked Marchmont.

'It's vital, as for at least six hours, the body was cooling in the mortuary, no doubt much colder than the flat in St Paul's, which distorts the cooling curve. We should really find out whether the place was air-conditioned, as some big city mortuaries are, which would increase the cooling even more. I've actually heard of a case where the body was put in the refrigerator for some hours until the post-mortem and then the pathologist took a temperature!'

'So you can castigate any attempt at arriving at an accurate result?' asked Penelope.

'Certainly, I can! Even when the best procedures have been followed, the accuracy is poor and cannot be narrowed down to less than a couple of hours either side of the calculated time. It's traditional to use a rule of thumb that a body cools at about one and half degrees Fahrenheit per hour, but all one can say about that is that if the answer turns out to be correct, it must be sheer luck!'

He paused for breath and then carried on.

'The size of the body, the amount of fat insulation under the skin, amount of clothing, fever, hypothermia, the environmental temperature, draughts, humidity and other factors make this little better than guesswork.'

Paul Marchmont leaned back in his chair. 'So you can confidently go into the witness box and declare that at the trial, the pathologist had been in error when he claimed that Arthur Shaw must have died between eleven and twelve o'clock that night?'

'Absolutely. I'm sure he was just agreeing with the prosecution who were maintaining that the man was killed during that short window of opportunity when Millie Wilson was alone with the deceased.'

'If he had been challenged on that, do you think he would have admitted that death could have been outside those tight limits?'

Richard Pryor shrugged and turned up his hands in a Gallic gesture.

'It's not for me to say that, but I would have hoped that Doctor Mackintyre would have done so. However, as I said earlier, some well-entrenched expert witnesses dig their heels in hard, if they are challenged.'

Penelope Forbes pursued this issue. 'Would he have been aware of these caveats you've mentioned, which affect the accuracy of any estimate?'

'I don't know about would have known, but he certainly *should* have known, if he appears as an expert. There have been innumerable research papers in the journals for decades. In fact, only this year, one of the most important papers was published from Sri Lanka, where Doctor de Saram made a careful estimate using forty executed prisoners, where obviously the time of hanging was known to the minute. He found, amongst other things, that there was a "lag period", a variable delay in initial cooling of up to forty-five minutes. Others have shown an even longer "temperature plateau", as it's called, where the normal body temperature persists for a time after death. So already, we have an in-built error almost as long as the hour claimed by Doctor Mackintyre.'

Richard felt that he had browbeaten his listeners long enough with his potted course in forensic medicine, but there were a few more questions from the lawyers, who wanted to make sure that they understood this most important aspect of their campaign to save Millie Wilson from many more years in prison.

When they at last finished and had been given more details of the expected date of the court appearance in London, Richard and Angela bade the lawyers farewell and escaped into the chilly street.

'Well, I think we've more than earned a gin and tonic and a decent lunch somewhere!' said Richard firmly, taking his partner's arm as they made their way back to the black Humber.

TWELVE

Markby Road in Winson Green was one in a series of long parallel streets lined with terraced houses, branching off Handsworth New Road like ribs from a spine. They were tidy dwellings, most with small front bay windows and were a cut above many of the streets in less attractive parts of the area.

At ten o'clock that morning, the two detectives drove their grey Standard Vanguard slowly down the street, looking at the numbers on the doors. They found No. 183 almost at the end, a slightly shabbier house, but otherwise indistinguishable from scores of others. Sergeant Rickman had to park outside the house next door, as there was an old green van in front of their destination. It was a large Bedford of pre-war vintage, with 'Franklin's Fish and Chips' painted on the side and a tin chimney poking from the roof.

'Looks as if he's swapped inn-keeping to become a chippie,' grunted DI Hartnell, as they went through a rusted gate into the small concreted area in front of the door. There was no bell or knocker, so Rickman rapped on the glass pane with the edge of a half-crown coin.

After a delay, a large shadow appeared inside and a disgruntled face appeared in the gap when the door was opened a bare six inches. Long experience told the sergeant that a direct approach was best in these circumstances and he thrust his warrant card towards the beefy, red features.

'Oliver Franklin?' he said briskly. 'Police, we'd like a word with you.'

The door opened a little wider, revealing a very large, pot-bellied man dressed in baggy trousers and a zip-fronted corduroy lumberjacket. He had a round, flabby face with sagging pouches under his watery eyes and a bulbous red nose. His coarse cheeks had the scars of old acne and Hartnell thought that he had rarely seen such an unattractive man.

Franklin glared at the officers with undisguised dislike.

'Bloody rozzers, is it? Look, if it's about the van out there, I sent for the tax disc last week, but bugger all's come back yet.'

The sergeant put a large hand on the door and pushed it further open. 'Nothing to do with your licence – not yet, anyway.' There was a hint of a threat in his words.

The detective inspector spoke again. 'We'd better come in, sir, unless you'd like to answer some questions on your doorstep.'

'Or down at the police station,' added Rickman, menacingly.

Olly Franklin got the message that these particular coppers were not ones to be messed with and opened the door wider.

'Come on then,' he growled grudgingly and shuffled back down the passage, his swollen feet encased in plaid slippers, the backs trodden flat by his heels. They squeezed past an old-fashioned bicycle propped against the stairs and walked down the worn linoleum to the kitchen at the end of the passage. Franklin went to stand with his back to a blackleaded fireplace, in which a small pile of coal was burning with more smoke than heat.

'What's all this about, then?' he demanded, standing with his brawny arms folded defiantly across his chest.

Hartnell took his time in answering, looking around first at the gloomy kitchen lit by a grimy window that looked out on to a brick wall. The room had a table and chairs, the former carrying a couple of used teacups and a half-full bottle of milk, together with several newspapers opened at the racing pages. There was another door in the corner leading into a scullery, from which came an intermittent chopping noise.

'Who's that in there?' he asked, being cautious about who might overhear their conversation.

'Only the missus, cutting spuds for today's frying,' grunted Franklin. 'I hope you ain't going to keep me long, I got a living to make!'

'You don't make it now from being a licensee, I hear,' said the sergeant. 'Fish and chips pays better, does it?'

'Does it hell!' snarled Olly, his face suffusing with anger. 'One pub knocked down from under me, then the bloody brewery fired me from the other, thanks to you lot who objected to the renewal of my tenancy.'

'That's partly what we've come about, your career in the local pubs,' said the detective inspector.

'What the hell for, that was years ago? Water under the bridge!' snapped Franklin.

Hartnell decided to chance his arm a little. 'We've been hearing that you were a bit too pally with Mickey Doyle,' he said. 'There's a real villain for you!'

Olly's hooded eyes flicked from one to the other. 'Mickey Doyle? What the hell's he got to do with anything? Haven't seen him in years, honest.'

His denial sounded genuine to the detectives, but Hartnell persisted.

'So you say, Olly. But we want to know about the famous head you used to keep for him.' Again he was making a guess, but it seemed to strike home, given the confused flush that spread over Olly's unlovely features.

'What head would that be?' he growled unconvincingly. 'I don't know nothing about no head!'

'The head you used to keep in the cellar of the old Barley Mow,' snapped Tom Rickman. 'Did you take it with you to the other pub when you moved?'

'I dunno what you're talking about,' replied Franklin, but the slight quaver in his voice and the way his piggy eyes flicked from one officer to the other gave the lie to his denial.

'Listen, we know you had a head pickled in a bucket,' rasped the DI. 'Whose was it – and where is it now, eh?'

'How the 'ell would I know who it belonged to? And anyway, it weren't in a bucket.' The former publican was not over-endowed with intelligence and his reply caused the two officers to grin at each other in triumph.

As Franklin slumped on to one of the hard chairs, a woman suddenly appeared at the door from the scullery.

'Best tell them, Olly! That bloody thing has plagued us for years.' His wife was a hard-faced woman with straggling grey hair falling about her shoulders. She wore a faded wraparound pinafore and her thick legs ended in a pair of man's boots. In one hand she carried a wicked-looking knife and in the other, a large King Edward potato.

'Tell us what, missus?' demanded the sergeant, seizing the moment.

'About that 'orrible thing in the shed out the back,' she grated. 'I told him, he should have got rid of it down the council dump years ago.'

Trevor Hartnell stepped towards Franklin and grabbed him by the arm. 'Come on, Olly, show us where it is.'

Muttering under his breath and giving his wife a poisonous glare as he passed her, the man led the way through the scullery, the floor piled with pans full of raw chipped potatoes. The back door opened into a small yard cluttered with junk, where a heap of coal lay next to a dog kennel, in which a grubby Alsatian was chained. The houses were all back to back, with no lane separating them from an identical street beyond. A dilapidated shed stood against the dividing wall, with a rusted car engine leaning against its side.

With leaden feet, Olly took them to its door and went in first, throwing an empty potato sack with what he hoped was a nonchalant gesture over a pile of new-looking cartons of Gold Flake cigarettes which lay on a workbench. The rest of the space was filled with a chaotic collection of tools, discarded domestic items and assorted junk.

'Go on, show them, Olly!' shouted his wife, waving her knife dangerously as she stood behind the policemen, as they stood in the doorway.

Reluctantly, he pulled aside a broken Ewbank carpet-sweeper, a gas-mask case and an ARP steel helmet.

Beneath the pile of old newspapers below was a metal drum about a foot wide and eighteen inches high. The remnants of a label stuck on the lid alleged it contained cooking oil, but the sloshing sound when Olly dragged it out suggested that there was a more watery fluid inside.

'What about possible prints?' murmured the sergeant to his senior officer, as Franklin appeared to be about to pull off the lid. However, a shrill voice from Olly's wife solved the problem.

'You're not opening that here!' she shrieked. 'I had

nightmares for weeks last time I saw it. Take the bloody thing away!'

Hartnell laid a hand again on Franklin's sleeve.

'Leave it to us,' he said. 'Better get your coat, Olly. You're coming to the station with us. I'm afraid it's your wife that will be doing the frying tonight!'

They found an empty cell back at the station where they put the drum while Tom Rickman went to get a pair of rubber gloves from the scenes-of-crime bag that they kept in the CID room. The former publican was placed in an interview room and given a cup of station tea, while Hartnell and his sergeant decided what to do about investigating the container. They had carried it carefully to and from the car by holding the drum with fingertips under the rim that ran around the top, though Hartnell felt that probably so many people had handled the thing already, that fingerprints would not be all that important.

Now they sat it on the bare bench that served as a bed in the cell and stared at it while deciding what to do.

'Should we open it or wait for the forensic lab to come?' asked Rickman.

His boss was of a more impulsive nature, anxious to get on with matters.

'We've got to have a look, Tom,' he said decisively. 'For all we know there may only be a dead cat inside – or even just a few pints of home brew!'

The sloshing sound certainly confirmed that there was some sort of liquid in the container, which was obviously of some age, as its greenish paint was badly scratched and there were several small dents in the side. Rickman felt in his pocket for a large clasp knife and pulled out a blade like a screwdriver. With the DI holding the drum in his gloved hands, the sergeant levered off the lid, which was held on firmly, but not too tightly.

'Phew, what the hell is that smell?' demanded Hartnell, recoiling more from surprise than from nausea.

'That's methylated spirits, surely,' replied Rickman, who ran a Scout Troop in his spare time and was used to lighting Primus stoves which were primed with the stuff.

They looked into the drum, which was almost full of a murky, pale purple liquid. Beneath the surface was a layer of fabric, which looked like a coarse dishcloth.

Cautiously, the inspector pushed it aside with his rubber-covered fingers and looked below the surface.

'That's hair, surely,' muttered the sergeant, pointing at some floating black strands. Gingerly, Hartnell slid his hands down each side of the container and lifted the contents above the level of the fluid.

'Jesus, it's horrible!' he muttered, echoing Mrs Franklin's opinion, as he held a human head between his fingers. It felt hard, like a motor tyre, and the colour was a washed-out grey. The features were like those of a shop-window dummy, apart from the eye sockets, which had sunk back under the collapsed lids.

The two detectives stared at it for a long moment, then Hartnell let it subside back into the liquid, where the black hair again swirled under the surface.

'Anyone you know?' asked Rickman, only half-joking.

His inspector put the metal lid back on the drum and, peeling off his gloves, made for the door.

'Let's have a few words with Olly,' he said grimly. As they went out of the cell corridor towards the interview room, he told the custody sergeant to lock the cell door and let no one inside without his permission.

'Right, Olly, let's be having you,' he snapped, as they entered the room where the flabby ex-publican was sitting at the table, smoking a Player's Navy Cut.

He looked up owlishly at Hartnell, trying to paste a look of innocence on his coarse features.

'Look, I don't know nothing about that thing. It was in the cellar at the Barley Mow, then got took to the White Rose when I was moved, along with a load of other stuff. When I got kicked out of there, everything was just dumped in my shed.'

'Tell that to the Marines!' sneered the sergeant. 'Your missus knew damn well what was in the drum.'

'Nothing to do with me. Some blokes left it with me in the Barley Mow years ago,' said Olly stubbornly.

The two officers sat down heavily opposite the man, where

Tom Rickman ostentatiously took out his notebook as his DI began the interview.

'Olly, you're in deep shit already, so don't dig yourself in any deeper.'

'But I ain't done nothing!' said Franklin in an aggrieved tone.

Hartnell extemporized as to the nature of the offences, as he was not sure himself what they were.

'You have concealed knowledge of a death, you have obstructed the coroner in the furtherance of his inquest and you have offended against the Death Registration and Burial Acts – and are probably an accessory to a felony, perhaps a murder!'

Franklin's usually red face blanched and beads of sweat suddenly appeared on his forehead as he realized the implications of what he could be charged with.

'I tell you, I don't know nothing about it!' he croaked.

'Come off it, Olly! How did this head come to be in your possession? Who gave it you and why? And who is it, anyway?'

The former innkeeper looked wildly about the room, as if either looking for escape or someone to help him in this sudden crisis. 'Why you asking me all this, after all these years?' he moaned.

'Because the rest of this bloke may have turned up, that's why!' snapped the inspector. 'Now stop messing me about and answer the questions. Who is he?'

'I don't know, guv! I swear to God that's true. It was already in the pub when I took over. I was in the Merchant Navy until forty-six and when I went to the Barley Mow, that drum was already there. It must have been there when the previous licensee ran the place.'

'Who was that?' demanded Rickman.

'Fred Mansell – but he's been dead for years.'

Hartnell looked at his sergeant, then murmured into his ear. 'I think this is getting too heavy for us. Better kick it upstairs for now, see how the brass want to play it.'

He turned to Franklin, whose shaking fingers were groping for another cigarette.

'Right, Olly. For starters, you're going to be charged with concealing a death, so you'll be locked up for tonight, until it's decided tomorrow what's to be done with you. We'll notify your wife; maybe she can bring in some fish and chips for you!'

THIRTEEN

On Saturday morning, Richard Pryor was alone in Garth House, with Angela gone to Berkshire, Sian at home and even Moira having a day off to go shopping in Newport.

She had left him a ham salad for his lunch in the old Kelvin refrigerator and he ate this quite early, as he wanted to get off to his appointment at the vineyard, forty miles away.

Picking up the A48 at Chepstow, he drove on it through Newport and Cardiff to the small country town of Cowbridge, an old Roman station twelve miles west of the capital city. It was now the market town of the lush Vale of Glamorgan, which lay between the hills of north Glamorgan and the sea. Here he followed the instructions given to him by Louis Dumas, supplemented by one of his one-inch Ordnance Survey maps. Richard loved maps and atlases, being happy to pore over them for hours as if he was reading a novel.

He turned off at the solitary traffic lights in Cowbridge and meandered through a few lanes until he came to the tiny village of St Mary Church, not far from the huge RAF station at St Athan. On a narrow lane beyond the village, he found a gateway in a high hedge with a discreet notice proclaiming 'Saint Illtyd's Vineyard', named after the fifth-century founder of the first monastic 'university' at Llantwit Major, a few miles away on the coast.

Driving in through the open gate, a gravel track took him to a nicely renovated farmhouse, with extensive outbuildings visible behind. He stopped on a wide turning area in front of the house and was greeted by a friendly golden retriever which ambled out of the open front door, wagging its tail as it came to have its neck patted. The dog was followed by a slim man in his mid-fifties. He wore a tweed suit with a waistcoat and a paisley-pattern cravat at his throat, his silver-grey hair covered with a matching tweed cap. Richard thought he looked very much the gentleman farmer, perhaps more typical of the Home Counties than South Wales. However, as soon as he spoke, his French origins were clear, though his English was perfect – perhaps too perfect for a native Briton.

'Doctor Pryor, welcome to my house. It is a pleasure to meet you.' He extended his hand and shook it warmly.

'We get very few vine enthusiasts here, though hopefully the number will increase as more people like yourself see the light!'

He escorted Richard into the house, where he introduced his wife as they settled themselves in an elegant sitting room. Emily Dumas was a small, neat woman, some years younger than her husband, even though her hair was quite white. Dressed in a dark blue dress with a prim lace collar, she was the epitome of a quiet, respectable housewife, yet somehow Richard felt that there was deep sadness in the eyes of both her and her husband. He sensed that they shared some deep unhappiness, but it was none of his business to probe.

After some polite small-talk about the improving weather, their amiable dog and the imminent approach of Christmas, Madame Dumas vanished, then returned with a tray bearing biscuits and coffee in exquisite Limoges crockery.

'We'll give you taste of good Welsh wine before you leave,' promised the husband. 'But have this before I take you on a tour of the estate.'

As they sat and enjoyed the coffee, Richard learned that they had lived in the house for twelve years, the vines having been planted the year after their arrival.

'Only half an acre to start with, as it was very difficult to find any vine stock during the war. We scoured market gardens to get enough, until the war ended and we could import from France,' explained Louis.

Emily Dumas took up the story.

'We came to Britain at the fall of France in 1940, as my husband was a senior staff-officer in the army and we escaped to London with Charles de Gaulle,' she explained. 'Louis worked at the Free French headquarters in Carlton Terrace, but unfortunately fell ill two years later.'

'It was a recurrence of a tropical disease I suffered when we were in Indo-China in the thirties,' explained her husband. 'But I was invalided out of the army in forty-three and we ended up here soon afterwards.'

At this, Richard caught a covert glance between the man and wife, which obviously had some private significance. Then briskly, Louis Dumas stood up, full of affability, and suggested that they go outside to talk about viniculture. The next hour was a fascinating one for the pathologist, who forgot all about headless bodies and lethal stab wounds during the Frenchman's lucid explanation of the secrets of vine-growing and winemaking. What Richard really learned was the extent of his ignorance, confirming Jimmy Jenkins' contempt for trying to become an expert by reading books. In the winter sunshine, they toured the acres of vines, now bare of leaves and looking like desiccated twigs as they clung to the wires that supported them.

'It's hard to believe that in a few months, these will spring back to life and by next autumn will be loaded with fruit,' enthused Dumas. 'We are the first to try winemaking in Wales since the twenties, when the last vines were grubbed up not far from here.'

When Richard sought encouragement that viniculture was a practical proposition in Wales, Louis Dumas reminded him that in the past, a great deal of wine had been made all over southern Britain, by both the Romans and the monasteries.

'That was until the climate changed for the worse in the later Middle Ages, and of course, Henry the Eighth abolished the monasteries, who were the main producers,' he explained. 'There was then a hiatus for centuries until the Marquis of Bute, one of the richest men in the world, thanks to Welsh coal, started a vineyard in the late nineteenth century at Castle Coch, near Cardiff. He even sent his head gardener to France to learn the secrets, though I don't understand how he could benefit much, as he didn't understand French! The marquis's son planted two more vineyards in the Vale, one at St Quentin's, just a few miles from here. They made quite a lot of wine for a few years, producing twelve thousand bottles in 1893, being the only commercial vineyard in Britain at that time. But alas, they gave up soon after the Great War.'

'Why was that, if they were making a decent vintage?' asked

Richard, eager to learn all he could, even if only to confound Jimmy's pessimism.

'It was too expensive to compete with imports,' replied Louis. 'And they chose the wrong grape variety for this cooler, wetter climate, as their Gamay Noir was better suited to Burgundy. They should have stuck to a white wine, rather than attempt to make a good red.'

As they walked towards the end of the first row of vines, Richard saw a figure ahead of them, bending over the wires. He wore green dungarees under a brown leather jacket and had a pair of strong secateurs in one hand.

'That's my son Victor, checking on the ties, ready for the winter gales,' said his father.

As they came up to him, Richard saw a tall young man in his early twenties, who straightened up when they approached. He had an angular face with a marked cleft chin and prominent cheekbones.

'Victor, this is Doctor Pryor, who I told you about. He's going to join the ranks of the Welsh wine makers.'

The younger man shook hands and gave Richard a pleasant smile.

'I'm glad to hear it! Then the ranks will consist of two of us!' he said heartily. He had none of the accent of his parents, though Richard realized that he must have been born in France before the war.

They chatted for a few moments, Victor explaining what he was doing. The vines had recently been pruned after the leaf fall, but needed tidying up and securing while dormant.

He walked back with them towards the outbuildings where the wine was made and Richard's head began to spin as he assimilated information of the double-Guyot training system, varieties of grape and the basic principles of making the wine once the grapes had been grown.

'Did you grow up in a winemaking area of France?' he asked Louis, when he had a chance to get a word in.

'I did indeed. My family came from the Loire region where the conditions are not all that unlike Britain. My father was a winemaker, but as I left to join the army when I was eighteen, I had to relearn the trade when we came here.'

From various bits of information, Richard gathered that the family still had land in France and that though the vineyard here was successful, it was far from being their only means of support. In fact, from the furnishings and many fine paintings and ornaments in the house, he felt that they were more than comfortably off. He wondered why they had chosen to remain in Britain after the war, when they could have made wine more easily in their native country. It was none of his business and he was not a nosy person by nature, though the thought occurred to him that perhaps there were political issues involved, as General de Gaulle was a controversial figure.

The next hour was spent blissfully in the outbuildings, where Louis had his equipment and the storage for his wines. Though some of the vats, presses and other arcane machinery looked old, the place was almost clinically clean.

'I brought most of this over from France later,' said Louis, with a sweep of his hand around the sheds. Though becoming bewildered with an overload of information from both father and son, Richard listened to the explanations of all the processes with fascination, determined that in a year or two, he would be doing the same thing on a much smaller scale.

The high point was a wine tasting in a small room which was almost a laboratory. Emily Dumas came out to join them with a plate of plain biscuits, so that they could enjoy several different wines from the previous year's vintage.

'Of course, we only make white,' said Victor. 'As I said, I don't think this climate is the right one for reds.'

It was almost dusk when, reluctantly, Richard left them, happy that his afternoon had been so pleasant and informative. As he drove home through the dark lanes and then the busier main roads, he felt that his odd, almost obsessional interest in vines had been greatly strengthened, in spite of the rather pitying way in which his friends and colleagues seemed to humour him over the idea.

'A man has to have a hobby,' he muttered to himself, as he stared down the tunnel of his headlights. 'Especially when he has such a damned morbid job as mine!'

He rather envied the Dumases' way of life at that idyllic estate, though he still had the impression that there was some sort of serpent in that Garden of Eden that prevented them from being totally contented.

Just as the orders to investigate the pickled head had cascaded down through the Birmingham police hierarchy, the fact that it had been found climbed back up the same route. When it reached the ACC early that afternoon, he called in his chief superintendent, Simon Black, and asked him what they were going to do about it.

'Is it a murder or not?' he demanded. 'So far, we have no evidence at all to show that this head belongs to this body in Wales.'

The CID chief agreed. 'But the Welsh corpse has to be a murder, according to the local force. Their pathologist down there says the chap was strangled . . . and anyway, who's going to bury a headless corpse unless it was unlawfully killed?'

'What does this fellow who kept the head in his shed have to say about it? Has he coughed as to its identity?'

The chief super shrugged. 'The DI started on him this morning, but in view of the strange nature of the whole affair, he decided to refer it up here to see how we wanted to play it.'

'What do you think, Simon? Do you want to handle it yourself or send a DS or a DCI down there?'

Simon Black shook his head. 'The local DI, Trevor Hartnell, is a sound man, plenty of experience. And he knows his own patch best. It would be a pity to take it off him now, at least until we know where we are with it.'

'Getting that damned head examined is the obvious priority, to see if it does belong to that corpse in sheep-shagger country.'

His chief detective agreed. 'Seems most sensible to ask the same pathologist to come up and have a look at it. He's in the best position to know if they match.'

The orders went out, one down to Hartnell telling him to get on with grilling Olly Franklin and the other to the police in Cardiganshire, informing them of the latest developments and asking them to arrange for Doctor Pryor to come up to Birmingham at his earliest convenience.

In Aberystwyth, David John Jones called Meirion into his office as soon as he had put the phone down.

'They've found the head! Good thing Gwyn Parry's brother-in-law has such good contacts. It had been in some pub as was suspected, but turned up in the licensee's shed, of all places.'

'What happens now?' asked his detective inspector.

'Birmingham suggest, quite sensibly, that Doctor Pryor goes up there to examine it, so can you ring him and fix a time. You'd better be there yourself, I think, to keep up to date on our behalf. The head is being taken to the central mortuary behind the coroner's court in Newton Street, so they said.'

This sparked a question in Meirion's mind. 'Which coroner will have to deal with the death, I wonder?'

The DCC turned up his hands in doubt. 'Beats me! We've got the biggest bit – that's assuming they belong together. I still can't understand how they came to be a hundred miles apart!'

Meirion Thomas made for the door, going back to his office to start phoning around. Then he stopped for a last question.

'What about the Yard? Do we have to tell them?'

David Jones growled something under his breath, then sighed. 'Have to, I suppose. Maybe they won't bother to come back here, if a big force like Birmingham is involved.'

When his DI had gone out, he swung round in his chair and glowered through his window at the inoffensive Irish Sea outside.

'Why the hell should the damned English use our bog as a cemetery?' he muttered.

In the police station in Winson Green, DI Hartnell and his sergeant were hard at it, trying to prise information out of Olly Franklin. A night in the cells had done little to soften his stubborn truculence, but Trevor Hartnell had been flattered by the trust his seniors had shown in his abilities and was determined to get something out of the ex-publican, even if it meant reaching down his throat.

They sat in a dismal interview room, with damp-stained green walls looking down on a bare table and chairs.

Tom Rickman sat alongside his 'guv'nor', notebook and pencil on the table before him, as Hartnell began all over again.

'Look, Olly, whatever happens, you're in the shit over this. But if you come clean, it'll be in your favour, right?'

'You don't want an accessory-to-murder charge slapped on

you, do you?' contributed the sergeant. 'So far, you're up for concealing a death and obstructing the coroner, but they're not exactly hanging offences. Why don't you keep it that way?'

'I don't know nothing – well, hardly nothing,' growled the red-faced man opposite. 'There was just this old drum in the pub cellar and I got stuck with it.'

'You could have gone round the nick next day and reported it,' snapped Hartnell.

Franklin sneered at this. 'Oh yes, I'm likely to have done that, after Mickey Doyle told me to hang on to it. That would earn a beating or even a shiv across my face.'

'Well, you're here in the nick now, so you may as well cough for us,' snapped Hartnell. 'Why did Doyle want you to keep the thing?'

Olly stared down at the scarred table-top for a long moment, then sighed and leaned back in his chair.

'OK, I'll tell you what I know, but it ain't much, honest. And it was years ago now.'

Rickman opened his notebook and poised his pencil in anticipation, as the other man began to speak.

'Look, you know as well as I do that Mickey Doyle was a villain – and he ran a gang of villains. You knocked off a few of them now and then, but others just popped up in their place.'

The DI nodded. 'We know that, what's your point?'

'He was into all sorts of things – theft, protection rackets, running tarts, illegal gambling – though I never heard he was into drugs. Then until things eased off after the war, black market was the big earner and Doyle was a big player in that.'

'Thanks for the lecture, Olly,' said the sergeant sarcastically. 'Now tell us something we don't know!'

The chippie scowled at him. 'I'm getting to that, ain't I? There was one thing about Mickey, he was a stickler for discipline among those who worked for him. He was a big bugger and I've seen him punch a guy to the floor in the pub, just for some fault in working the rackets. I even heard he had some guy's legs broken years ago, for holding back some of the loot in a black-market scam.'

The two detectives waited, as Olly seemed to be painfully approaching something of use to them.

'So where does this head come into it?' demanded Hartnell.

'It was before my time at the Barley Mow, but I heard that one of his thugs was actually topped for trying to rip Mickey off, big time! I don't know how, nor who, nor if it was Mickey himself that did it, but he ended up dead.'

'When was this?' rasped Rickman, lifting his pencil.

'Must have been when the war was still on, but towards the end. Anyway, what I heard from gossip between the villains in my bar was that part of this fellow's job was to go round the illegal gambling joints run by Doyle and collect the takings. Turned out that he had a fiddle going on with some of the guys who ran the dens, so that they creamed off a part of the collection for themselves.'

'And Doyle eventually found out?' said Hartnell.

'Yes, so the story goes. Mickey had him done away with, but as a warning to the rest of his foot soldiers, he had the head kept and used to display it now and then to keep them in line.'

The sergeant threw down his pencil. 'Sounds a bloody farfetched yarn to me!' he growled. 'Like something out of a Mickey Spillane novel.'

The former licensee shrugged. 'You asked me, mate, so I'm telling you what I heard. Doyle wouldn't let me get rid of the thing in case he wanted to use it again.'

Trevor Hartnell fixed Franklin with his hard blue eyes.

'And you say he used to parade this horrible thing in front of his men in your pub?'

Olly nodded his ponderous head. 'A few times, when I first went to the Barley Mow after the war. He used the function room upstairs for a booze-up now and then. It was usually after they made a good haul after some big heist. I remember one was after they had nicked a couple of lorry-loads of sheep from somewhere down in the country – couldn't get much good meat during rationing.'

'Did you see him showing off this head?'

'No, he didn't let anyone in the room. I had to leave a barrel of beer and a stack of food and spirits in there for them.'

'And you claim you've no idea who this bloke was that he had topped?' demanded Hartnell.

Olly shook his head and replied vehemently. 'Not a clue – and

I damned well didn't want to know, either! Keep a tight mouth anywhere around Mickey Doyle, that was the golden rule.'

'So who would know, Olly?'

The burly publican toyed nervously with the lid of a cocoa tin that served as an ashtray on the table in front of him.

'Well, Doyle himself, I suppose. I don't know who's in his gang these days, I keep well clear.'

'Mickey did a bunk to the Costa del Sol last year, Olly, things were getting a bit hot for him here. And there's no extradition from Spain. So who else can we ask, eh?'

Franklin looked furtively around the room, as if some criminal eavesdropper might be lurking in a corner.

'The only bloke from the old days still around is Billy Blair,' he confided.

Tom Rickman threw down his pencil with a clatter.

'Billy Blair! Well, at least we know where to find that bastard! He's a quarter of a mile away, inside Winson Green Prison.'

FOURTEEN

Richard Pryor took the call from Aberystwyth in his room and, after listening for a few moments, called out to Moira in the office next door. They had no intercom, but a good shout seemed to work equally well. When her neat, dark head appeared around the door, he asked if there were any local cases for him the next day.

'There's a sudden death at Chepstow, doctor, that's all.'

'I can leave that until Wednesday, can't I?' he reassured himself and, speaking into the phone again, arranged with Meirion Thomas to meet him in Birmingham the next day. The DI had already confirmed that noon would be a convenient time for them to descend on the mortuary there and after some amiable banter in Welsh, Richard put the phone down and followed Moira back to the laboratory, where the three women in his life were regaled with the news he had just had from the Midlands.

'They've found the missing head!' he told them. 'In some

chap's shed in Birmingham, of all places.' When he had repeated
the sparse information that he had heard on the phone, he asked
Angela if she would like to come with him in the morning when
he went to examine it, but she gracefully declined.

'No thanks, Richard. I've seen many horrid things, but unless
you really need me, I think I'll pass on looking at a ten-year-old
head in a bucket!'

Later, he wondered if his astute partner had realized that it
was possible that her former fiancé, Paul Vickers, might also be
present, as he was also involved in the investigation of the bog
body.

Richard retired to his room to look at a road atlas to see the
best way to get to Birmingham, as this was a part of the country
which was unfamiliar to him. It was a good excuse for him to
have a few minutes with one of his favourite books but he soon
exhausted his quest, as the route from the Wye Valley was all
too obvious.

'Up to Ross, then Malvern, Worcester, Bromsgrove and then
into B'rum,' he murmured to himself.

When they assembled in the staff room for their afternoon tea
and biscuits, Jimmy Jenkins came in from the vineyard where
he had been hoeing the last of the weeds from around the roots
before winter set in. When he heard that 'the doctor' was off to
Birmingham next day, he immediately volunteered his services
as a chauffeur and Richard could find no reason to disappoint
him. Jimmy had acted as his driver from time to time, usually
on long journeys and, despite being such a laid-back character,
was actually very alert on the road.

They both agreed that it would be best to allow at least three
hours for the journey and so at half-past eight next morning
they set out, stopping in Monmouth to fill the Humber's
tank with National Benzole. Jimmy was incensed by the recent
price increase, which took a gallon up to four shillings and
threepence.

The going was easy on such a fine but chilly morning and the
climb up over the Malvern Hills gave a superb view over the
Midland Plain, which stretched away to the horizon.

'First hills that way are the Urals, Jimmy!' said Richard in a
euphoric mood, but the geographic allusion was lost on his

handyman. They stopped at a roadside café near Droitwich for a cup of tea, where Jimmy demolished a doorstep ham sandwich while Richard bought a copy of the *Daily Telegraph*. He scanned the news while his driver champed his way through his snack. Clement Attlee's resignation from his chairmanship of the Labour Party, a black boycott of buses in Alabama, a patent taken out for something called a 'hovercraft' and sixteen new member countries admitted to the United Nations. None of it thrilling stuff, Richard decided and as soon as Jimmy had finished, they were back on the road again.

The last few miles into Birmingham itself were more difficult than the previous hundred, but using a street plan in the back of his atlas and then asking a police constable, they arrived in Newton Street with a few minutes to spare. The coroner's court and mortuary were in this narrow side-street, near the centre of the city, not far from the main railway station and very close to the large children's hospital. Courts, police stations and other civic buildings crowded the area, but to Jimmy's satisfaction there were also several pubs within sight.

They cruised slowly down the short street until they saw the red-brick coroner's court. It had a gate to a narrow lane at the side, from which a hearse appeared, marking it as the entrance to the mortuary.

There was no room to park in the lane, but Jimmy found a space further down the street. He declared his intention of finding the nearest boozer and promised to be back at the car in two hours' time, happy to wait for his boss for as long as necessary.

Richard hauled his black bag out of the Humber's boot and made his way back to the entrance of the court. Here a coroner's officer showed him into a waiting room where DI Thomas from Cardiganshire was standing with several other plain-clothes officers from Birmingham.

Meirion Thomas introduced him to the Winson Green detectives, Trevor Hartnell and Tom Rickman. They brought him up to date with the finding of the head and the meagre information they had prised from the former publican of the Barley Mow.

'We're seeing another villain later this afternoon,' explained Hartnell. 'He's banged up in prison, but we hope he can tell us a bit more, possibly even give us an identity.'

After a little more chat, the coroner's officer, a middle-aged constable whose developing arthritis made him unfit to pound a beat, asked Richard if he would have a word with the coroner. He took him through into an inner sanctum, where he met Doctor Theobald Priestly, a dapper man in his fifties, who had qualified as a barrister at Lincoln's Inn some years after becoming a medical practitioner. Richard knew that in some of the larger cities, such as London and Birmingham, doubly qualified men were preferred as coroners.

Doctor Priestly had greying ginger hair with a matching Van Dyke beard and Richard felt that with a lace collar and a rapier on his belt, he could have walked straight out of a Restoration portrait. He came around his desk and shook hands, motioning his visitor to a chair.

'Damned odd affair this, doctor!' he remarked, in what Richard's mother would call a cut-glass accent. 'Two coroners each with part of a body in two different countries!'

'Well, we're not yet sure that they are parts of the same body, but I'll do my best to find out,' replied Richard. 'If it seems likely, which way will the parts go?'

The coroner gave his beard a brief massage.

'I'll have to discuss this with my counterpart at your end, but if what our CID fellows suggest may be true, then the cause of his death sounds as if it's more a matter for this city than Aberystwyth. No hope of deciding where he died, I suppose?'

Richard shook his head. 'I don't see how that could be established, given the length of time that's elapsed. With no known scene of death to examine, it seems impossible, unless some solid new evidence comes to light. But that's a matter for the police, rather than me.'

A few minutes of chat established that they had several mutual acquaintances in the Royal Army Medical Corps, as Doctor Priestly had spent most of the war in a Field Ambulance, ending up commanding one in the Italian campaign. When Richard left his office, he felt pleased with this new contact, as the coroner had promised to keep him in mind whenever he need someone to stand in for one of his regular pathologists.

Outside, the coroner's officer led him and the detectives down a passage and out into the body store of the mortuary, a busy place with a large throughput of bodies from the central part of the huge city. The outer area was where the hearses and plain vans loaded and unloaded coffins into a hall lined on one side by a bank of refrigerators. Beyond this was the mortuary assistants' office, which housed the registers and the inevitable electric kettle and tray of chipped mugs and cups.

An amiable senior technician welcomed them and promised tea and biscuits as soon as they had finished.

'A bit out of the usual run of "pee-ems", doctor!' he observed. 'A body in a bucket, almost! I thought we could do the necessary on one of the tables, if that suits you.'

They trooped into the main post-mortem room, a large, bare chamber with a partial glass roof and half a dozen porcelain autopsy tables in a row down the centre. Waiting there was a police photographer with a large camera and flashgun.

Three of the slabs had corpses on them, one being in the process of being sewn up and made presentable by another mortuary attendant. On one of the empty tables stood a metal container with a police exhibits label tied to its handle with string. The photographer began by taking a few shots of it, the flashes from the bulbs illuminating the whole room.

'What do you need, doctor?' asked the senior technician solicitously. 'Will just an apron and gloves do, or do you want a gown as well?

Richard settled for a green rubber apron and some rubber gloves and approached the table with the canister. Close behind came the two CID men, Trevor Hartnell already lighting up a cigarette. 'Can't stand the stink in these places,' he said apologetically. 'Blood and Lysol, I reckon!'

His detective sergeant seemed immune to smells and stood impassively on the opposite side of the white table, still wearing his belted mackintosh and wide-brimmed trilby.

'Right, sir, I'd better identify this properly to you.' Hartnell, who wore a heavy grey overcoat, tapped the label on the handle. 'This is the container we recovered yesterday from a shed at 183 Markby Road, Handsworth. It's been dusted for prints, not that I think that will help after it's been knocking about for all these years.'

Richard took a stainless-steel T-bar from the assortment of

mortuary tools left on the table. This was like a short, wide screwdriver with a crossbar, used for levering off skullcaps after they had been sawn through. He used it now to pop off the lid, which he laid to one side, allowing a pungent aroma to arise from the interior of the drum.

'That's mainly methylated spirit, by its smell,' he remarked. Peering inside, he saw strands of hair floating under the surface, but resisted the temptation to use them to lift out the head, in case they detached from the scalp. Sliding both gloved hands down the sides, he carefully hoisted it out and laid it on the table.

The head was covered in shrivelled skin of a pale greyish colour, with a wizened caricature of a face. It seemed to have collapsed in on itself, the cheeks hollow and the eyelids lying back in sunken sockets. There was no sign of decomposition and the hair, which was still black, lay in wisps across the scalp. The lips had contracted back in a bizarre grin, showing irregular teeth in grey gums.

Richard stood back to allow the photographer to take a series of pictures from various angles.

'Why the pale colour, Doc?' asked Tom Rickman, who seemed unmoved by the gruesome object.

'Alcohol fixes the tissue like that, making them hard, not like formaldehyde. It used to be used for preserving specimens many years ago and some of the pots in old medical museums are full of it.'

'The head has lasted well, if it really is ten or more years old,' observed Hartnell.

The pathologist agreed. 'It also tells us that the head was put into preservative quite soon after death, as there's no sign at all of decomposition.'

'How soon, doctor?'

'Depends on the environment and even the season. A head will last much better than the belly, but in cold weather like this December, it would keep fresh for a week at least, but left in a warm house or during hot summer weather, a couple of days would see it going off quickly.'

The two detectives peered intently at the face.

'I haven't been around our manor for very long, so I wouldn't expect to recognize him, even if that horrible face was in better shape,' said the inspector. 'What about you, Tom? You've been in Winson Green for a long time.'

The sergeant leaned closer, then shook his head. 'Doesn't ring a bell with me. But I doubt his own mother would recognize him, all shrivelled like that.'

Richard got to work, taking the head in his hands and studying it closely from every angle. He lifted the stiff eyelids and saw the globes inside had collapsed completely. The jaw was immobile, due to the fixation of the muscles by the alcohol, but he could see almost a full set of teeth, even though some were chipped and discoloured.

'Plenty for a dentist to get his teeth into, so to speak,' he said. 'I can see some metal fillings at the back and there's one canine tooth missing.'

'Is that going to tell us who he is, Doc?' asked Rickman.

Richard shrugged. 'Only if we get a name by some other means, so that you might be able to find a dentist who treated him and has some records.'

He had left his black bag on a table nearby and now opened it to take out a glass jar in which a piece of bone was padded in cotton wool. Fishing it out, he held it out to the watchers.

'Now for the crunch question!' he said lightly. 'This is a vertebra from the top end of the spine of our friend in Borth Bog. It's got tiny cuts on it where the head was detached, so I want to see if it matches up with the stump of spine on the head.'

The helpful attendant, himself aproned and gloved, held the grisly exhibit upside down on the table so that the ragged undersurface was uppermost. Amongst the tatters of grey muscle, the lower end of the spine was visible, with a central hole where the shrunken spinal cord lay. With a dissecting knife, Richard cut away some of the muscle and, with his fingers, delved down towards the base of the skull.

'Three vertebrae left, which corresponds with being next to this one, which is number four of the seven bones in the neck.' He pointed down at the dried specimen from Wales, which he had laid on the porcelain table.

'Does that clinch it, doctor?' asked Hartnell.

'Suggestive, but not definite. I'd like to see some similar cut marks on the upper one, proving that a knife or something sharp had been used to sever the neck. I need to take it off and have it back in our laboratory for a good look under magnification, after cleaning all the tissue gubbins from it.'

The inspector looked disappointed at not getting a quick answer. 'Nothing else you can do today, doctor?'

Richard grinned at him. 'Fear not, Mr Hartnell! I've got one more trick up my sleeve.'

He turned the head right way up again and set it on the slab, its ghastly rictus of a smile beaming at the three police officers. Then he looked across at the mortuary technician.

'Do you think you could saw the skull off for me, please? It'll be a bit difficult, not being attached to a body.'

The man seemed pleased to have a challenge. 'No problem, sir. I'll get Reg to hold it for me.'

The other attendant, a much younger man, left his stitching tasks and came across to grip the head in his strong hands, while his senior took a knife and slit the scalp across the top of the head, from ear to ear. When he had peeled it back, a more difficult job than usual due to the stiffness of the tissues, he took a silvery handsaw and prepared to attack the exposed bone.

'Don't you use an electric saw?' asked Richard.

'The younger lads do, but I'm of the old school, doctor, I like to use a bit of muscle on it.'

Richard concealed a smile, as if he was right about the identity, quite a lot of muscle would be needed.

The technician laid the saw blade against the skull and began sawing almost horizontally around the circumference, with a slight V-shaped dip on each side to allow a good fit when it was replaced. However, as Richard watched his face, he was gratified to see a frown appear as the man's efforts seemed abnormally strenuous.

After a few moments, he stopped for a rest. 'Bloody hell, sir, this is as hard as flint!' He tapped the top of the skull with the back of the saw, producing a dull, almost metallic sound.

Richard, with some relief, turned to the detectives.

'I think we can take it that the rest of this fellow is lying in Aberystwyth mortuary. I'll get it X-rayed to make certain and do some other tests, but I don't think there's any doubt at all now.'

*   *   *

An hour later, they were back in the coroner's office where Richard gave his provisional findings to Theobald Priestly.

'The head must be from the body in the bog,' he said firmly. 'It would be a remarkable coincidence if they both had the same very rare disease. The number of spinal vertebrae match up, three on the head, four on the body, which gives the correct total of seven.' He added this for the benefit of the police, rather than a medical coroner.

'You say you would like the head X-rayed, just to check on the bone density?' asked Priestly.

'Belt and braces, really, just to make sure. The skull thickness was hardly above average, but it certainly was abnormally dense. I'm afraid your mortuary technician had to swallow his pride and send for the electric saw!'

'Fine, I can arrange to have it taken to the hospital for an X-ray,' agreed the coroner. 'One of the radiologists is a friend of mine, so he can look at the films. I'm sure he'd be interested in seeing an Albers-Schonberg, it's so rare. You know, I've never seen one in my thirty years as a doctor.' He sounded quite pensive, as if this had made his life incomplete.

'Perhaps you could ask him if he knows of any cases reported in the Birmingham area,' suggested Richard. 'It might help to put a name to this chap.'

The group soon broke up, the coroner needing to contact his opposite number in Cardiganshire and the CID men going off to report to their seniors, before making their way to Winson Green prison.

For Richard, his priority was getting back to Jimmy Jenkins at the car and finding somewhere to have a late lunch, before setting off for the Wye Valley.

With some relief, he dumped his bag into the waiting Humber, complete with an extra vertebra and a fragment of skull for Sian to decalcify.

'Home, James, and don't spare the horses until we come to a café!'

FIFTEEN

Winson Green Prison was a huge and forbidding Victorian structure stretching along the A4040 in the centre of the suburb of the same name. It had a high stone wall and an entrance which looked as if it should have 'Abandon Hope All Ye Who Enter Here' carved above it. With a bad reputation even among English prisons, both for the prisoners' living conditions and the degree of violence of both inmates and warders, it was often in the news for one scandal or other.

Given the now major status of the death of the bog man – and the possible involvement of one of Birmingham's most notorious gang leaders – the Assistant Chief Constable had pulled enough strings with the prison authorities to get a rapid approval for his detectives to interview Billy Blair that day.

As DI Hartnell and Sergeant Rickman waited in the cold outside the wicket gate in the massive main doors, the inspector asked Tom if he knew Blair, as the convict had been incarcerated before Hartnell had arrived in this part of the city.

'Yes, a real toerag is Billy Blair,' growled the sergeant. 'One of Doyle's gang from way back. He's done a couple of stretches before, mainly for assault and obtaining money by menaces. This time he's doing six years for robbery with violence. He must be getting near time for release; he lost his chance of parole because of an attack on a warder.'

'Sounds a nice chap,' said Hartnell sarcastically, as the door opened and they began the laborious process of being admitted, with much signing of passes and jangling of keys as they were escorted through half a dozen gates and doors.

Eventually they came to an interview room, the bleakness of which made their similar facility in the police station look like a luxury boudoir. The bare concrete chamber was divided in half by a heavy wooden counter, above which was a high barrier of steel mesh.

A few hard stools stood on their side and as they sat down, a
door opened in the far wall beyond the screen and a sullen-looking
warder led in a man in grey prison overalls, who he pushed
towards a single stool opposite the policemen, before moving
back to lean against the wall. 'This is your William Blair,' he
announced in a surly voice.

'I'm Detective Inspector Hartnell and this is DS Rickman,'
began Trevor.

'I know that bastard Rickman, he nicked me once . . . and I
got off!' sneered the convict, setting the tone for the interview.
He was a wiry, pugnacious-looking man of about forty, with
cropped blond hair and a square, ugly face, which had a scar
running down from the left eyebrow, part closing the eyelid in
a permanent droop.

'We just want to ask you a few questions, nothing to do with
why you're in here now,' continued the DI, trying to avoid
antagonizing the man.

Billy Blair looked at him suspiciously through the wire.

'Why should I bother? What's in it for me?'

Hartnell shrugged. 'If you're helpful, it'll be noted on your
record. I hear you've already lost your chance of parole, but a
few Brownie points can't do you any harm.'

The prisoner continued to glower at them. 'Whadd'yer want
to know?'

The sergeant had less patience than his senior, especially as
Blair had got off to a bad start by insulting him.

'We want you to tell us about this head. The one that used to
be in the old Barley Mow.'

This must have been about the last question on earth that Blair
had expected and his genuine surprise was apparent to the two
detectives. But he rapidly covered up and growled his denial of
any knowledge of the matter.

'I don't know what the 'ell you're on about!'

'Come off it, Billy!' snapped Rickman. 'We've just taken it
from Olly Franklin's shed.'

Blair's face suffused with anger. 'That fat, drunken bastard!
Was he the one who set you on to me?'

His tone suggested that if he was at liberty, Olly would rapidly
suffer for his treachery.

'Never mind about that! Tell us about this head,' demanded the inspector.

'Never heard of it! Don't know what you're talking about,' replied the convict, defiantly.

'Listen, Billy, we've not only got the head, we've got the rest of the body too. It's a murder investigation now and at the moment, you're the only one in the frame for it.' Hartnell was not averse to stretching the truth when it seemed useful.

Blair's red face rapidly paled at this threat.

'Don't be bloody silly! What would I know about that?'

Tom Rickman took up the questioning again.

'Come off it, chum! You were one of Mickey Doyle's lads before you were locked up. He's done a runner to the Costa del Crime, so you're the next best thing.'

Blair's small eyes flicked from one officer to the other as he sized up his position. 'Doyle's mob broke up a coupla years ago, after I came in here.'

'This bloke's been dead a damned sight longer than that,' snapped Hartnell. 'He copped it when you were still on the loose, so unless you start talking, we might be looking at you for a Murder One – or at the least, an accessory to murder.'

'You're trying to stitch me up, ain't you?' snarled the other man.

'Tell us what you know about this head,' said the DI implacably.

'Look, I heard about this head years ago, like all the other guys did in this part of Birmingham,' he said in an attempt to be dismissive. 'And yeah, it was in the Barley Mow at one time. I'd forgotten all about it; it was no big deal.'

'No big deal!' said Rickman in derision. 'A feller's head in a bucket of meths?'

Now that they had prised his mouth open, the convict seemed more willing to speak.

'It was a gag that Mickey Doyle used to pull,' he said sullenly. 'When he got the lads together for a few pints, he would get Fred Mansell, the previous landlord, to bring this tub up from somewhere. Then he'd haul it out by the hair and show it to the room, saying that he had plenty more tubs for anyone who crossed him up. Everyone was half-pissed by then, including Doyle. It was a bit of a joke, really, a sort of tradition.'

Even the hardened CID men thought that waving a murdered man's head about was hardly a 'bit of a joke'.

'So why did this charming old tradition come about, Billy?' asked Hartnell, but Blair seemed to be having second thoughts about being helpful and sat sullenly on his stool beyond the screen.

The detective inspector looked across at his sergeant and gave a slight wink with the eye away from the screen.

'Tom, he's admitted knowing about the head, so if he's not going to tell us any more, I think we're obliged to charge him with being an accessory, just for starters.'

Rickman nodded gravely. 'Sure, boss. At least we won't have to drag him down to the station, as he's already banged up here.'

Hartnell turned back to the glowering, but now very uneasy man on the other side of the barrier.

'Last chance, Billy! Two things and I'll let you off the hook for now. First, why did Doyle hold these frightener sessions? And who was the dead chap, anyway?'

Blair shifted on his stool and, after some thought, came to a decision.

'Look, I was never at one of these shindigs at the Barley Mow, right? We all heard about them, but it was before my time. I never saw the bloody head, so I don't know who it belonged to.'

'But you must have heard the gossip, being one of Doyle's mob,' retorted Rickman. 'What was he trying to prove?'

Blair shrugged. 'It was a frightener, like I said. I did hear that this bloke had been a collector for Doyle, going around for the takings from his gambling joints and knocking shops, as well doing pick-ups from the protection rackets. There were a few of these guys, but this one was caught ripping Doyle off big time, so he had him creased as a warning to the others.'

They were getting somewhere at last, thought Trevor Hartnell.

'And hoisting his head out at these booze-ups was a way of reminding everyone, is that it?'

Billy made a face and shrugged again. 'Your guess is as good as mine, mate! But it seems to fit the bill.'

'And you're sure you don't know who it was?' rumbled the

sergeant. 'There must have been a whisper going around, some of the gang are bound to have known him.'

'You'd better ask them then. I told you, it was before my time.'

Blair decided to seize up at this point, having come too close to incriminating himself in these old felonies. He refused to say any more and after another five minutes of fruitless badgering, the two police officers called it a day.

'You'll be hearing from us, Billy,' promised Hartnell as they left their stools. 'Don't think you're walking away clean from this affair.'

With this rather empty threat, they watched as the warder pushed the convict out through the door opposite. When it had closed behind him, Hartnell turned to his sergeant with a scowl.

'That bastard knows more than he's letting on! We need to find some of the old Doyle gang to see if we can sweat a bit more out of them.'

They went off to the station, only a few hundred yards away, to report their meagre findings to the top brass at headquarters.

Next day, the forensic routines down in the Wye Valley were going on as usual. Christmas was fast approaching, now little over a week away. Angela was planning to have a full week at home in Berkshire, family gatherings having become more important now that there was always the fear of another stroke hovering above her mother. Richard had promised to spend a couple of days with his parents in Merthyr, though he had also agreed to stand in as Home Office pathologist for the Gloucester police over the holiday period, as their local man wanted to take his wife and three children up to their grandparents in Derby for Christmas.

The autopsy rate was having its usual festive period surge, as unfortunately it was always a bad time for both suicides and road traffic accidents. Richard was busy every day at Monmouth and Chepstow mortuaries and had several forays down to Newport for 'Section Eight' cases, the shorthand for road deaths where it was possible that a charge of 'causing death by dangerous driving' might be brought by the police. It was usual to ask a Home Office man to deal with these, as the hospital pathologists who did the routine coroner's cases were never keen to get involved in potential criminal cases, partly because they disliked being called to the Magistrates and Assize courts.

Sian was consequently busy with her alcohol estimations, both with post-mortem bloods and with some defence cases where the accused was seeking to contest the clinical diagnosis over 'unfit to drive' by a police surgeon. All in all, the Garth House partnership was thriving, as their reputation spread by word of mouth, cases coming in from a wide area in Wales, the West and the adjacent part of the Midlands. Angela's paternity testing was flourishing, but there was still not enough income to warrant considering an increase in staff.

On that cold but sunny day, they were all in the kitchen, taking a rest from their labours at the afternoon tea-break, when they heard a car zoom up the steep drive and stop in the yard with an impatient squeal of brakes. Richard, who knew most of the vehicles that called here by the sound of their engines, did not recognize this one and stood up to look through the window.

'It's an MG-TC,' he exclaimed, looking out at a small low-slung sports car. It was bright red, with a black fabric hood hoisted against the blustery weather. 'Who do we know who has one of those?'

He was soon given the answer, as a shapely leg emerged from the driver's door, followed by the rest of Priscilla Chambers' shapely body, swathed in a heavy car coat, her auburn hair half-hidden by a colourful Hermès silk scarf.

By now they had all seen her. 'It's Pris, what on earth is she doing here in a car?' exclaimed Angela, as they all moved towards the back door to greet her.

She hugged them all and gave Richard a full-blown kiss on the lips that made his toes tingle.

'I'm frozen,' she cried gaily. 'That car's great, but I need a new hood, there's a gale blowing through it!'

After she had been plied with hot tea and biscuits, she told them her news.

'Thank God for your dismembered body, Richard,' she began. 'I've got a job already, thanks to digging in that blasted bog!'

She explained that having hit it off so well with the Hungarian archaeologist, Doctor Boross had phoned her a week ago and asked if she would be interested in a temporary lectureship in her department at the university in Aberystwyth.

'It's for a year in the first instance and has cropped up as they've got a rescue dig on an old abbey,' she explained. They all pressed their congratulations on her and wanted more details.

'Have you got the job actually in the bag?' asked the more cautious Angela.

'Eva Boross was quite definite about it, said my experience was just right for the post,' answered Priscilla happily. 'I'm on my way down there now for a formal interview tomorrow afternoon.'

'What's with the car, then?' enquired Richard, looking out of the window again at the MG, which was one of the first models manufactured after the end of the war and which was looking its age a little.

'I decided I couldn't survive down in the wilds without transport,' replied the ebullient redhead. 'It's a bit of a banger at seven years old, but it was cheap and it goes well.'

'You can't drive down to Cardiganshire tonight,' protested Moira. 'It'll be dark in an hour or so. You must stay with me tonight and set off first thing in the morning.'

After some token protestations, Priscilla gladly accepted and then Richard stepped in to trump Moira.

'We need to celebrate this, folks,' he said amiably. 'I'll treat you all to a meal down in the village.'

Work was abandoned for the rest of the afternoon, as Priscilla was brought up to date on happenings in Garth House, especially the news that the head of her bog body had been found in Birmingham.

Richard went out for a good look at her 'new' car, admiring what was under the bonnet and assuring Priscilla that a good garage in Aberystwyth could work wonders on its rather shabby appearance.

That evening, they went again to the hotel in Tintern Parva, though Jimmy was not with them this time as he had gone off on one of his mysterious absences, which Richard suspected was some form of organized poaching.

The meal was excellent and they all talked about the delights of leaving rationing and shortages behind.

'It only seems yesterday that we were living on dried egg powder and Spam,' said Angela.

'And the kids had concentrated orange juice and cod-liver oil and malt shoved down their throats every day,' laughed Sian.

'You were all healthier for it, though,' claimed Richard, until he was shouted down for spending much of the war in Ceylon, where he was accused of living on the fat of the land in an officer's mess.

Over coffee, they wanted to know more about Priscilla's new job. 'What's this abbey business?' asked Moira.

'Apparently, approval has just come through for the flooding of a valley up in the hills, for a new reservoir to supply the Midlands. The ruins of a Cistercian abbey will be submerged, along with a large monastic cemetery, so there's a rush to exhume the burials and record anything of historical interest.'

'That won't be popular with the locals,' prophesied Richard. 'You'd better get yourself a steel helmet in case there's a riot!'

'It's a year's appointment, you said?' asked Angela.

'Yes, it also carries a temporary lectureship, and if I'm a good girl and don't offend too many people, Doctor Boross says it may well be extended.'

Everyone was happy for Priscilla, including Richard. As he looked at her across the table, he saw a beautiful, extrovert woman, warm-natured and, as far as he knew, unattached. It occurred to him that Aberystwyth was only a few hours' drive away, easily accessible for a weekend trip. Then his eyes moved to Angela, cool, elegant and highly intelligent, with so much in common with him professionally – and living under the same roof. As he picked up his cup to drain the last of the coffee, he saw Moira looking at him and felt that she was well aware of his appraisal of the two other women. He winked at her, wondering what was going through her mind and received a conspiratorial smile in return.

The Birmingham coroner telephoned Richard the following day, to let him know that he had arranged for the head to be X-rayed in one of the hospitals and that the radiologist had confirmed that the skull did indeed show the presence of Albers-Schonberg disease.

'He says it was not very severe, but definite enough,' said Doctor Priestly. 'Sometimes the head can be enlarged or deformed, but the density was markedly increased, so I'm happy to accept that the head came from your body down in Cardiganshire.'

'But we still have no idea who he was?' observed Richard.

'The police here are "pursuing their enquiries", as they like to call it,' said the coroner wryly. 'They've promised to keep me informed and I'll let you know when I have any more news. Meanwhile, I've arranged with the coroner in Aberystwyth to take over jurisdiction and have the body sent up here, as it seems obvious that Birmingham must hold the key to his murder.'

Barely ten minutes after Richard had rung off, Moira came into his office to say that Meirion Thomas was on the phone and when he spoke to the detective inspector, he had much the same news as he had had from the coroner, but with a small addition.

'My contact in the Birmingham CID also told me that they had been interviewing some thug in prison there and it seems apparent that the mystery man was mixed up in the gangs and rackets during and soon after the war. Some arch-villain called Doyle kept the head as a warning to other gangsters not to step out of line and try to rip him off!'

Having lived and worked in Singapore for almost a decade, such a bloodthirsty situation was not all that strange to Richard, as the antics of the underworld Chinese and the Triad wars were more than capable of such excesses. He thanked Meirion for ringing and said that presumably this was pretty much the end of the matter, as far as they were concerned.

'What's left of the body is going back to Birmingham, so I suppose you'll be closing down your end of the investigation?' he suggested.

'Nothing more we can do – in fact, there was virtually nothing we could do before, as we've not had a whisper of information this end,' said the DI. 'At least the Yard isn't coming back here. I doubt a big force like B'rum will need them, either.'

Richard was glad to hear that, for he didn't want Angela upset by the unexpected arrival of Paul Vickers, as had happened some months ago.

After he had told Meirion about Doctor Chambers' good fortune in getting a job in Aberystwyth – perhaps the one good thing to come out of the bog body discovery – he wished him well with his sheep-rustling investigations and rung off. Almost immediately, it rang again, Moira having left it switched through from her office.

This time, rather to Richard's surprise, it was Louis Dumas, from the Vale of Glamorgan. After a few conventional greetings, the vineyard owner rather diffidently wondered whether he could call to see the doctor.

'I'd be very interested to see the ground you are using and to look at that new vine stock you said you had recently planted,' he said. 'But I must admit that I have another reason for wishing to meet you again.'

He cleared his throat nervously. 'I have a private, family matter which concerns me and after hearing what kind of investigations you and your associates are involved in, I wondered if I might have your advice. It is possible that I might need your professional services.'

Richard was intrigued and made encouraging noises, hoping to hear the nature of Monsieur Dumas's problem.

However, the Frenchman was rather reticent. 'It is difficult to explain over the telephone, doctor. Would it be at all possible for me to come up to see you, perhaps this weekend, if you are not going away?'

Richard, conscious of the kindness and hospitality they had shown him at St Mary Church, readily agreed and they arranged that Louis would call at Garth House on the coming Saturday afternoon, two days away.

Richard reported all this to Angela and she was as intrigued as he about the nature of Dumas's problem.

'Either he's being sued for fathering an illegitimate child and wants a paternity test – or he wants his wine analysed to see how much alcohol is in it,' she suggested, with a rare show of facetiousness that she might have caught from Richard.

Her partner shook his head solemnly. 'No, I reckon he's murdered someone, buried him under his vines and wants to know how he can dispose of the body!'

If they had but known it, something near the truth was in one of those light-hearted suggestions.

*   *   *

The Assistant Commissioner (Crime) of Birmingham City Police had pulled out all the necessary stops when, after discussions with other senior officers, he had considered the news delivered by the CID from Winson Green. He instructed his Detective Chief Superintendent to use whatever resources were needed to follow up this bizarre homicide and a number of Headquarters staff were immediately set to research the background of the wartime gangs and Michael Doyle in particular. Some records from wartime had been destroyed in the blitzes and others seem to have vanished, but there was enough information to put together an overview of the situation ten to twelve years ago, added to by personal recollections of some older officers who had been around at the time. Due to retirements and transfer to other divisions or even other forces, these were not numerous, but overall, when the Head of CID had a meeting with a few divisional detectives later that day, they had a general picture of the villainy that had abounded a decade earlier. Trevor Hartnell was one of those present and though only an inspector, his central position in the case so far caused the others to defer to his more immediate knowledge.

'Do you reckon that this chap Blair has anything else to tell us?' asked the chief.

'Yes, he's holding out on something, sir,' said Hartnell.

'But probably he's trying to distance himself from having been one of Doyle's outfit. I don't think he knows who the dead man was or what happened to him. He says it was before his time and I suspect he's telling the truth there.'

'No chance of getting Doyle back, I suppose?' asked one of the DCIs from an adjacent division.

The chief superintendent shook his large head. 'Not a hope! We've been down that route before and it's a dead end. No extradition with Spain, that's why all these damned crooks make a beeline for it.'

'What was it that sent him scooting down there?' asked another chief inspector, who was relatively new to the city.

'It had been building up; we were gunning for him,' said the chief. 'The final thing was when one of his men decided to save his own skin by squealing about a series of big house robberies in Worcestershire and the Welsh border. For the first time, we had a chance to hang them on Doyle, but he got wind of it and scarpered to Malaga.'

The DCI scratched his chin thoughtfully.

'He operated down in Wales as well? Any possible connection with the body being found down there?'

The Chief was dubious. 'A possibility, I suppose. But the crooks from our fair city have always had long arms and the big houses and sparse population down there have always been a happy hunting ground for them. Burglary was the main occupation, though in the days of food shortages, they fed their black-market rackets with a lot of rustled sheep and even cattle from Mid-Wales.'

The discussion went on for a time, but no definite plan of action was drawn up, apart from the exhortation to find and grill as many former members of Doyle's nefarious outfit as possible. In the meanwhile, the ACC decided on issuing a press release which would give all the details they had, including the Batman tattoo, with the hope that someone in or around the huge city might turn in some information that would help identify their mysterious corpse.

In expectation of the visit of the Dumas pair on Saturday, Moira had made a jam-and-cream sponge for them, one of her specialities. She was an excellent cook, mainly because she enjoyed the kitchen so much. Richard and Angela had talked about her talents many times, deciding that her late husband must have been a lucky man for the short time he was married to Moira, before the tragic accident.

Their visitors arrived on time, Louis driving an MK VII Jaguar, which confirmed Richard's conviction that his income was derived from far more than the profit from a small vineyard. Angela entertained Emily Dumas in her pleasant lounge overlooking the valley, while Richard took her husband on a tour of his 'estate' to proudly show off his two rows of recently-planted vines. While Louis Dumas politely admired them and commented on the excellent south-east-facing site, the two women chatted quietly, avoiding the mysterious subject which had brought them to Garth House that day. Angela found her companion a gentle and charming woman, but as Richard had sensed, she felt that there was an underlying sadness in the French woman.

When the two men returned from the hillside, Richard's head full of wise advice on the arcane mysteries of viniculture, Angela went off to make tea and returned with a trolley complete with their best – and only – tea service, of Noritake china brought back from Singapore by Richard. Sandwiches were made with local salmon from the Wye, covertly produced by Jimmy with a meaningful wink, followed by Moira's classic sponge.

When the ritual hospitality had been completed, with every sign of genuine appreciation on the part of the pair from St Mary Church, Angela stood up to push the tea trolley towards the door.

'If you have something confidential to discuss with Richard, perhaps I should leave you in peace?' she offered. Immediately, Louis jumped to his feet and raised his hands in a Gallic gesture.

'No, please stay, Doctor Bray!' he pleaded. 'From what I understand of your expertise here, you may well be able to advise and perhaps assist.'

Quite happy to hear what all this was about, Angela abandoned her trolley and sat down again in one of the armchairs, the two visitors occupying the settee, with Richard in the remaining part of his late aunt's three-piece suite. Louis sat forward, his hands clasped between his knees as he broached the sensitive reason for his visit.

'I am afraid we have a family problem. It goes back a long way – in fact, about twenty-five years!'

His story was quite long and Angela found it very sad, certainly explaining the unhappiness that both Richard and she had sensed in the pair opposite.

Louis described how he had been commissioned into the French army in the mid-1920s. Soon afterwards, he married Emily and she accompanied him when in 1928 he was posted to Indo-China, which was part of the then extensive French colonial empire. They were sent to the relatively remote garrison town of Yen Bai in the north of Vietnam where Emily, a teacher by profession, taught part-time in the small garrison school. She soon became pregnant and rather than having her live in the bleak garrison quarters, Louis rented a pleasant bungalow a couple of miles outside the town. There was no lack of servants to look after them and when their son Maurice was born, he had a devoted baby amah, a Siamese woman named Sukhon.

Unfortunately for the Dumas family, they came to Yen Bai when political trouble was brewing, an upsurge of feeling against the French colonialists. On the tenth of February 1930, about fifty soldiers from the locally-recruited regiment revolted and joined an equal number of nationalist party members in a sudden attack on the French officers and troops.

On the day of the uprising, Captain Dumas was already on duty in the town, his wife being in her school. All officers and men were recalled into the garrison, where they had to organize a defence, then a counter-attack. Unfortunately, in spite of desperate concern for their nine-month-old son at home, they were besieged for most of the day and quite unable to leave to bring him into the safety of the garrison. When the short-lived revolt was crushed, apparently with great ferocity, Louis with a troop of his men, rushed back to his home to find it completely destroyed, along with several other nearby residences.

'It was burnt to the ground, just a heap of smouldering ashes!' he said, with a bleak resignation still in his voice, a quarter of a century after the awful event. 'One of our servants was lying dead nearby, beaten to death as he presumably attempted to escape into the trees. There was no trace of the other three servants, including the amah – nor of our baby son, Maurice!'

There was a sob from the settee as Emily Dumas put a handkerchief to her eyes. Angela laid a compassionate hand on her shoulder. 'What a terrible thing to have happened,' she said softly.

Louis nodded. 'We were naturally utterly distraught,' he continued, in his rather formal English. 'Emily was so ill that the doctors soon sent her back to France to live with her parents in Paris. I stayed behind in Yen Bai to make all the enquiries I possibly could, before also being repatriated to France on compassionate grounds.'

'Was there no better information as to what had actually taken place?' said Richard, choosing his words carefully. What he really meant was whether any bodies had been recovered from the fire and Dumas understood and appreciated his delicacy.

'You will appreciate that this was a time of political turmoil, with violent anti-colonial unrest and a hostile, uncooperative population. One other body was found in the ashes, but it was an adult male. The regiment scoured the countryside for miles around, sometimes brutalizing the locals in their anger at the revolt and the loss of French lives, but of the amah and our child, there was no sign. I spent two months contacting every organization I could – embassies, military and the Red Cross, all without avail. There was no news nor sighting of either Maurice or Sukhon. Then I was sent home and although I never ceased to seek information, nothing was ever forthcoming.'

Both Richard and Angela were beginning to wonder where this tragic story was leading and how it could possibly involve them, when Monsieur Dumas continued his story.

'I was posted to a staff position in the War Ministry, probably out of sympathy for our loss in the line of duty. Emily and I lived in Paris and slowly she recovered, though the catastrophe undoubtedly put a strain on our marriage for some time. Eventually in 1934, our second son, Victor, was born and after what had happened, he was cherished perhaps even more than was good for him. Gradually our lives returned to what passed for normality, until the war came and in 1940 we had to flee to London. The rest I think I have mentioned to you before, that I fell ill and was pensioned off on medical grounds. Somehow, when peace came, France had lost its attraction for us, as both my parents had been killed during the war. Eventually I became the beneficiary of their estate and became financially independent.'

Richard thought that this was a considerable understatement, but it was none of his concern.

'So you came to Wales and went back to your traditional family roots – making wine?' he said, to lighten the rather sombre atmosphere.

Louis Dumas nodded. 'Yes, and we have settled into a quiet, peaceful mode of life for the past ten years. Now Victor is twenty-one and, thankfully, is very interested in the vineyard. He is keen to take over the management as I get older and he has ambitious plans for its extension.'

Angela began to wonder what their problems could be, as it sounded as if they were living an idyllic life, being well off, with a pleasant house, a satisfying occupation and what sounded like a devoted son. However, Richard was beginning to guess the direction in which the story was leading, but he made no attempt to anticipate Louis's narrative.

'We heard no more for many years, until about four weeks ago, when I had a telephone call from London. It was a man calling himself Pierre Fouret and claiming to be my long-lost son Maurice!'

There was a strained silence for a moment, broken only by a stifled sob from Madame Dumas.

'You must have been shocked!' exclaimed Angela, with spontaneous sympathy. 'What did you say?'

Louis ran a hand slowly over his brushed-back hair. 'I was not so much shocked as a little angry – and curious as to how he had obtained my address. Though for years I had desperately sought out information about Maurice, this was the first time that anyone had approached me on the matter.'

'Did he explain himself?' asked Richard.

'He was very polite and restrained, apologizing for springing such a momentous matter on me without warning, but said he could explain all the circumstances, if I would be willing to meet him.'

'Did he not give you at least an idea of his story?' asked Angela. 'It sounds very much like some kind of confidence trick.'

Louis shook his head. 'He said it was too complicated to explain on the telephone, but he was sure that he could satisfy any doubts I may have. He asked if we could meet at any location that I cared to suggest.'

'What did he sound like?' asked Angela, fascinated by the strange story. 'And what language were you using?'

'He had excellent French, but with a strange accent that had a North American twang, but I was sure it also had an Asian element in it – which was partly why I didn't dismiss him as an obvious impostor and slam the phone down.'

Monsieur Dumas looked across at his wife, who was sitting bolt upright on the settee, agitatedly twisting a small handkerchief between her fingers.

'I told the man that I would consider meeting him after discussing the matter with my wife and asked him to call back later that day. I was almost afraid to tell Emily, in case it aroused false hopes which would almost certainly come to nothing.' The French woman spoke for the first time since the story began unfolding. 'I'm now sure that he is genuinely my son Maurice, but Louis is still very cautious,' she said very quietly, before he continued.

'On that first day, both of us were naturally extremely dubious, suspecting that we were dealing with some form of scam, as I think the Americans call it. But after a long talk, we felt we could not risk rejecting any further contact with the caller in case he had some genuine information, so when he phoned later that day, I arranged to meet him on neutral ground, so to speak.'

Louis Dumas went on to relate the rest of this remarkable story, which Richard felt was highly ingenious and detailed, even if it eventually proved to be a tissue of lies. He arranged to meet the alleged Maurice in the lounge bar of the Angel Hotel in Cardiff, an easy place for both to rendezvous, the stranger coming by train from Paddington and Louis driving the dozen miles from his vineyard.

'It was obviously going to be a fraught meeting, but the young man handled it impeccably. He did not throw his arms about me and cry "Father", but offered a polite handshake and an invitation to take lunch after a drink.'

'Did his physical appearance offer any help?' asked Angela, now completely hooked by the drama.

'Not really. He was a pleasant, but ordinary-looking young man, of an apparent age that matched what Maurice would have been now, just twenty-six years old. He was quite well dressed, though not ostentatiously so.'

'Did you recognize any family resemblance at all?' asked Richard.

Louis replied that there seemed to be no features that resembled either his wife or himself, but equally nothing to suggest any exclusion. 'You've seen Victor, our other son, Doctor Pryor. He also has no marked resemblance to either Emily or me.'

He continued his account of the strange meeting in the Angel

Hotel. The young man said that he was a French-Canadian, living in Montreal under the name Pierre Fouret. He said that he would explain the different name shortly and that actually he had grown up thinking that his name was Annan Thongchai!'

A tortuous story emerged, which Louis said made it almost believable, for how else could such a fantasy be constructed without a basis of truth?

'Pierre' was less than a year old when he vanished from Yen Bai and his first memories were of living in a remote village with his 'mother', Sukhon Thongchai. Later it emerged that this was in eastern Siam, a region flooded with refugees from the war across the frontier in French Indo-China. Though he had jet-black hair, it was obvious that he was European, but he was accepted by the village community and was brought up in infancy as a Siamese, the only language he knew apart from a smattering of French that Sukhon had picked up in Yen Bai. She eked out a living as a seamstress and with the charity of her extensive family, as this was her home village before she went away to work. Pierre Fouret did not know how his appearance was explained, but later assumed that the village accepted that some virile French soldier had 'put her in the family way', in spite of his lack of any Asian features. He accepted Sukhon as his mother and only in later childhood did he become curious as to his different appearance, about which his mother was always evasive. In retrospect, it was apparent that the barren woman had always been yearning for a child of her own and the flight from the rebellion had given her an opportunity to abduct Maurice and make her way home to her village in Siam.

Louis broke off his long explanation to ask for more tea and Angela took the opportunity to fill up all around.

'But how did this Pierre get to know all this detail?' asked Richard, as fascinated as his partner with the story.

'Be patient with me, doctor,' replied Louis with a wan smile. 'I will be coming to that very soon.'

When he resumed, he explained how this potentially unstable situation was again thrown into chaos in 1940, when the Japanese occupied Indo-China, now administered by Vichy-France. Sukhon and her family knew that it was only a matter of time before the

Japanese invaded Thailand, as Siam was called after the 1934 revolution. Realizing that such an obviously European boy might become a target for the invaders, she reluctantly took her adopted son to a Catholic orphanage near Bangkok, persuading the Thai sisters to shelter him.

'They were unwilling at first,' declared Louis, 'but Sukhon claimed that he was the child of a French soldier and his wife, who were killed in the insurrections of a decade earlier. She was deliberately vague as to how she had saved the child, but said she had found him abandoned during the turmoil, and escaped with him to her village over the border.'

Being French, and hence a Catholic, the sisters were persuaded and they kept him in the convent for several months, until they managed to place him with an expatriate French-Canadian couple who were patrons of the orphanage. Lucas Fouret and his wife, Angelique, had lived in Bangkok for several years, as he was the senior representative of a Canadian farm machinery company. Childless, they agreed to unofficially adopt Annan Thongchai and as this was patently not his birth name, they decided to call him Pierre. But yet again, total disruption descended upon them, as soon after being taken into the Fouret household in a suburb of Bangkok, Japan attacked Pearl Harbor and immediately demanded that Thailand allowed their armies to cross the country to invade British Malaya and Burma. The Thai government capitulated after only eight hours' armed resistance and the Fourets lost no time in catching a train from Bangkok down to Penang and then on to Singapore.

'Thankfully, they kept ahead of the invading Japanese,' said Louis Dumas. 'They were lucky enough to get a ship to Australia and then another onward to the United States, from where they reached their home city of Montreal. From then on, Pierre led the life of a normal French-Canadian youth, soon becoming fluent in French.

'He now looked on the Fourets as his parents and, when he left school, his adopted father found him a job in the tractor company, where he flourished so that now he is one of the European sales team.'

Monsieur Dumas seemed to come to a turning point in his narrative and, putting his cup and saucer back on the low table, he continued more briskly, as if he was determined to put sadness aside and get to the point of this meeting.

'You might be wondering how Pierre tracked us down after all these years. He explained that when he became a teenager, the Fourets gradually told him what they knew of his past, having learned all there was from the nuns in Thailand, who in turn had been given a sketchy version by the amah, Sukhon. She had never divulged where she 'found' the child nor who the true parents were and Pierre suspected that she had hoped to reclaim him from the orphanage, if no problems had arisen from the Japanese occupation. He happily accepted his new life in Canada and it was only when he began working that the urge to seek his past roots developed. He began making enquiries, hoping to trace Sukhon, but the orphanage had closed down during the war and the nuns were dispersed.

Then he was sent for several months to Paris as a sales representative for his company and took the opportunity to seek information from the relevant newspapers of the time and the archives of the Ministry of Defence. Many of the army records had been lost during the various wars, but eventually he tracked down the siege of Yen Bai, which would have been when he was a small infant.

Then his researches at last came upon the tragedy of the missing child of Captain and Madame Louis Dumas. Convinced that he must be the missing boy, he then had to trace them and further problems arose from the reluctance of the military authorities to divulge personal information. However, with the help of the Red Cross, they were tracked first to London and then, through Louis's pension payments, to the address in South Wales.

He managed to get a temporary transfer to the British sales office in Slough and made his first contact by telephone.

'And that is where our bittersweet problems began!' said Louis Dumas, pensively.

SIXTEEN

On the first day of Christmas week, there was a development in the efforts of the Birmingham police to move forward their investigation into the Winson Green murder, as it had become known. A period of frustrating stagnation had occurred since the head had been matched to the bog body. Attempts to find Mickey Doyle's former gangsters and winkle information out of them had proved futile. A couple of minor thugs had been unearthed who had once been associated with his felonies, but they steadfastly denied knowing anything about the bizarre corpse, other than that, years ago, the head had occasionally been exhibited during drunken revels at the Barley Mow.

Then on that Monday, a letter addressed 'To Whom it May Concern' arrived at the police headquarters and rapidly filtered down to the detective chief superintendent. After reading the short message, he hurried to the ACC's office and within an hour, a conference was being held in his room, to which DI Trevor Hartnell had hastened up from Winson Green.

Several other senior CID men were present and their chief lost no time in passing around copies of the letter that had arrived in the morning's post. Eyebrows were raised as they scanned the brief note and a DCI muttered, 'Well, I'll be damned!' as his comment on the news.

'May be a red herring, of course,' cautioned the chief. 'There may have been more than one Batman tattoo in Britain at that time!'

He cleared his throat and read the letter aloud, to impress it on his listeners. 'He says, "I am an antiques dealer in Ludlow, having been in business there for many years. Yesterday, I happened to see in a copy of the *Birmingham Post*, which was wrapped around a delivery, a request for any information about a man with a Batman tattoo, of which there was a sketch in the article. I recall seeing a man in late 1944, who had an identical tattoo on his upper arm. I could give some further details if they were of interest to you . . . Yours sincerely, Bertram Tomlinson."'

He looked around at his audience for a response.

'Seems that the Chief Constable's idea about publicity paid off,' offered a DCI from the Division adjacent to Hartnell's.

'But why the hell didn't he give us the details he mentioned?'

Lively speculation followed, but the chief super cut it short with a decisive order. 'Hartnell, you're still the prime investigating officer, so get yourself down to Ludlow straight away to see this chap. I'll fix it with the Shropshire force, to tell them you are on their territory. Squeeze what you can from this fellow and let me know what you find.'

Inside another hour, Trevor Hartnell was in a plain black Ford Consul with Sergeant Rickman driving him south-west towards Kidderminster and onward to Ludlow, which was almost on the Welsh border. Hartnell had never been there before and was impressed by the medieval feel of the little town, perched on a hill alongside a huge castle, its narrow streets abounding with half-timbered buildings. Tom Rickman manoeuvred the Ford through the congested lanes to find Broad Street, which was the address on the copy of the letter which Hartnell held on his knee.

'Tomlinson's Antiques . . . there's the place,' he pointed out. Broad Street lived up to its name as there were some empty parking spaces and, moments later, the bell inside the double-fronted shop tinkled as they went in. A gloomy cavern, half-filled with furniture and scattered remnants of past years, led back to an area partitioned off by frosted glass panels. As they approached, a figure came out warned by the bell. It was a cadaverous old man, stooped and slow-moving. Fancifully, Trevor felt he had been transported back into a Dickens novel – the shopkeeper was not actually wearing woollen mittens and round spectacles, but he did have a long, shapeless brown cardigan over a waistcoat.

The policemen displayed their identifying warrant cards and Hartnell explained that they had come in response to his letter, thanking him for his public-spiritedness. Bertram Tomlinson seemed amazed at the rapid reaction and invited them into his glassed-in den, which was awash with papers and documents overflowing from a large desk. He found two hard chairs for them and sat behind the desk, after they had politely refused his offer to make them a cup of tea.

'We were most interested in your statement that you recall seeing a man with that unique tattoo, sir.'

Tomlinson's scraggy head bobbed, his thin grey hair becoming even more dishevelled. 'I had no idea it was something called "Batman" until I read that newspaper on Friday,' he said.

'It's from an American cartoon character, sir. But tell me, in what circumstances did you see this device?'

The old man explained that towards the end of the war, he was visiting the weekly market in Castle Square in the centre of the town, always on the lookout for articles for his shop.

'Most of the stalls were for produce and used clothing, but there were some bric-a-brac dealers who sometimes had items of interest to me. This day, I saw a nice Georgian card table and, rather to my surprise, the stallholder accepted a low offer that I made without too much haggling.'

'Was he the man with the tattoo?' asked Rickman.

'No, he was a heavily built man with a strong foreign accent. I paid cash for it – twenty pounds, I recall – but as it was too awkward for me to carry away, the man offered to drop it from his van when they closed up for the day.'

He went on to describe how the purchase was delivered to Broad Street just after five o'clock. 'It was a very hot day and when the van arrived outside, the driver got out and carried the table into the shop. After exerting himself, he took off his shirt to cool down and as I gave him a half-crown tip for the delivery, I noticed this very odd tattoo on his arm.'

He paused and frowned. 'That was not the end of the story, because a few weeks later, a policeman came around with a list and photographs of recently stolen goods and one of the items was the card table. It was part of a robbery from a large manor house near Oswestry. There were many such thefts in those days, I'm afraid.'

'There still are, sir,' replied Rickman, rather bitterly.

'So what happened then?' asked Hartnell.

'The police took the table away, and though I eventually had

a few pounds compensation from an insurance company, I
certainly came off badly.'

The detectives were beginning to think that they were also
getting a poor return for their journey from Birmingham, but the
DI tried to squeeze as much as he could from the old dealer.

'The man you bought the table from, was he also in the van?'

'Yes, in the passenger seat. The tattooed man did the driving
and carrying.'

'Can you recall anything about the van, sir?' asked the sergeant.
'Its make or even its colour?'

Bertram Tomlinson gave a crafty smile and reached for a
battered notebook that lay amidst the confusion on his desk.

'I can do better than that, Officer!' he said as he opened the
dog-eared book at a point where a piece of paper marked the
page. 'I can give you the registration number!'

'The crafty old fox! I'll bet he suspected that his Georgian table
was stolen, if it was that cheap. Pity for him that he hadn't sold
it on, before it was circulated,' said Tom Rickman, as they drove
back towards Birmingham.

'Just as well he was suspicious of the seller,' observed Hartnell.
'He was afraid that the chap would do a runner after being paid,
so he took down the registration of the van parked alongside his
stall.'

'Amazing that he's still got the number, but I saw that he had
all his purchases and sales written down in that old book. I doubt
it tallies with the one he shows to the Inland Revenue!'

The detective inspector looked at the notes he had made in
the shop. 'I hope the number will still get us somewhere. It's
over eleven years ago, according to Tomlinson's records. The
van may well have been scrapped by now, though the name
of the registered owner at that time should be on record
somewhere.'

'I don't recognize the index letters, do you, guv?' replied the
sergeant. 'EJ 2652 isn't a local one, anyway. I know most of
those in the Midlands.'

When they got back to Winson Green, Trevor Hartnell got
straight on the telephone to an inspector he knew in the Traffic
Department, who rang back an hour later.

'Trevor, that number originated in Cardiganshire. I chased up the Licensing Authority there and the van was a 1939 Bedford 30 hundredweight K-Model, registered to a Jaroslav Beran in Aberystwyth.'

Hartnell and his sergeant had a hurried consultation with their Divisional DCI, who on hearing the latest news, telephoned their boss in headquarters. He wanted instructions on how to proceed, as this looked like another issue that crossed police-force boundaries.

'The Welsh lads had better follow this up,' directed the chief superintendent. 'The ball seems to have bounced back into their court for the moment. Who the hell is this Jaroslav chap?'

'It's a Czechoslovakian name, sir. We had a few Czechs in the army when I was serving. He probably stayed behind at the end of the war.'

'Well, get on to your contact in Aberystwyth and follow it up! Maybe this van is still around somewhere. If you can find it, it had better be impounded for the forensic lab to give it a going over.'

The DCI relayed this to Hartnell, who, though it was getting late in the day, managed to find Meirion Thomas still at his desk in Aberystwyth. After telling him what they had just discovered, he added a caution. 'Of course, it may all be a wild-goose chase! We can't be sure this chap with the tattoo is our lad from the bog.'

A chuckle came over the wires from West Wales. 'I'll put money on it being him! If he was associated with Jaroslav Beran, he must have been involved in something illegal. Beran is "known to us", as they say!'

He went on to explain that the Czech had several convictions in the past for receiving stolen goods and had done two stretches of six months and eighteen months in Swansea Prison.

'I nicked him myself the last time,' he said. 'We tried to get him for the actual burglary, but he wriggled out of it on some legal technicality.'

'Any connections with Birmingham that you know of?' asked Hartnell.

'Not specifically, but it was suspected that he was on the

fringes of a gang who came down from the Midlands in the Forties, knocking off isolated country houses. They were probably also involved in a bit of sheep rustling during the black market days.'

'Is he still around your neck of the woods?'

'Haven't heard of him since he came out of Swansea a few years back, but the probation people must surely have kept tabs on him for a bit. He used to have a sort of bric-a-brac shop down in a back street here, obviously fencing some of the stuff that was nicked elsewhere.'

Hartnell digested this information. 'No hope of identifying this driver chap, the one with the tattoo?'

Meirion Thomas, sitting with his feet up on a chair, staring out at the sea, shook his head at the telephone. 'It's a long time ago. I was only a DC then. I can ask around with the older or retired CID men, but that would have been before he first got arrested, so he wouldn't have come to our notice all that much.'

'What about this van, then? Thankfully, this dealer in Ludlow took down its registration, otherwise we wouldn't have had this break. Is it likely to be still around? Plenty of pre-war vehicles are still on the road.'

The local DI swung his feet down to the floor, ready for action.

'I'll check that with our County Road Tax Office – they're in the same building as us, as it happens. Unless they're too busy with their Christmas parties, I'll ring you tomorrow about it. And I'll get on with trying to find this damned Jaroslav fellow.'

After he had rung off, he clumped down the stairs and followed some passages to the other side of the big building, which still seemed reluctant to shed its atmosphere of an old hotel.

As it was past five o'clock, he expected everyone to have gone home, but found a middle-aged man and a couple of young ladies busy decorating the main office, standing on the public counter to pin up paper chains to the ceiling beams. A cardboard Father Christmas stood on a filing cabinet and a sprig of mistletoe hung from one of the lights. A bottle of Cyprus sherry was surrounded by three half-empty glasses on the counter and it seemed from their jovial and cooperative manner as if the Yuletide festivities had already started.

One of the girls found another glass and pressed a sherry upon Meirion. As he had no intention of more detecting that evening, he accepted, then announced his mission, laying on the urgency of the quest, as it 'was related to a murder investigation'. As the Borth body was the first murder in the area for several years, they knew perfectly well what he was referring to and, with rather giggly excitement, the other young lady took his piece of paper with the registration number and went across to a long bank of metal cabinets, with scores of small drawers, each carrying index numbers.

Within a couple of moments, she returned with a card and laid it on the counter, topping up his glass at the same time.

'There we are, Inspector! That's all we've got on EJ 2652. Merry Christmas!'

He studied the details on the card, which gave the specifications of the vehicle and the list of owners since new. There were six and the last but one was Jaroslav Beran. Meirion pointed to this final name, and asked the girl, who was hovering over the counter, consumed with curiosity, 'Does this mean he sold it on to the last chap?'

She nodded. 'Yes, in July 1952. The current registered owner is Myrddin Evans of Ty Ganol Farm, Comins Coch.'

'Does that mean he still has it?'

The clerk shrugged. 'Can't tell from that. There's no scrapping notification and no further transfer of ownership, but often they don't bother to tell us if it's been taken off the road.'

'You can't tell if it's still got a current Road Fund Licence, then?'

She shook her head. 'You'd have to see the vehicle for that – or at least look at the logbook, to see if it's been stamped to show a current payment.'

With seasonal greetings all round, he thanked them and went back to his office. First job tomorrow, he thought, was to go up to Comins Coch to see if this damned van is still there.

SEVENTEEN

In the house in the Wye Valley, there was as yet no sign of an anticipation of Christmas and work went on as usual. On Tuesday, the solicitor in Bristol phoned to confirm that the date for the Appeal was the tenth of January. After returning from his morning visit to the mortuary in Chepstow, Richard invaded Angela's sanctum across the hall to discuss the arrangements.

'We'll have to stay in London for at least the previous night, as the kick-off is ten thirty in the morning,' he said. 'A pity it's a Thursday.'

She looked at him enquiringly. 'Why is it a pity?'

'Means no chance of a dirty weekend, partner!' he replied with one of his facetious grins.

'You're like an overgrown schoolboy sometimes, Richard!' she replied with mock disgust, though she had to hide a smile of her own. 'If I have to put up with you for a night, I suppose we could stay again at the Great Western in Paddington. It seemed so convenient for the train.'

Serious again, he nodded. 'I'll get Moira to ring up and make a booking. I wonder how it will turn out?'

He was referring to the Appeal itself, as until today they had heard no more from the lawyers since the conference in Bristol.

'Are you happy with our side of the evidence?' asked Angela, motioning to him to sit down in a swivel chair on the other side of her desk.

'I'm quite sure that I can debunk the ridiculously over-accurate estimate of Anthony Claridge about the time of death. What about your end?'

His partner shrugged. 'I'm absolutely sure that the blood splatter couldn't have come from the knife; it had to be the injury to the nose. Whether or not they believe me is out of my hands.'

Richard nodded. 'That's not our problem. We just present the scientific truth as best we can. After that it's up to the lawyers.'

She fixed him with her brown eyes. 'Do you think she was guilty, Richard?'

He thought for a moment. 'It would be wrong to say that I don't care, as any miscarriage of justice is an affront to society, especially if it arises from bigoted minds who are more concerned with their own reputation than with the truth. But what matters to me is offering the best scientific opinion I can, without any influence from sympathy or compassion for the client. Perhaps she did kill him, but on the evidence that was presented to the trial jury, she shouldn't have been convicted, given the alibi she had. That's what matters to me.'

Angela nodded. 'That's how I feel, too. At least Millie won't hang, whatever happens next month.'

There was silence for a time, as they both looked out across the valley, where the trees now wore their grey winter uniform. Richard, conscious of an air of sadness that had descended on them, decided to change the subject.

'What did you think about the last part of the Dumas saga last weekend? A pity if the family get divided because of the return of the prodigal son.'

Recognizing that he was trying to divert her, Angela was grateful for his sensitivity.

'Do you feel this chap from Thailand is genuine?' she asked.

The final chapter of the strange story related to them by Louis Dumas was that the arrival of the alleged missing son had created a serious rift in the family. Though the father maintained a neutral scepticism until more proof was forthcoming, Emily Dumas was convinced that Pierre Fouret was her long-lost son, Maurice. When the younger Dumas, Victor, learned of the extraordinary reappearance of his brother, he exploded into a tirade of denial, both because of what he claimed was the cruel deception being played upon his parents, especially his mother, but also with an eye to his inheritance. Apart from the house and vineyard, his father had extensive property in France and the prospect of having to share it with an alleged elder brother incensed him beyond measure. He had denounced the man as a scheming impostor and every argument put forward by his parents was met with a contemptuous dismissal.

'If he could find those facts from the army records and the old newspapers, so could anyone else, especially a confidence trickster intent on swindling you!' he had declared, according to Louis. He refused to take part in any medical tests or to meet Pierre, threatening that if he came to the house, he would walk out on him.

The Dumases had consulted lawyers and employed an investigative agency, but they were not helpful, saying that as far as they could determine, the facts advanced by Pierre Fouret were true, but repeated what Victor had pointed out, that such public information was available to anyone who had the incentive and patience to dig deeply enough. They had contacted the Fourets in Montreal and confirmed that Pierre's story was true as far back as his being taken by them from the orphanage, but there was no corroboration of what had happened in the years prior to that.

'We even made enquiries through the British Embassy in Thailand,' Louis had said. 'But it was impossible to locate any of the nuns in the former orphanage as it had long been disbanded. Enquiries in Vietnam were out of the question, as since the contentious splitting of that country into two by the Geneva Accord of 1954, the northern part containing Yen Bai was now communist, making a search for Sukhon impossible, even if she were still alive in war-torn Indo-China.'

Angela and Richard had discussed this before and the obvious direction of the Dumases' concern was whether any biological tests could determine whether Pierre Fouret was really Maurice Dumas.

Angela sighed. 'I told them time and again that there was no technique based on blood tests or anything else that could absolutely prove that any child was the offspring of a particular person. All that can be done is to exclude that possibility – but it sometimes seems hard, even with intelligent, educated people, to get them to believe it.'

Her partner ran a hand through his springy hair.

'I know, it's like a doctor telling a patient some important fact about their illness, then finding that however well you explain it, their mind seems reluctant to accept it if it doesn't fit with what they want to know.'

'I can give them probability results, which sometimes can be pretty near a positive answer,' agreed Angela. 'But you can never get to the hundred per cent mark, even if you get lucky with all the blood subgroups and the other factors that are being discovered all the time.'

'What about the genetic stuff that these people discovered in Oxford the year before last?' asked Richard. 'Will there be any hope of this DNA being useful?'

'You mean Crick and Watson?' she replied. 'Well, who knows what may come out of it in years to come. But at the moment, it's just a nice toy for geneticists. It's not going to help the Dumas family.'

He stretched and hauled himself out of the chair. 'Well, anyway. I'm sorry for them, as until this is settled one way or the other, there'll be no peace in the family.'

That same morning, Meirion Thomas and his sergeant, Gwyn Parry, drove north out of Aberystwyth for a few miles on the A487 until they reached the village of Comins Coch.

'Do you know where Ty Canol is?' asked Meirion, as Parry swung the Wolseley off the main road and drove through the village back out into the countryside to the south.

'Yes, and you should too! It's where we had that stake-out for almost a week, about five years ago. Remember, we had a tip-off about rustlers and damn-all happened.'

There had been so many of those attempts to foil the sheep thieves that the DI had forgotten this one, but when the white-washed farmhouse came into view after a couple of miles, it all came back to him.

'Myrddin Evans, he was the farmer, wasn't he?' he recalled.

'Yes, and there he is!' said the sergeant, pulling up at the gate to the yard. A man wearing the inevitable flat cap perched on one side was dragging the gate open for them. Gwyn Parry drove across to the other side of the cobbled yard, into the shelter of a rusty corrugated French barn. There was a strong east wind and chaff was blowing around their legs as they got out of the car.

Myrddin Evans had closed the gate again and advanced on them, the skirts of his grubby raincoat flapping, even though he had several turns of binder twine wrapped around his waist. He came near and glowered at the two policemen.

'Don't tell me there's another tip-off about rustlers! I've got all my ewes up in the pound behind the house, so there's no chance of them being pinched!'

He spoke in Welsh, but with a few choice English obscenities mixed in. Meirion always thought that the expression 'swear like a trooper' was nonsense, as they couldn't hold a candle to farmers when it came to foul language.

'Nothing to do with that, Mr Evans,' said Parry, placatingly. 'We called to ask about your van, that's all.'

The weather-beaten face registered surprise. His mouth opened, revealing totally toothless gums.

'I haven't got a bloody van! I use a Land Rover with a big trailer these days.'

Meirion Thomas hauled out a piece of paper from his breast pocket and held it fluttering in the cold wind.

'According to the Vehicle Registration people, you've got a green Ford thirty-hundredweight, number EJ 2652.'

'Oh, that old thing! It's not been on the road for years. The crankshaft went and the body's so rusty it wasn't worth fixing. What d'you want to know for?'

'Have you still got it?' asked the sergeant.

The farmer waved a hand vaguely in the direction of a row of stone-built cowsheds on the other side of the yard. 'Bloody thing is rotting away behind there. I keep fence posts and rolls of wire in it.'

'Is it the one you bought from Jaroslav Beran down in town?'

Myrddin Evans' bewilderment became more obvious.

'Yes, that foreign bugger sold me a pup; I paid forty quid for a heap of rust. Didn't last more than a year before the engine blew up. What's all this about, anyway?'

'That man you bought it from was a crook, Myrddin. We're looking into some of his past activities, for which he may have used the van,' said Meirion evasively.

'Needn't tell me he was crooked,' growled the farmer. 'He sold me that heap of rubbish for a start!'

The DI started to walk across the yard. 'Let's have a look at it, then.'

Behind the grey-slated roof of the cowshed, they found a green van nestling in a patch of dead nettles. All the tyres were flat and it seemed to be sinking slowly into the Welsh countryside. The rusted bonnet was against the wall of the building, so that the back doors were accessible, being kept closed by yet more binder twine being wrapped around the handles.

'Want to look inside?' demanded the owner.

'Yes, it may be that we have to take the whole van away for examination. But let's see what it's like first.'

Evans reluctantly unwound the hairy cord that bound the handles together and with a squeal of rusty hinges, dragged the two doors apart. Inside, the detectives saw a layer of six-foot fencing posts on the floor, covered with rolls of pig-wire and spools of barbed wire. Both being from farming stock, they saw nothing odd in old vehicles being used in this way. The countryside was peppered with old railway wagons, which made cheap and useful shelter for animals, feedstuff and equipment.

They advanced on the old Ford and looked at as much of the floor as was visible. Then they trampled through the nettle stems and dragged open the side doors to look at the sodden, rotting upholstery of the seats.

'Think forensic can do anything with this?' asked Parry.

The DI shrugged. 'Amazing what they can find, sometimes.'

He turned back to Myrddin Evans, who was regarding them with a scowl at this waste of time.

'Have you ever carried meat in this – or killed any animals in it, chickens and the like?'

He shook his head. 'No, never! I used to collect feed sacks from the Farmers' Co-op in it – and sometimes hauled a few sheep or pigs. But never slaughtered in it, I was never into black-marketing, not like some I could mention around here.'

Meirion had his doubts about that, but he was not interested in that now. 'We might have to either take this van away or perhaps have a team of experts up here to examine it. We'll let you know.'

The farmer's scowl deepened. 'Bloody nuisance! Any compo in it for me?'

Meirion pleaded ignorance on that one, but before they left he had one last question.

'Do you know if this chap Beran is still around?'

Myrddin pushed his cap back on his head to scratch his grey bristles with a forefinger. 'He was keeping that old shop he had in Vulcan Street when I bought that damned van off him. But I did hear later that he lived somewhere out of town. Bow Street, I think it was.'

After failing to find Beran in the telephone directory, the legwork that followed was delegated by Meirion Thomas to a couple of detective constables. They were sent to comb the Electoral Roll and question the Rates Department in the County Hall for any address of the elusive Czech. Nothing at all was found in the name of Jaroslav Beran and by mid-afternoon, the DI had sought the advice of the Deputy Chief Constable, David John Jones.

'How the hell did a fellow with a name like that ever come to be in Aberystwyth?' demanded Jones.

His senior – and only – ranking officer in the CID looked down at his boss.

'At the trial that sent him down for eighteen months, it was said that he was a member of the Free Czech Army during the first part of the war, but he was invalided out in 'forty-two, on account of being accidentally shot in the foot.'

'Did it himself, I'll bet,' grunted the DCC. 'That's an old dodge. But someone must know where the damned man is?'

'He's certainly not around here. That farmer who has his old van thought he had moved to Bow Street, but there's no mention of him being there in the county records. I'm waiting to have a call back from someone in the Parole Board in Swansea. They must surely have kept tabs on him, or he'd be back behind bars by now.'

When he went back to his own cubbyhole of an office, there was indeed a call from Swansea, with interesting information about the missing man.

'He changed his name, that's why you can't find him,' said a man identifying himself as Beran's probation officer.

'Can an ex-con do that?' demanded the DI.

'Yes, he can these days. He claimed that his foreign name was a hindrance to him getting a job and like many of his Czech and Polish ex-forces friends, he wanted an English-sounding name.

As long as we could still keep track of him, we had no reason to object, so now he's officially called James Brown. We've got an address for him, it's Gelli Derwen, Llancynfelyn, near Borth.'

The detective inspector almost fell off his chair with astonishment. Llancynfelyn was within bowshot of the part of Borth Bog where the body had been buried. In fact, it was there that the police vehicles had parked when they went to dig it up.

He hurried back to David Jones' room with the news.

'This fellow has to be involved, somehow! It's far too much of a coincidence that the tattooed bloke drove Beran's van years ago in some crooked scheme involving stolen goods from houses robbed by Midland gangsters.'

The DCC, usually a placid man more concerned with staff rosters and overtime claims, became almost animated.

'You're right, *bach*! But why the hell would he go back to live on the edge of the bog?'

'Morbid interest or a guilty conscience?' suggested Meirion. 'So what do we do now? Bring in Birmingham – or even the Met?'

David Jones scowled. 'Nothing those London blokes can do that the Midlands and ourselves can't. Best tell Birmingham straight away – and you'd better get the forensic people to go over that van you told me about.'

Once again, Meirion beat a retreat downstairs, where he first phoned the liaison officer at the Home Office Forensic Science Laboratory in Llanishen, on the outskirts of Cardiff. They already knew about the case, as they had dealt with some of the material from the bog exhumation, but Meirion explained the new developments and the DCI who acted as a go-between between police forces and the lab, promised to come up next day with one of the scientific officers, to have a preliminary look at the old van.

The next call was to Trevor Hartnell in Winson Green, who was still nominally the Investigating Officer in the death of the tattooed man. He was delighted to hear of the progress made in Aberystwyth and wanted to be in on any interview with Jaroslav Beran, presumably now to be known as 'James Brown'.

'At least it's less of a mouthful – and we can call him Jimmy,' he said cheerfully. 'I'll talk to my DCI and probably the chief super first, but I'll have to come down there. Can't get there until tonight, I'm afraid.'

Meirion could see a risk of his Christmas going down the pan, but there was nothing new in that for a policeman.

'No problem, he's been here for years, so another day won't matter. He's hardly likely to do a runner after all this time.'

That same Tuesday afternoon, a violent altercation took place at the side of the main A49 road between Hereford and Leominster, a few miles north of the city.

An elegant two-tone Alvis saloon was pulled up close behind a large green Post Office Telephones van which had extending ladders secured to the near side.

The driver of the GPO vehicle descended from his cab and stomped angrily back to the car, where the driver had wound down his window, ready to engage in a shouting match.

'What d'you mean by blowing your bloody horn at me all the time?' snarled the man from the van, a large, pugnacious fellow dressed in dungarees.

The car driver, a portly man in his fifties, glared red-faced up at him. 'Because you cut me up back there, pulled right across in front of me. I want to see if you've scratched my offside wing!'

The van man put his hands on the roof of the Alvis and bent down so that his face was almost in the window opening.

'Don't be damned silly, mister. I had to pull in because of oncoming traffic, but I didn't come within feet of you!'

Another higher-pitched voice came from inside the car, where a woman was sitting in the passenger seat.

'Oh yes, you did! I'm sure I heard a scraping noise as you passed!'

The car driver pulled at his inside door handle and tried to open it against the bulk of the GPO man.

'Get out of the way, I want to see if there's any damage,' he snapped, his fleshy face now suffused with angry indignation. He struggled out and pushed past the bigger man, who was at least a dozen years younger, and half a foot taller. Bending down near the front of the sweeping front wing, he stared at it, then ran a hand over the lower offside edge.

'Yes, I thought so!' he shrieked. 'Those are new scratches. Now the whole wing will have to be resprayed!'

It was the van driver's turn to push him side, as he bent to make his own inspection.

'I didn't do those. They must have been there already. There's none of my green paint in them. I told you, I didn't come near your damned car!'

'You must have!' screeched the Alvis driver. 'I'm going to have a look at your nearside.' He padded away between the vehicles to the grass verge and scanned the side of the van. With a howl of triumph, he pointed to the skirt of the rear part of the body, where low down behind the rear wheel, the green panelling had a comb-like series of grey lines. 'I told you so! You did scrape across my front. Those are the same colour grey as my paintwork!'

The van driver ran a perfunctory hand across the offending area of metal.

'Get away with you! Those were there before. You're just a bloody troublemaker. I'm off, can't waste time with the likes of you.'

Without further ado, he walked round the front of the green van and opened the driver's door. Almost gibbering with righteous anger, the tubby Alvis-owner hurried around him and, reaching into the cab, snatched the ignition keys from the dashboard.

'You're not going until we settle this!' he said quaveringly, holding the bunch of keys defiantly behind his back.

'Give me those flaming keys, blast you!' roared the other man, who was not used to being crossed by posh little men who criticized his driving skills. He advanced on his antagonist, who made the mistake of throwing the keys into the winter undergrowth of the verge, where they vanished into a tangle of brittle stems and briars.

'You can look for them once you've admitted being in the wrong and given me your name and address,' retorted the car owner, his voice almost squeaking with tremulous emotion.

With a howl of rage, the GPO driver gave him a push in the chest, which sent him staggering back against the gleaming radiator of the Alvis. He lost his balance and slid down to sit momentarily on the chrome bumper, then slowly subsided on to the road surface, where he toppled over and lay still.

At this, his wife erupted from the front of the car, followed by another woman who had been sitting in the rear seat. They crouched over the fallen man, whose face was now pale, with sweat beading his forehead, in marked contrast to the purple enragement of a few moments earlier.

'You've killed him!' screamed his wife. 'Get an ambulance!'

EIGHTEEN

Samuel Jackson was in fact not dead at the scene, but he died an hour later in the Casualty Department of Hereford County Hospital.

He had only been admitted a few minutes earlier and the junior doctor who saw him had time only to administer oxygen and give a few last-hope injections to try to bolster the feeble, irregular heartbeat. Then the SHO had sent urgently for his registrar, but it was too late and after talking to the distraught widow and her fellow passenger, both doctors were in a quandary as to the cause of death.

Over a hasty cup of tea in the sister's office, they discussed what they should do.

'Do the police know about it, Tim?' asked the registrar.

'There were two constables who came behind the ambulance,' replied the young doctor. 'They were talking to the driver of the van outside, then they came in to see the wife and sister, who were carrying on about manslaughter!'

The registrar rolled his eyes heavenward. 'Let's keep out of that! He didn't have any injuries, did he?'

The SHO shook his head. 'Nothing worth talking about. A few trivial scratches on his back, that's all. The wife said that he had been struck in the chest and fell back against the car, then fell to the ground.'

'Nothing on his chest?'

'A bit of reddening over his sternum, but no bruises.'

The registrar looked at his watch anxiously. 'I've got to be off. I've told Mrs Jackson that we think the cause of death was a heart attack, but that in view of the circumstances, we have to report it to the coroner.'

As he made for the door, the sister hurried in and grabbed the harassed younger doctor and hustled him out to see another emergency, a farm worker who had cut his wrist half-through with a billhook.

That evening, Richard Pryor was in Angela's upstairs sitting-room, watching their newest acquisition, a Bush TV-53 with a fourteen-inch screen in a wooden cabinet. He had decided to treat themselves to a Christmas present and only that day a dealer from Chepstow had installed the device and erected an aerial on a long pole attached to a chimney. He warned that reception in the Wye Valley was 'a bit dodgy' due to the hills on either side, but to a novice like Richard, the slightly blurred black-and-white images were enthralling. Angela's family home in flatter Berkshire boasted much better reception, but she kept it to herself, not wanting to spoil her partner's obvious pleasure.

However, someone else soon spoiled his enjoyment of the end of *Panorama*, as the telephone extension in her room began ringing. It was the Hereford coroner's officer wanting to speak to Richard about the death of Samuel Jackson.

'Both the coroner and the police feel that we should have a Home Office pathologist on this one, doctor,' he explained. 'The relatives are screaming blue murder – or at least manslaughter, as the chap collapsed after a scuffle. And the hospital would prefer an outside opinion, as he died on their premises and the wife is hinting at their failure to save him.'

It was common after any death in a hospital where there was even a possibility of an allegation of negligence, for the post-mortem not to be performed by their own pathologist, to avoid any accusation of prejudice.

Richard agreed to come up the next day, after he had dealt with a couple of cases in Monmouth, then went back to the start of the *Benny Hill Show*.

When he arrived at Hereford next morning, he found the

coroner's officer waiting for him, together with a detective inspector and a police photographer.

They stood in the little office as the DI explained the position.

'The wife and two sons, one of whom is a solicitor in Worcester, are raising a stink about this, sir. There's no doubt that Frederick Holmes, the Post Office driver, pushed the deceased, as both the wife and her cousin are solid witnesses and Holmes doesn't deny it, though he says he was provoked by Jackson throwing his bunch of keys away.'

'But it was nothing more than a push in the chest, not an actual heavy blow?' asked Richard.

The inspector shrugged. 'Well, the wife is making the most of it, quite naturally. But the hospital doctor says there was nothing significant in the way of injuries.'

'And he died within an hour of this incident?' persisted the pathologist.

'Yes, he was alive when the ambulance reached him. It got there about thirty minutes after the incident. A passing AA man on his yellow bike and sidecar had stopped to see what was going on and he drove off to phone from the nearest box.'

'Do we know if Mr Jackson was conscious after the collapse?'

'He was according to the wife. Groaning on the ground and complaining of a pain in his chest, but then he slipped into a coma by the time the ambulance arrived.'

The coroner's officer, a bluff police-officer nearing retirement, added a little more.

'I spoke to the senior house officer and his registrar, sir. They had told the relatives that they felt that coronary artery disease was the cause of death, but the wife and sons were emphatic that the assault, as they called it, had led to the heart attack.'

Richard trod carefully here, as an incautious word, even to policemen, might come back to haunt him.

'Well, it's true that any stress, emotional or physical, can precipitate a sudden cardiac arrest in people with heart diseases, but it certainly can't cause coronary artery disease. I think we should keep an open mind until the results of the post-mortem. Eventually, it may be a matter for the lawyers, rather than doctors.'

With this hopefully diplomatic remark, he hung up his jacket and went into the post-mortem room next door, to put on his boots and apron. He found Samuel Jackson to be a rather short, plump man of fifty, who looked as if his main form of exercise was going to good restaurants. The coroner's officer said that he was a successful businessman from Worcester, owning a brewery and a chain of shops.

The only signs of injury were the slight scratches on the back of his neck and between the shoulder blades, consistent with sliding down the front of his Alvis, rather than significant evidence of impact. The reddening of the front of the chest seen by the Casualty Officer was no longer visible to Richard's eye.

The internal examination revealed no injuries whatsoever and the only positive findings were an over-abundance of fatty tissue and generalized arteriosclerosis. Most significant of all was severe narrowing of all the coronary arteries, with thrombosis of the main branch of the left artery.

'Could that have occurred in the hour between the incident and the death, doctor?' asked the detective inspector, with a firm eye upon cause and effect.

'I doubt it, as this looks firm and well established,' replied Richard, cautiously. 'But I'll need to look at it under the microscope to make sure. That'll take a few days, but I'll try to get it done before Christmas.'

Mentally he kept his fingers crossed, as Sian would only have until Saturday to make the sections.

The last thing he did was to cut a number of incisions into the muscle of the heart itself, looking for evidence of infarction, but it looked normal, in spite of the blockage of the supplying artery.

The examination over, he stood at the sink to wash his hands and give a summary to the inspector and the coroner's officer.

'There's no doubt that he had potentially fatal heart disease. This must have been developing for years and could have killed him at any time. But I'm well aware that he died within an hour of a stressful argument and a mild blow on the chest, which caused him to fall backwards.'

'So did that lead to his death, doctor?' demanded the CID man, with a terrier-like tenacity.

'To be frank, I don't know. I will have to do some tests to try to find out. If he has severe damage to his heart muscle which arose before the incident, then my opinion is that the argument and very slight physical trauma did not significantly contribute to death, which may have been inevitable. But I'm willing to bet that a lawyer might have a different view.'

'So you don't feel it's justifiable to charge the van driver with causing the death?'

'Let's wait a few days until I do all that I can to clarify the situation,' suggested Richard, not wanting to unnecessarily condemn a man to spending Christmas in police custody.

'He's presumably not going to flee the country over this, so if we hold our horses until we get all the evidence that's available, it will be best for everyone concerned.'

As he drove home with his samples, including the complete heart in a large glass jar, he fervently hoped that some articles he had read recently in the specialist medical journals might help him to arrive at the most just solution.

That same Wednesday was proving a busy one for the usually placid Aberystwyth CID. Trevor Hartnell had arrived following a very early start from Birmingham and, after a late breakfast in the canteen, was going off with Meirion Thomas to seek the elusive Jaroslav Beran, now officially known as James Brown.

The local sergeant, Gwyn Parry, was detailed to accompany the pair that had arrived from the forensic laboratory in Cardiff to look at the old van in Comins Coch.

He sat in the front of their Morris Oxford estate, the rear luggage space filled with the paraphernalia needed at a scene of crime. When he piloted them to Ty Canol farm and led them into the weedy wilderness behind the cowsheds, the two men from Cardiff looked with distaste at the rusting van filled with mouldering agricultural devices.

'What are we supposed to be doing with this?' asked Larry McCoughlin, the liaison officer. 'It's full of junk.'

'There's a faint possibility it was used to move a dead body, maybe around ten years ago,' explained Parry. 'Can you find bloodstains after all this time?'

'Depends on where they are,' replied Philip Rees, the biologist. 'Not much chance if they were exposed to the weather for all that time, but if some has seeped into protected cracks, we may get lucky.'

He was just going to ask if they were supposed to shift hundred-weights of stakes and fencing wire, when the sound of a police Land Rover was heard coming into the yard and two uniformed constables appeared.

'I thought that might be a problem,' said the detective sergeant. 'So I've organized some muscle for you.'

The back of the Ford van was soon cleared and the floor became visible, albeit cracked, dirty and covered with an assortment of debris.

'Made of nine-ply board, that!' growled Myrddin Evans. The farmer had come to watch the desecration of his vehicle and his scowl deepened as Philip Rees levered up the rotting floor with a case-opener.

'I'll be putting a claim for compensation, mind!' he threatened. 'Damaging my property like this.'

Gwyn Parry grinned at him. 'You do that, Myrddin. About five bob should cover it!'

With McCoughlin holding the floor away from the battered side panels and the rusted bearers underneath, the forensic scientist scraped off sludge and debris from along the edges of the plywood. Then he dug a sharp probe into the cracks in several areas of the floor and removed more concealed material, which he put into some specimen tubes. With a few circles of filter paper which he pressed against suspect areas, he did some magic with fluids from bottles out of his case and then viewed the results with interest.

'We've got a positive screening test for blood here. That's by no means conclusive, and it might well be animal, but I'll take this stuff back to Cardiff and get back to you tomorrow.'

The two uniformed constables found a tarpaulin in the back of their vehicle and spread it to protect the floor of the van before putting Myrddin's fencing materials back inside.

'We may need to have that bit of floor taken down to Cardiff, depending on what's found,' said the scientist. 'Until then, it should be OK like this, given it's already been sitting here for years.'

As they all drove away, leaving a bemused farmer wondering what all the fuss was about, a few miles away Meirion Thomas was pulling up in the CID Vauxhall outside a small cottage near Llancynfelyn. Trevor Hartnell got out the other side and was rather overawed by the surroundings, which contrasted so greatly with the seedier part of Birmingham where he spent his working life. Below the road, the ground sloped down to the great expanse of the bog, beyond which the sea sparkled in the sunshine. Looking the other way, the purple line of the hills formed the horizon, whilst near at hand, the whitewashed *bwythyn* of Gelli Derwen was like something from a Grimm's fairy tale, against its background of trees.

They walked towards it and closer inspection took some of the romance from the scene, as the walls were stained with green mould and the window frames showed peeling paint over rotting wood. The front garden was overgrown and a rusty bicycle was on its side near the corner of the single-storey cottage. The door was set between the two small windows, inside which were yellowed net curtains.

There was no bell or knocker, so Meirion rapped on the upper panel. A dog began barking and was followed by a muffled curse and a yelp.

'At least somebody's home,' said Hartnell, feeling in his breast pocket for his warrant card.

There was a rattle of a chain and then the door was pulled open, the bottom grinding against uneven floor tiles. A beery, unshaven face appeared, an unwelcoming scowl fixed in place.

'Who are you? What you want?'

The heavy features, chin and cheeks part-hidden by several days' growth of stubble, glowered at them. Trevor, accustomed to such meetings over many years, was certain that one glance had told the man that these were two police officers standing on his doorstep. They both flashed their proof of identity at him and his dark eyes under the beetling grey bows seized upon Hartnell's card.

'Birmingham? What you want coming from there?'

His central European accent was still strong.

'We want to talk to you, sir. You are James Brown, formerly Jaroslav Beran?'

'Don't use that name no more. James Brown is me.'

'Can we come in and talk, Mr Brown?' said Meirion, easily. 'We're hoping you can help us with our enquiries.'

That ominous phrase seemed familiar to the Czech and his scowl deepened even more.

'Never let us go, do you, once we've been inside? But I done nothing, you ask my parole officer.'

'We already have, sir,' retorted the local DI. 'Now can we come in and talk, please? Unless you want to come down to the police station instead.'

Reluctantly, Brown dragged the door open wider and without a word, turned away to lead the way into the room on the right of a short passage. As Hartnell followed him, he got a glimpse through the other door, where greyish sheets were tumbled on an unmade bed. A dog began whining somewhere in the back of the cottage as the two detectives went into a living room, where a small log fire smouldered in the hearth. Facing it was a sagging settee covered in American cloth and a couple of hard chairs stood by a table near the window, on which was a pre-war Marconi radio and a couple of half-empty bottles of whiskey and gin. The floor was covered in faded linoleum, worn right through near the fire and at the door. Both officers were large men and Brown was also over six feet and equally broad-shouldered, so the small room seemed full of bodies.

'What you want with me?' repeated the householder, not inviting them to be seated.

Meirion pulled a notebook and consulted it. 'You used to own a Ford van, registration number EJ 2652?'

Surprise tinged with unease passed over Brown's coarse-skinned face. He raised a hand to his head and scratched his cropped, bristly hair in a classical gesture of puzzlement.

'Sure, years ago I did. What's the problem, you just discovered I made parking offence?'

His attempt at levity or sarcasm fell flat.

'What did you use it for?' asked Hartnell.

Brown failed to see where this was leading and his beetle-brows came together like two hairy caterpillars above his eyes.

'I had business in Aberystwyth, everybody knows that. I carried furnitures in it.'

'Sometimes stolen furniture?'

James Brown made a sweeping gesture of annoyance.

'Christ, why you bring that up again? Look, sure there were some misunderstandings; I got landed with hot stuff. But I paid twice in the prison for that, now for years I am clean!'

'Did you carry anything else in that van apart from furniture?' asked Meirion.

The man looked shiftily from one officer to the other.

'It's a long time ago. Sure, I used to move all sorts of stuff, sort of transport business for others when they wanted small things moved.'

'Did you ever carry meat of any sort?' persisted Hartnell.

This was a difficult one for their victim. Rationing in Britain had only finished very recently – ironically, long after it had been abolished in Germany. To admit to carrying meat was tantamount to owning up to black-market activities – or even rustling, a crime well established in West Wales.

'No, I never carried no meat! Look, why you asking me all this?'

Ignoring this, Meirion went off on another tack.

'You live within sight of Borth Bog. You must know about the body found there recently.'

Brown grabbed the back of one of the hard chairs and Hartnell tensed himself slightly – but the man was only leaning his weight on it.

'Sure, I heard something about it.'

'Come on, it's almost on your doorstep!' snapped Trevor. 'You must have read or heard that he was man with a Batman tattoo on his shoulder?'

Brown shrugged. 'I don' recall, no.'

'Who used to drive your van when you were in business?' asked Trevor, smoothly.

Brown stared at him suspiciously. 'I had a few guys, different times.'

'And what was the name of the one with a Batman tattoo on his shoulder?'

The Czech stared blankly at Trevor Hartnell.

'What the hell you talking about, mister?' he demanded aggressively. 'You come here, push into my house and talk bloody nonsense!'

'You had an assistant – or more likely, an accomplice – about ten or eleven years ago,' interposed Meirion. He drove for you and carried furniture for you, when you had the shop in Aber. We want to know his name.'

'I don' remember. I had plenty working for me then,' replied Brown, stubbornly.

'We can find out, if you won't tell us,' said Meirion complacently. 'Didn't you keep records, paying their tax and National Insurance?' He said this with his tongue in his cheek and was rewarded with a scornful laugh.

'You making joke? This was in war still, nobody did those damn things. I just paid cash in the hand.'

The local DI nodded. 'OK, have it your own way. Your shop was in Vulcan Street, wasn't it? We can soon ask around that area, plenty of people can still remember ten years back.'

Brown shrugged and stayed silent.

'How long have you lived here?' asked Hartnell.

'Since before end of war – except when I was on holiday in Swansea.' Again the attempt at humour fell on deaf ears.

'Where were you before that?'

'In army, Czech battalion. I got invalided out, now live on little pension.'

Meirion seized on this straight away. 'I looked up your Probation Service records. You left the military in 1942, but you didn't come here until 1944. So where were you in between?'

James Brown looked from one to the other, in a troubled, hunted fashion.

'I was here and there . . . travelling to get job.'

Trevor Hartnell took a chance.

'You were in Birmingham, weren't you? Ever heard of Mickey Doyle?'

'I was in Midlands sometimes, yes. Who this Doyle fellow?'

From then on, the Czech stubbornly refused to admit anything, denying any knowledge of Birmingham gangs or any involvement in organized crime. Eventually, the two detectives decided they were wasting their time until they had better evidence and left the cottage, with a promise – or a threat – that they would be returning, probably the next day.

Their farewell from Brown was a final bellow at the whining dog, then the door was slammed behind them.

'Nice chap!' remarked Trevor, as they walked back to the car. 'I'll bet he was up to something back in my manor in Birmingham. I'll get a check run on him now that we've got a name.'

As Meirion drove away, he looked down at the bog, where there was still a muddy scar where the body had been hoisted from the peat.

'Too much of a coincidence for this fellow to be here, within spitting distance of where we found Batman,' he said ruminatively. 'And we still haven't even got a name for him!'

'You haven't put the heart in formalin, doctor,' admonished Sian. She was looking over his shoulder as he sat at the big table in the bay window of the laboratory, where the light was strongest.

He had a large stainless-steel tray in front of him and, wearing a pair of rubber gloves, was using a forceps and scalpel to cut small postage-stamp-size squares of heart muscle and coronary artery. These went into pots of formaldehyde-saline, to fix the proteins in the tissue, ready for Sian to process them into sections for viewing under his microscope.

'No, and I'll tell you why in minute, Sian. Meanwhile, can you get these blocks processed and give me fibrin stains, an acridine orange and a PTAH, as well as the usual H and E stains, please.' These were special stains, intended to reveal different defects in the heart muscle.

'What's the problem with this case, doctor?' said the technician, being as insatiable as usual in her search for knowledge.

'There's a thrombus in the descending branch of the left coronary artery and I'm anxious to know how long it's been there. The family are claiming that the shove in the chest that this poor man suffered was the cause of his coronary episode and hence his death.'

'And was it?' she demanded, always ready to take the side of the downtrodden masses, even though this particular victim was a rich brewer with a very expensive Alvis motor car.

'Well, his coronary artery disease certainly wasn't, as it must have been there for years. And I don't think the thrombus was either, as he died within an hour of the squabble. But I'd like to know if his heart muscle was already damaged from lack of blood supply, which is why I've got the heart in this tray.'

Sian looked at the organ phlegmatically, unlike Moira, who though she had got used to typing descriptions of unpleasant things, was not keen to view them in the flesh.

'Why have you already sliced across it?' she asked.

'I want to try some new techniques that I've read about in the pathology journals, mainly from the other side of Europe,' he explained. 'The trouble with conventional histology is that it can't show the very early stages of cell death in the heart muscle, just by staining fixed tissue.'

Sian was already ahead of him. 'You're into histochemistry, then. But we haven't got the equipment. You need frozen sections and all sorts of fancy reagents.'

He nodded, pleased at her quick mind and wide knowledge of what was going on in the technical world.

'There are some cut-price methods being tried, where a large slice of tissue, as opposed to little bits for the microscope, can be processed for enzyme content.'

She settled on a stool next to him and put her chin in her hand, prepared to listen to his explanation.

'We're doing enzymes now in my biochemistry course. But how can that help you with this problem?'

Richard settled back to give a lecture, always ready to impart knowledge to those who wanted to hear it.

'Muscles need energy and they get this through turning carbo-hydrates and other nutrients in the blood into carbon dioxide and water, using enzymes, especially the dehydrogenases.'

Sian nodded, in a slightly superior manner. 'Yes, the Krebs cycle and all that!'

'Well, those enzymes are inside the muscle cells, but if those get killed or injured by cutting off their blood supply, as with a coronary thrombosis, then the enzymes leak out through the damaged cell walls.'

Again his technician was ahead of him. 'That's the basis of the SGOT tests we used to do in the hospital. The enzymes became raised in the serum, because they were leaking out of the heart.'

Richard gave one of his impish grins. 'I don't need to tell you anything, do I, Einstein? So you'll appreciate that if the enzymes increase in the blood, they must decrease in the muscle – and that's where these tests are useful.'

At this point, Angela came in from the office clutching a sheaf of papers, but she diverted to the window area to hear what was going on.

'I'm getting taught some biochemistry by Sian here,' said Richard. 'Damned good she is, too!'

The young blonde made a face at him, but she flushed with pleasure at his praise.

'How's it done, then?' demanded Angela.

As she joined the audience, he explained. 'As you said, it can be done now on a microscopic scale using live tissue in frozen sections, but we haven't got the equipment. The same can be done using the same reagents on big slices like these, but it's prohibitively expensive to use large volumes of stuff like nitro-BT. However, recently there have been attempts to use cheaper chemicals, which is what I'm going to try.'

Intrigued, Angela wanted to know what they were.

'According to some chaps in Czechoslovakia and Germany, potassium tellurite and TTC can react with dehydrogenase enzymes and show up deficiencies. I messed about with tellurite a bit just before I left Singapore, but it was too unreliable to be of much use, so I turned to TTC. That's why we've got some here. I brought it back with me.'

'What's TTC?' demanded Sian, determined to be able to show off the next time she went to her biochemistry session.

'Triphenyl-tetrazolium chloride,' he replied. 'A long name, but relatively cheap stuff.' He reached across the table and picked up a small bottle containing white powder and placed it in front of Sian.

'If you would be kind enough to make up a one per cent solution in a slightly alkaline phosphate buffer and – if we can borrow space in Angela's incubator for half an hour – we'll see what happens.'

* * *

As soon as Trevor Hartnell got back to the police headquarters in Aberystwyth, he sat in an empty office offered by Meirion Thomas and did some urgent telephoning. First, he rang his wife to say he wouldn't be home that night, but would be staying in a bed and breakfast place on the seafront, organized by the local CID. He wanted to be on hand if the forensic report, promised by next morning, added any weight to their enquiries, so it was not worth trekking back to Birmingham, only to have to return. After assuring his wife that he would do all he could to be back home before Christmas Eve, to go shopping for presents for their two kids, he spoke at length to his Chief Inspector in Winson Green. He brought him up to date with the visit to the derelict van and the interview with the former Czech soldier, then asked for some digging into the antecedents of 'James Brown'.

'I've got a suspicion that he may have been on our patch towards the end of the war,' he explained. 'Can you organize a search to see if a Jaroslav Beran shows up anywhere in the records for that time, especially if there's any connection with Mickey Doyle?'

His DCI promised to get some men on to it straight away, and with nothing more he could do that day, decided to go for a bracing walk along the promenade in the chill December wind.

After Sian had made up a fresh solution of TTC and Richard had submerged a centimetre-thick slice of the heart in it, the shallow glass dish was placed in the body-heat incubator and left in peace for twenty minutes.

'Leave it too long and there can be a non-specific deposition of the tetrazolium all over the tissue,' cautioned Richard.

'What's the actual basis of the test?' asked Angela, curious about something outside her usual expertise.

'The dehydrogenase enzymes in the muscle convert the colourless TTC to a red dye which precipitates out on to the surface. If there's no enzyme present – or a marked reduction – then nothing happens in that area and the tissue remains unstained.'

They watched the bench timer, bought in a kitchen sundries shop, and when the time was up, there was a feeling of anticipation, as even Moira, aware of something unusual going on, came to watch. Though earlier she had baulked at the fresh heart lying in the tray, the circle of muscle in its glass dish seemed much less repulsive as Richard laid it on the big table.

'There's a pale patch there!' exclaimed Sian, proud that her efforts in making up the solution had contributed to success.

'Yep, just where it should be,' agreed Richard, pointing with forceps at one side of the thick circle of ventricle. 'Blockage of the descending branch of the left coronary artery would cause an infarct of that part of the heart.'

'So what's the significance in this case, Doctor Pryor?' asked Moira.

'It takes some time for the death of the muscle to become apparent. How long depends on the way you look at it . . . just naked eye, with no fancy techniques like this would show nothing for many hours, even a day or two after the blockage. Using ordinary histology would shorten that time, but this is the most sensitive, together with the microscopic techniques that we can't do here yet.'

'So you feel that this rules out the possibility that the push on the chest caused the death?' persisted Moira.

Richard shook his head. 'I can't go that far. But it shows that the infarct – the dead tissue – must have been present well before the incident at the side of the road. This was a man with severe coronary disease, who had already suffered an infarct, so that he was in danger of dropping dead at any time.'

Angela joined the discussion. 'But you can't rule out the possibility that the squabble pushed him over the edge, so to speak?'

'No, I can't. I'm pretty sure that the physical act of pushing him in the chest, which has not left any mark whatsoever, is not relevant. But anyone in a dispute gets an adrenalin release – the old "fight or flight" reaction. Their blood pressure goes up, their heart rate increases and this could well trigger an abnormality of its rhythm, which in a damaged heart, could cause it to stop altogether.'

'So where does that leave the lorry driver – and the family?' queried Moira, who was more interested in the legal liability than the pathology.

'That's a legal matter, not medical. On past experience, I would think that a criminal prosecution would be unlikely, as if it came to trial, the defence would have a field day with the fact that the deceased had already had a recent, potentially fatal myocardial infarct. Still, you never know, there's another legal axiom, which is that "you have to take your victims as you find them".'

Moira's smooth brow wrinkled in puzzlement at this.

'I don't really follow that, doctor.'

Richard did his best to illustrate the point.

'Look, if someone hits another on the head with a blow that normally would not be expected to kill him, but that person has an abnormally thin skull and dies of a brain haemorrhage, it's not a valid excuse to claim that the attacker did not know of the thin skull. Actually, in practice, it's a good point for the defence in mitigation, but the principle is the same as someone with a heart condition.'

Angela, also familiar with many legal dilemmas, pointed out to Moira the difference between criminal and civil actions.

'The standard of proof in a criminal trial has to be "beyond reasonable doubt", but in a civil action for damages, it only has to be a "balance of probabilities" which means that it only has to be proved that it was more likely than not that the outcome was due to the alleged cause. So if the police don't take any action, maybe the family will sue the driver.'

Their secretary was looking bemused by now, but found it all fascinating. 'I'll have to go away and think about this,' she said with a sigh. 'I wish I knew a lot more about these things.'

As she went back to her typewriter, Richard went off to telephone the Hereford coroner to give him much the same opinion as he had offered to Moira.

NINETEEN

On Thursday morning, Trevor Hartnell was sitting in Meirion Thomas's room when a phone call came through for him from Birmingham. His DCI, a gaunt Scotsman nearing retirement, had news for him about Jaroslav Beran.

'We've turned up something about him from way back in 1944. He's never actually been convicted of anything serious up here – just a few drunk and disorderlies and a couple of minor assaults – but he was pulled in a couple of times for questioning on bigger stuff, then released for want of evidence.'

'What sort of thing was he involved in?' asked Trevor, giving a thumbs-up sign to the Welsh DI sitting across the desk.

'He was suspected of being the driver in a smash-and-grab on a jeweller's in Aston, but the main witness conveniently vanished before trial. Then there was a big black-market meat investigation that he was certainly involved in, but again it all fizzled out for lack of evidence. That one was almost certainly a Mickey Doyle enterprise, as it was known that it was he who had put the frighteners on some of the witnesses. Oddly enough, some of the lamb and mutton involved was known to have been rustled from Wales.'

'Anything else known about him?'

'His background was very dodgy. He was virtually kicked out of the Czech Free Forces after deliberately injuring himself, though again they couldn't prove it. He turned up in Handsworth in forty-three, but after the black-market case, he vanished from the scene altogether.'

Trevor Hartnell shifted the receiver to his other hand, as he made some notes on a pad.

'Does anybody actually remember him from those days, boss?'

His DCI told him that a couple of older uniformed officers from Handsworth recalled 'this Czech bastard', as they called him. 'A real hard case, they said. Heavy drinker and violent at the drop of a hat, often involved in punch-ups with other toerags. One of them says he used to frequent the Barley Mow pub, which is interesting, as it was one of Doyle's hang-outs.'

There was nothing more the DCI could pass on, but he promised to keep a couple of men asking around about Jaroslav Beran. When he had rung off, Trevor repeated what he'd heard to Meirion Thomas.

'Sounds as if he was a low-level crook up in your place,' was the Welshman's response. 'A getaway driver and an enforcer, presumably working for this Doyle character.'

'Odd that he suddenly disappeared from Birmingham and

turned up in Aberystwyth. His convictions for receiving were since he came down here, according to the probation people.'

Meirion leaned back in his chair and looked out at his favourite view, the cold sea now choppy in the winter wind.

'Maybe things were getting too warm for him in Birmingham – or perhaps this Doyle wanted him as a sort of lookout man down here. A lot of the country house thefts were in Mid-Wales and along the Marches.'

'You never got a whiff of him in your sheep stealing cases, did you?' asked Trevor. 'It seems he was involved in the black-market meat racket up in B'rum.'

The stocky DI shook his head. 'I never knew he existed until this week. He's kept his head down pretty well.'

One of the youngest detective constables came in with two cups of tea and a plate of McVitie's digestive biscuits.

'I like a proper cup and saucer,' declared Meirion, lifting a yellow cup with Royal Welsh Show 1927 emblazoned on it. 'Can't be doing with this new fad for thick mugs . . . like drinking with a lot of navvies on a building site.'

Trevor grinned to himself at this unsuspected fad from a policeman who looked as if he could wrestle an ox, but then brought his mind back to the current problem.

'So what do we do next? Knowing this chap Beran used to be a gangster doesn't take us any further forward in our murder without more evidence.'

It was Thursday afternoon before some help in that direction arrived. Hartnell and his fellow DI were treated to lunch by David John Jones, going down the promenade to a small hotel which had one of the few restaurants open in the depths of winter. After a couple of pints of Felinfoel bitter, they sat down to a leek soup, which the other two said was *cawl*. It was followed by a good steak and three veg. A rich bread-and-butter pudding made Trevor suspect that the rigours of a decade of rationing may not have been so severe in Cardiganshire as in Birmingham and by the time he had walked back to the police headquarters and climbed all those stairs, he was glad to be able to drop into a chair in the office he had borrowed.

However, his rest was short-lived, as within minutes, Meirion Thomas appeared at the door.

'Just had the forensic people on the line from Cardiff,' he announced. 'They've found human blood in the samples they took from the van! No doubt about it, they said, it certainly wasn't just animal. Not only that, but it's Group B, Rhesus negative, whatever that means. Doctor Rees says that B negative is relatively unusual. Only about eight per cent of the population are B, but only two per cent are B-negative.'

'Are you going to tell me what I hope you're going to tell me?' asked Hartnell, rising from his chair.

'Yes, Philip Rees confirmed that the corpse in the bog was also B-negative! Doesn't prove it was his blood in the van, but it's a damn good bet that it was!'

Though after a decade or so, urgency was not really a prime consideration, the looming imminence of Christmas sent the detectives back out to Beran's cottage that same afternoon. Trevor Hartnell was especially anxious to get home next day, to avoid his wife's exasperation, though after eight years as a policeman's wife she was getting used to his inconvenient absences.

Sergeant Parry drove them in a black Wolseley 6/80, the archetypal post-war British police car, and parked it across the front of Gelli Derwen cottage. He sat in the car with a uniformed constable in the front passenger seat, while Meirion and Hartnell went to the door, where once again a dog's bark turned to a whine after they had banged on the panels. After a delay, James Brown dragged the door open and scowled at them.

'Now what you want?' he growled through the crack allowed by the length of security chain on the inside.

'We want you to come with us to the police station in Aberystwyth to answer some questions,' announced Meirion Thomas.

'Go to hell, I done nothing!' was the response. 'I told you last time, I know nothing about what you talk.'

'That was before we found blood soaked into the floor of your old van,' snapped Thomas.

There was a coarse laugh from behind the door. 'What the hell you talk about? That damn farmer had my van for years. He carry all sorts of animals in it, plenty of blood.'

'Not human blood, the same type as the man buried down in

the bog there!' Hartnell gestured over his shoulder at the huge marsh in the distance behind him.

Beran's response was unexpected. He closed the door, his visitors expecting him to unhook the chain inside, but instead there was a click as the lock engaged.

'The bugger's shut it on us!' snapped Meirion and hammered on the panel. There was a momentary silence, then a muffled whine of pain from the dog inside, but the door remained obstinately closed.

'He may be doing a runner!' shouted Trevor. 'Let's get around the back.'

As they started to trot around the cracked cement path that went around one side of the cottage, there was the sudden roar of a motorcycle engine starting up. By the time they reached the back corner of the building, they saw Beran flying past them on the other side of a straggling hedge, where a side lane ran out towards the road.

'He can't get far, the number of his bike will be on record,' shouted Meirion.

Beran didn't get far, for as soon as he heard the engine start up, Gwyn Parry had moved the Wolseley forward so that it blocked the narrow exit to the lane. He reached it just before Beran's BSA, which skidded in a desperate attempt to squeeze through the closing gap and fell on its side. The sergeant and constable were on him before he could get his leg from under the bike and in seconds, the PC's handcuffs were snapped around his wrists.

The two detective inspectors hurried up, just as Gwyn hauled the would-be fugitive to his feet.

'Put him in the car, sergeant, we'll take him back to Aber.'

Meirion turned to the constable. 'You'd better stay here and keep an eye on the place until we get back. And look after that poor dog, will you?'

Jaroslav Beran – neither of the detectives could think of him as James Brown now – stood glowering at them, but was keeping his mouth firmly closed. Dressed in a grubby pair of canvas trousers and a thick navy-blue jumper, he offered no resistance as he was pushed into the back of the police car. Meirion sat alongside him and Trevor went into the front alongside Gwyn Parry as they drove back to Aberystwyth.

'Where were you thinking of going on that bike?' asked Meirion, conversationally. 'Back to Birmingham, was it?'

Beran remained mute, as he did when he was taken to a dismal interview room on the ground floor of the police station on the Esplanade. However, after being given a cup of tea and a cigarette, he unbent enough to complain that he had done nothing wrong and that they had kidnapped him unlawfully.

'I reckon your parole has gone down the tubes now,' advised Trevor Hartnell. 'Obstructing the police in the course of their duties is enough for that. And now we want an explanation of how you happened to have had a van which has traces of human blood in the back.'

Vehemently, Beran argued that he knew nothing about it. 'The bloody van had many owners before me, you find the log book and see their names,' he snarled. 'Then I sold it to a farmer, they all carried black-market meat for years.'

Meirion for once felt the urge to be facetious.

'I know this is Cardiganshire, but even so, there's not many cannibals around these parts. This was human blood, of a rare group which was the same as that body found less than half a mile from your cottage.'

Hartnell took up the questioning. 'Funny you should mention black-market meat. We know you were mixed up with Mickey Doyle in Birmingham years ago. He ran rustling and illegal meat rackets, didn't he? Is this all to do with that?'

For the first time, Jaroslav failed to deny anything. He sat staring down at the table, his cigarette burning down unheeded between his fingers.

'Listen, we want some answers,' continued the Birmingham DI. 'Firstly, who was this man in the bog? Secondly, how did he die – and finally, did you kill him?'

The last question jerked Beran into sudden animation.

'No, I not bloody kill him! Don't try to hang that on me!' he flared.

'Hang it on you might be quite near the mark, Jaroslav!' said Meirion heavily. 'You can still hang in this country, you know. Both for murder or even being an accessory to killing.'

Trevor Hartnell nodded his agreement. 'But you might be able to do yourself some good if you're helpful to us by telling us everything you know.'

For a moment, they thought the Czech might be about to 'cough'. But then the obstinate expression came back across his heavy features. Having learned about criminal proceedings from hard experience, he uttered the words he knew were his best defence.

'I want lawyer – now!' he muttered.

TWENTY

It was now Friday, the day before Christmas Eve, and as everyone at Garth House was planning to be away over the coming holiday, there seemed little point in hanging up festive decorations in an empty house. Moira was going to Newport to spend three days with her sister and Angela was off to Berkshire for the whole week. Sian was going home to her large family in Chepstow and Richard was off to his parents in Merthyr Tydfil, though as he had agreed to be on call for the police until Boxing Day, he was leaving his contact number with the forensic science laboratory in Cardiff. Though there were no chains of coloured paper festooning the rooms, Moira had put up several sprays of red-berried holly from a tree in her garden – and Sian had hopefully hung a sprig of mistletoe from a light in the staff room.

The following week was a barren one for getting much work done. Though more people died over this period, from road accidents, suicides and increased natural disease precipitated by cold weather, overeating and overdrinking, the legal machinery ground to a halt for quite a few days, as solicitors' offices were closed, coroners held no inquests and the other courts were suspended. However, the police and forensic pathologists had to carry on as usual – and in fact, the homicide rate increased slightly, mainly due to more alcohol-induced disputes. Richard had arranged with the several coroners' officers with whom he dealt to begin post-mortems again on Wednesday, as a Sunday

Christmas meant that an additional day's holiday was due after Boxing Day.

After lunch on Friday, they held a modest office party in the staff room, where they exchanged Christmas presents and spent an hour in pleasant relaxation. Richard contributed a bottle of Harveys sherry and one of Mateus Rose, while Angela brought Gordon's gin, her favoured tipple, and a bottle of cherry brandy.

Moira had made mince pies and an iced cake with Santa and reindeer decorations. Jimmy came in long enough to drink two pint bottles of Rhymney Bitter, then vanished on one of his mysterious expeditions with friends 'up the valley', which Richard suspected involved shotguns and dogs.

They ate and drank in a convivial mood, looking back contentedly at the first seven months of their forensic venture and looking forward to even more success in the coming year. No one was driving that day, so the level in bottles dropped without challenge and as it did, so the level of chatter and gossip rose. Their more memorable cases were revisited and the star event was, of course, the Body in the Bog.

'Haven't heard a word from the cops about it lately,' said Richard, relaxing deeply into the sagging armchair that had once belonged to Aunt Gladys. It sounds as if the trail has gone cold – hardly surprising after more than ten years.'

He was about to add that even Scotland Yard had given up and gone home, but looking across at Angela, he decided to close his mouth, as he knew she did not want to be reminded of Paul Vickers.

'What happens when an investigation stalls like this?' asked Moira. 'Does the coroner just put the file on the top shelf and forget about it?'

Richard warmed to her abiding interest in legal matters.

'No, eventually he will have to hold an inquest, but inevitably there would be an "open verdict", which allows the body to be buried, but leaves the option for a later criminal trial or a reopened inquest, if further evidence ever comes to light.'

Moira, a couple of glasses of wine making her less reserved than usual, broached a subject that she had been nurturing for some time.

'My eyes have been opened since I've been with you all,' she said, rather emotionally. 'You all are experts in various things and I've just been stagnating, especially since I lost my husband. It's time I did something myself. Doctor Pryor, if I tried to start training as a lawyer next year, would you help me, please? You know so many solicitors, barristers and all about college applications and so on.'

Though it was hardly a Christmas party topic, Richard was immensely pleased that he seemed to have stimulated someone to move on to better things.

'Of course I would, Moira. I'd be delighted to do what I can. Let's talk about it after the holiday. It can be your New Year resolution!'

Angela and Sian also added their encouragement. 'Only on condition you find us someone who can cook as well as you!' chaffed Angela. 'Seriously, it's a great idea. I'm sure you'd do well. You could be a QC cross-examining me before very long!'

Sian came across and gave Moira a hug. 'You'll knock them out, a great girl like you!' she enthused. 'Why not go the whole hog and do a degree, like me? I know you've got double matriculation from your School Certificate, so you could apply to Cardiff or London. There are grants for mature students; you could start next October.'

Richard beamed like a benevolent father with his forensic family. 'That would give us time to scour the kingdom for a secretary almost as good as you!'

Moira, throwing caution to the winds, went over to Richard and kissed him on the cheek, her eyes moist with gratitude to these good friends. After a hug for Angela and another for Sian, she pulled herself together and demanded that they all tucked into her mince pies and iced cake.

As they ate, Richard proposed a few toasts, primarily to the continued success of Garth House Consultancy and all who sailed in her. Then Angela raised her glass to Millie Wilson, who was languishing in Holloway Prison. 'Let's hope we can do her some good at the Appeal,' she said sincerely. 'I'm afraid she won't be having much of a Christmas this year.'

They all drank to Millie, then Sian reminded them of another apparently stalled case.

'I expect that the Dumas family won't be too happy this year, either,' she said. 'I'm so sorry for the poor mother, yearning to believe that this chap from Siam really is her lost baby, but not knowing if it's true.'

'I think even worse is the rift it's caused between them and the younger son,' declared Angela. 'No sign of him agreeing to blood tests, Richard?'

He shook his head. 'Like the bog body, I haven't heard anything lately. That's the trouble with our business, we experts do our bit, then we're left out of the loop until we're wanted again.'

'Don't worry, doctor! I'll keep you fully informed when I'm a lawyer,' promised Moira, with a slight giggle.

In Aberystwyth, the police had something of a problem, in that the local solicitor who they had called at Beran's demand was doubtful if they had enough grounds for detaining his new client. He had certainly evaded questioning, but that was hardly an arrestable offence. The blood in a van which he had once owned was potentially very serious, but as the lawyer was keen to point out, Beran had been one owner amongst several others and there was no question of detaining them.

The Deputy Chief Constable, who was nominally in charge of the CID, was called in by Meirion Thomas as a more senior back-up to their discussions. David Jones quickly pointed out that neither had those owners ever been fingered by an antiques dealer in Ludlow as having employed a driver with a Batman tattoo identical with one found on a corpse buried very near Beran's place of residence and whose blood group tallied with those found in his old van. To clinch the last point, Meirion made a phone call to Ludlow and next morning sent a police car post-haste to the town, which brought back Bertram Tomlinson, who positively identified Beran as the man who had sold him the stolen card table and whose delivery man was the fellow with the distinctive tattoo on his shoulder.

Meirion promptly charged Beran with receiving stolen goods, which was enough of a holding offence to satisfy the solicitor and keep him in custody for at least a few days until things were sorted out after Christmas.

He was housed in the station cells and refused police bail, given his propensity to escape on motorcycles.

'He'll have a Christmas dinner there, anyway,' said Gwyn Parry, philosophically. 'Though I don't think we can run to paper hats.'

'What about that poor bloody lurcher?' asked Meirion, a confirmed dog lover.

'No problem! That PC we took with us says he'll take it home with him. If everything pans out, I doubt Jaroslav Beran will see the outside of a prison for many years, so probably Constable Lloyd will have got himself a free dog.'

As expected, there was a hiatus in most forensic activities over the Christmas period, but by the middle of the week, things slowly started moving again.

Richard's long weekend in Merthyr had not been interrupted by police calls after all and on Wednesday morning, he was back in Chepstow mortuary dealing with four sudden deaths and a traffic fatality. At Garth House, Moira came in to make him his lunch and leave a pie for him to warm for his evening meal. He had told her not to bother with typing the reports until next day and as he had already given Sian an extra day off, he was alone in the big old house. The weather had turned cold and grey, but it was dry, with a cutting east wind. They had no central heating and he couldn't be bothered to light a fire in the staff room, even with the attraction of their new television set. Instead, he spent the time either in the kitchen, warmed by the big coke-fired Aga, or in his study where he had an electric fire.

It was here that in the afternoon he took a phone call from Aberystwyth. It was DI Thomas, who gave him an update on what had been happening both there and in Birmingham.

'I had a talk with Doctor Rees from the Cardiff forensic lab. He said there was no more they could do to refine that blood type from the floor of the van, mainly due to the long time since the sample was shed and the effects of the weather. I suppose your lady, Doctor Bray, would say the same thing?' he asked hopefully.

'She's away this week, so I can't definitely speak for her, Mr Thomas. But I suspect she'd say that if the Home Office scientists can't do any more, then no one can. Mind you, I think they were very fortunate to get even a blood group out of that stuff, after all this time in those conditions.'

'I suppose there's nothing more that can be done in the pathology line to narrow down the identity?' asked Meirion hopefully.

'Can't see what, really,' said Richard sadly. 'We had no joy with finding anyone with that marble-bone disease, even though it's very rare. Presumably it wasn't bad enough for him to complain about it, so there may be no medical record of it anywhere. That suggests that he might not have been in the Forces, as probably a medical officer would have picked it up.'

'Maybe he was foreign, like this Czech chap we've got in custody,' suggested the inspector.

'I wonder if a dentist might be able to help,' mused Richard. 'I'm not an expert on teeth, but I understand that some dental work, like fillings and bridges, can be recognized as having been done abroad.'

So far, because there was not the slightest hint as to who the bog body was or even where he might have come from, no forensic dentist had looked at the teeth to match them with a prospective individual. There were a few dentists, usually in hospital or university practice, who offered forensic expertise in addition to their usual duties, but the subject was only just beginning to become recognized as a separate speciality.

'I can probably find an expert who might take a look at the teeth in that head. I'd have to discuss it with the Birmingham coroner first, as he'd have to pay him a fee.'

Meirion said that he thought it was worth a try.

'Unless we can get this Beran fellow to spill the beans, we're stumped. Without an identity, it's virtually impossible to bring anyone to trial for his death.'

After they had finished speaking, Richard rang the Dental School in Bristol University, hoping to find someone to give him advice, but as he had half-expected, everywhere there was shut down for the rest of the week.

He looked at his calendar and confirmed that New Year's Day was the following Sunday.

'Thank God, life gets back to normal on Tuesday,' he

murmured, after realizing that the New Year holiday would be pushed on to Monday. His eye moved further along the calendar and saw that the Appeal was written in for 10th January, just a couple of weeks away. He decided to start revising all the notes and data he had prepared for his evidence, as he needed to be word-perfect to make any impression upon the three Lord Justices of Appeal.

He was deeply immersed in this for the next hour until the telephone again rang. Rather to his surprise, it was Louis Dumas, speaking from his house in the vineyard. After some rather strained small talk about the holiday season and the cold weather, Louis came to the point.

'After failing to get my son Victor to consent to meet Pierre Fouret, my wife and I have decided to go ahead with the blood tests without his agreement. Are you still willing to proceed with them, doctor?'

Richard heard the resigned sadness in his voice and suspected that, as Angela had forecast, Christmas in the Dumas household had not been very merry.

'Certainly, if that is definitely what you want. I must emphasize again, though, that the blood tests can only positively exclude Maurice being your son. They can never confirm it, even though the results may be very persuasive.'

Louis confirmed that he understood this perfectly.

'It is mainly the desire of my wife, doctor. She says she cannot rest until we have done all that is possible to resolve this matter. She says she would prefer to know that he is not our true son, rather than be forever in doubt.'

As he seemed firmly committed to the decision, Richard agreed and they went on to arrange the practical details. He explained that because of the visit to London the following week, it would have to be when they returned and they fixed on the following Tuesday.

'As you know, my partner Doctor Bray is the expert in this field. We could come down to you at St Mary Church to take the blood samples, if that would be convenient for Mr Fouret, as well as yourselves.'

Louis confirmed that his putative elder son was still in London, returning to Canada in a few weeks' time, and that he had made it clear that he would be willing to come down to provide a blood sample at any time.

Richard put the phone down after polite good wishes for the New Year, though he wondered how happy it would be if the tests excluded Pierre Fouret from being a Dumas. With a sigh, he took down the calendar from the wall above his desk and wrote in the appointment for that January day.

In Birmingham, the detectives were also stirring themselves after the Christmas paralysis. DI Hartnell had had a meeting with his Chief Inspector and the head of CID, to report his visit to Cardiganshire and the arrest of Jaroslav Beran, as they preferred to call him.

'He's just on a holding charge of receiving, based on the identification of the guy from Ludlow, but it's not going to keep him locked up for long unless we get something a bit stronger on him.'

'I've still got men looking out for any former members of the Doyle gang,' said the chief superintendent. 'But they seem to be keeping their heads well down. I suspect that they're still wary of Doyle's long arm, even though the bastard is in Spain.'

'No hope of getting anything out of Doyle himself, I suppose?' asked the DCI, pessimistically.

'Not a chance! That's why he's sitting tight on the Costa del Crime. But what about this publican who had the head in his shed? Have we taxed him with knowing anything about Jaroslav Beran?'

The two CID officers from Winson Green looked at each other. 'No, we haven't had a chance to see him since this Beran fellow surfaced,' said Hartnell. 'We'd better have a word today.'

'He's out on bail, after being charged with obstructing the coroner and all that stuff,' said the chief. 'Anything else I should know about?'

'The DI in Aberystwyth told me he spoke to the pathologist today. He suggested getting a dentist to look at the teeth of our head to see if there was anything useful there that might tell where he was from. He's going to have a word with our coroner about it.'

The head of CID sniffed. 'Sounds as if we're scraping the

barrel now, lads. What a way to end the year. I'm sorry now that anyone ever dug this bloody body up!'

It was a sentiment that the two officers from Winson Green echoed as they made their way back to their dismal part of the city.

'I'd better get around to see Fat Olly and try to put the frighteners on him again,' said Trevor Hartnell. 'I'll pick up Tom Rickman at the station and go round there now.'

An hour later, he and his sergeant were knocking on the door in Markby Road. It was snatched opened by Olly's wife who stood glaring at them, her long grey hair straggling about her face and shoulders. Trevor's impression was of a bad-tempered Old English Sheepdog, which was heightened when she opened her mouth to bark at them.

'You've got a damned cheek coming round here again, when you got my husband into such trouble!' she snarled, lacing her complaint with a few choice blasphemies. The officers ignored her tirade, as after so many years on the city streets, to them abuse was like water off a duck's back.

'We need to talk to your husband,' said Tom Rickman impassively. 'Either here or back down at the station.'

Her response was cut short by the former licensee appearing in the passage behind her, his corpulent body dressed in a grubby vest under a shapeless brown cardigan. Unshaven and bleary-eyed, he was an unsavoury sight, but he pulled her out of the way and confronted the two policemen.

'What's it this time? I'm on bail until next Thursday.'

'A few questions about the old days, Olly,' said Hartnell. 'We'd better come in, unless you want another trip downtown.'

Reluctantly, the fat man waddled back down the passage to the kitchen, where his wife vanished into the scullery after a poisonous glare at the detectives. Preferring not to sit down in the scruffy room, the two officers stood to confront Franklin.

'Did you know a chap called Jaroslav Beran when you were running either of the pubs?' demanded Hartnell. 'He was a foreigner, had been in the Czech army.'

Expecting a sullen denial, Trevor was surprised when Olly nodded his head, the wattles under his chin bobbing up and down.

'Yes, "Johnny B'rum" they called him, easier to say. Real
rough bugger, Johnny was, always in fights.'

'What did he do? Any sort of work?' asked Rickman.

Olly leered. 'Work? Not many of Doyle's boys did any work,
other than thieving or coming the heavy on anybody Mickey
didn't like.'

'So he was one of Doyle's gang,' confirmed the DI. 'What
happened to him?'

Franklin shrugged his heavy shoulders. 'Dunno, he just disappeared, years ago. Mind, that's what happened to them all, they
came and they went. Some got banged up in jail, others went
off thieving somewhere else, I suppose. Mickey didn't keep them
around long enough for them to become serious competition to
him.'

'When was this Beran fellow around, d'you remember?'

Olly stared at the ground for inspiration. He didn't mind
answering this sort of question, which seemed remote from his
own troubles with the police.

'I came here in 'forty-four, he was here then. Can't recall
when he went, must have been a year or two later.' He suddenly
looked up at his interrogators. 'You're not thinking he was the
bloke with the head, are you? Couldn't be, nothing like him! I
know the head was a mess, but it wasn't Jimmy.'

Hartnell waved a hand at him. 'No, this chap is alive and well.
But did he have any special crony in those days, a chap quite a
bit smaller than him?'

Olly shook his head slowly. 'Not that I recall. There were up
to a dozen of Doyle's mob who used to come to the pub. I didn't
know the names of most of them – safer not to be too nosey, in
fact.'

'Any other foreigners?' ventured Rickman. 'We know about
the Czech, was he the only one? What about Americans, for
instance?'

Franklin scratched his bristly head. 'Half of them were Irish,
but there was a Pole as well – and they used to talk about a
bloke they called "The Yank", but I can't recall seeing him. I
think he was one of Doyle's collectors on the protection rackets.'

This interested the two detectives, but in spite of further
probing, it was clear that Olly's memory was not going to come

up with any more details. When they left him in peace to enjoy his bail and to wonder what was in store for him when he was hauled before the magistrates the following week, Hartnell and his sergeant went back to Winson Green station and sought out the chief inspector.

'All we could get from Franklin was the fact that one fellow he remembers from the Doyle days was known as "Yank",' reported Trevor.

'But he says he can't recall what he looked like and wasn't sure he ever saw him, sir,' added Rickman. 'He thought he might have been involved more as an enforcer, rather than an armed robbery man.'

The DCI mulled this over. 'It might fit with what we heard about the head being shown as a warning to anyone tempted to rip off Mickey Doyle, I suppose.'

'And a Yank is more likely to know about Batman,' said Hartnell. 'So what d'you want to do about it?'

What the CID top brass did was to send both of them back down to Aberystwyth very early next day.

The three-hour drive got them there before mid-morning and Meirion Thomas, who Trevor had warned of his coming, gave them a substantial canteen breakfast while Trevor told him of the rather vague information they had dragged out of Olly Franklin. The local DI had been tempted to order Welsh laver-bread to go with the eggs, sausage, bacon and beans, but decided that boiled seaweed might hamper the cordial relations between the two police forces.

'Any memories of a dodgy American around here in those days?' he enquired as he attacked the food.

'That's the problem,' said Meirion. 'It was so long ago, I wasn't even here then. And during and immediately after the war, the country was awash with Yanks.'

Hartnell sighed. 'We'll just have to play it by ear, then. Perhaps if he thinks that we know more than we really do, he'll throw in the towel.'

The Welsh inspector doubted it. 'Not if he thinks he's being put in the frame for the murder. The prospect of a long drop at the end of short rope is a powerful incentive to keeping his mouth shut!'

*   *   *

James Brown, the former Jaroslav Beran, was not pleased to
see them again, when they sat across the table from him in
the dismal interview room. With his rather inert solicitor
alongside him, he ranted in his fractured English about
illegal imprisonment, threatening to sue everyone from the
Queen downwards. Tom Rickman sat slightly behind the two
detective inspectors and stared intently at the prisoner. As soon
as there was a break in Beran's tirade, the sergeant pointed a
large forefinger towards the man.

'I remember your face; they called you "Jimmy" around
the boozers!' he boomed. 'When I was a beat constable in
Handsworth, I helped nick you one night for drunk and disorderly.
You were one of Mickey Doyle's gang of thugs.'

Brown-Beran scowled, but made no reply, as the sergeant
turned to Hartnell.

'It's him right enough, boss. A real nasty bit of work,
he was.'

The solicitor opened his mouth to protest, then decided to
close it again. Now Trevor Hartnell began the proceedings, referring to some brief notes before him.

'Brown – or whatever you want to call yourself – you're in
deep trouble! Known to have been a criminal associate of
Mickey Doyle in Birmingham, you're found living within sight
of a possible murder scene. In a van that belonged to you,
we've found human blood, of a rare group that matches the
dead body – and its head was found in the same part of
Birmingham as that which witnesses say it was displayed by
Doyle.'

He paused to let this sink in. 'Now we have reason to suspect
that the murdered man was another one of the same mob that
you ran with, known as "Yank", who seems to have vanished
from Birmingham at about the time you came here.'

The DI was massaging the truth a little, but nothing he had
said was actually false, and the lawyer found no objection to
offer.

'You attempted to escape from police questioning, which
doesn't fit well with your protests of innocence, so before you
dig yourself deeper into the shit, I suggest that you tell us what
you know.'

Beran chewed hard on his lower lip, staring down again at his big hands clasped before him on the table.

'I want speak with this lawyer,' he said abruptly.

Trevor Hartnell agreed, hopeful that this heralded a change of attitude. The police went into the corridor for a smoke, leaving him alone with the rather ineffectual young man who was supposed to be advising him on his legal rights.

'Think he's going to cough, boss?' asked Tom Rickman.

'He's obviously thinking of it, or he wouldn't be trying to find out from his brief which is the best way to jump.'

Meirion was scornful. 'He won't get much help from that chap – he's hardly the smartest egg in the nest!'

The consultation was certainly short, as a few moments later, the constable who was standing inside the door of the interview room poked his head out to call them back inside.

The podgy, bespectacled solicitor addressed them as they sat down again.

'Mr Brown is willing to make certain facts known, on the understanding that he denies any part in the death of the man found in Borth Bog.'

The Aberystwyth DI answered him, being the person technically the custodian of Jaroslav Beran.

'We'll hear what he has to say, but he can't qualify it in any way. Anything he tells us will go on the record, whether to his favour or otherwise.'

This was another way of saying there were no deals on offer, and he turned to the Czech.

'Right, just tell us what you know about this business. The sergeant here will be writing down all you say.'

Tom Rickman put his notebook and pen on the table before him and the solicitor had a yellow legal pad at the ready as Beran grudgingly began his story.

'OK, I did some jobs for Doyle when I lived in Birmingham. I knew some other guys there; one was the Yank, as we called him.'

'What was his name?' interrupted Hartnell. 'Was he really an American? '

'We knew him as Josh Andersen, though God knows if it was his real name. Said he was from New Jersey.'

'A deserter from the US forces?'

Beran shook his head.

'He was a sailor who jumped ship in Liverpool in 'forty-two. Said he wasn't going risk being killed on another convoy trip. So he just melted into wartime England.'

'And like you, he turned to crime, working for Doyle?'

Beran stared sourly at Hartnell.

'Not much crime, no heavy stuff. For two years, he was collector for Doyle, going round for protection money, tart's takings and the cash from his gaming clubs.'

'So where did you fit into all this?' demanded Meirion.

Jaroslav hesitated; this was where he was entering dangerous territory.

'Just before end of war, Doyle was easing off on the violent stuff like armed robbery and raiding shops. He went more for the black-market rackets and stealing from big houses out in countryside. He sent me down here to run a front business, with furnitures and stuff, so as to have an extra outlet for what was stolen.'

'Like your shop here in Aberystwyth?' suggested Hartnell.

'Yeah, before that, I was moving around, like in fairs and markets, to be harder to spot by you bloody police.'

His accent became more marked as he became agitated, and he broke off to fumble in his pocket for a packet of cigarettes and a lighter. When he had drawn down his first lungful of smoke, he continued at a rush.

'After a while, must have been late 'forty-four, Josh appeared here and I had to take him as assistant. I don' know why, but Doyle wanted him out of Birmingham. I think police were making it too hot for him over something to do with protection money, maybe some punter complained too hard. Anyway, he stayed with me for couple months, then one day vanished back to the big city.'

He glowered at Trevor Hartnell. 'You must know about his troubles, if you bobbies were breathing down his neck.'

The DI only wished he did and made a mental note to urgently get the records searched for the activities of a Josh Andersen eleven years earlier.

'What happened next?' growled Meirion Thomas, only half-willing to believe what Beran was telling them.

The Czech picked a shred of tobacco from his tongue as he considered his answer. He was getting perilously near the point of no return.

'I rented cottage and a barn ten miles away, where stolen stuffs were stashed. Doyle paid the rent and one of his guys came down now and then to bring me new heists and pick up the money I made by sales. I also arranged for them to buy black-market food from farms, and spot places to steal animals, maybe fifty miles around. I used the van for all that.'

'You were Doyle's agent, then?' summarized Hartnell. 'But we haven't heard a word about any dead body yet, so get to the point!'

This made Beran angry. 'Look, you want me to talk, so I talk! And I already done two stretches for dealing in stolen goods, so you got no reason to bring that up again! Anything else like black market is years ago, and you got no evidence, mister!'

The detectives were unimpressed by his outburst, though the lawyer moved himself sufficiently to hold up a warning hand to his client.

Trevor Hartnell continued. 'What about this Josh Andersen? How did he come to be dead, eh?'

Jaroslav seemed to deflate and he sank back on to his chair, then crushed out his half-smoked cigarette on the edge of the scarred table.

'I said he had gone back, but a month later, two guys from Handsworth came late one night to my house. They had old Mercedes, which they said they'd nicked from a car park in Dudley. In boot was a body, trussed up like chicken, but with no head. They didn't say anything much, except Mickey Doyle ordered me to get rid of it real good. They just dumped it in my back garden, and said that if it ever turned up again, Doyle would have me killed. Then they drove off and left me with the bloody thing.'

In spite of his earlier scepticism, Meirion Thomas felt that there was a ring of truth in the Czech's voice.

'So what did you do then?'

Beran looked sideways at the solicitor, who turned his palms up in despair, then plunged on with his confession.

'What could I do? The guys went away and left me. I heard

later they torched the Merc miles away, there must have been a pick-up car there for them.'

'Are you telling us you buried the body on your own?' grated Meirion.

'Sure I did, I had no choice! I dragged it further into the yard, covered it with sacks and kept the dog away. Next day, I went walking on the bog and worked out a route to a place that seemed OK. I did not want risk taking it far, in case I was stopped.'

'So you used the van, did you?' snapped Hartnell.

'Sure I did! It was too far to carry it all the way. Next night was dark, no moon. I lifted it into back of van, drove half mile on road, then dragged it down through field to bog. Spent bloody two hours digging hole with shovel, dropped it in, filled up and went home.'

His hands were shaking now, as he played with his cheap lighter, made from a brass bullet casing.

'And you expect us to believe that?' barked Meirion.

Beran shrugged indifferently. 'Take it or leave it. I got nothing else to tell you.'

'You killed him, didn't you?' snapped Hartnell. 'I'll buy the part about you burying the body, but all that about the two men and the Mercedes is a fairy story.'

Jaroslav shook his head, like a bull confronting matadors.

'Why I do that? I hardly knew the Yank, he was just a pair of hands sent down to me to get him out of the heat in Birmingham, so they said.'

'When did you stop working for Doyle?' asked Trevor.

'When I got nicked over some of his stuff from house robberies. Long time after this dead body shit, he didn't want anyone once they'd been fingered by you police.'

The interview ground on, going back over the story for dates and places, though Beran was conveniently vague about details. Eventually the solicitor, who had been silent most of the time, declared that his client had had enough for one session and they broke up the interview.

Upstairs in the DI's office, the three detectives were joined by Gwyn Parry and they reviewed what they had so far.

'He seems determined not to tell us who actually strangled this Josh fellow and cut off his head,' said Hartnell. 'But his admissions are enough to charge him as an accessory to murder, as well as all the stuff about obstructing the coroner and illegal disposal of a body.'

'Do we believe in these two mystery men from Birmingham?' asked Meirion.

His sergeant pointed out that the head had been found a hundred miles away, so perhaps Beran's claim to have been in Cardiganshire when the killing took place, possibly had some validity. 'And we should be able to trace police and fire service records if a Merc was burned out between here and the Midlands around that time.'

They kicked the evidence around for a time, until Meirion decided he had better go and tell David John Jones what had taken place.

'It's up to the brass to decide what happens next – especially who runs this prosecution, us or your lot, Trevor?'

Hartnell pondered this for a moment. 'I'll be ringing my boss in a minute, but I think it has to be a Birmingham case from here on. You've got an unlawful burial, but it looks as if the murder was in our patch.'

The local DI nodded his agreement. 'I'm sure you're right, and it's not our problem. But who the hell strangled him? Beran seems to have been down here, so either the two hoods who brought the corpse killed him – or even Mickey Doyle himself.'

'And until Spain signs an extradition treaty, we've not got a snowball's chance in hell of finding out,' said Trevor Hartnell with an air of finality.

TWENTY-ONE

After the first few days of January had come and gone, it felt in Garth House as if the festive season had never been. A faint air of anticlimax hovered over the staff as they settled down to pick up their routines.

Sian's microscope sections of the heart in the 'road rage'

dispute had allowed Richard to confirm his previous supposi-
tions. The thrombus in the coronary artery was seen to be at
least several days' old, certainly well before the incident
with the truck. This fitted with the suggestive results of the
TTC experiment that there was infarction of the heart muscle,
tissue damage which had to be well in excess of the one-hour
interval between the altercation on the road and the time of
death. Having explained all this to the Hereford coroner, that
worthy was able to placate the relatives sufficiently for them
to abandon their intention to bring a legal action against the
other driver.

Angela and Richard had two other matters coming up for their
attention. In a few days, they would be going to the Royal Courts
of Justice for the Millie Wilson Appeal – and soon after that,
they were to investigate the intriguing case of the vintner's
Prodigal Son.

On the tenth of the month, they found themselves at Newport
railway station, waiting for the Red Dragon express to Paddington.
Jimmy had driven them down in the Humber, as they would be
staying in London for at least one night, depending on how the
case went.

When the train thundered in behind the famous Caerphilly
Castle engine, they found their seats in a First Class carriage,
booked by the ever-efficient Moira.

There were four other people in the compartment, so they
were unable to talk shop. Richard was in one of his restless,
expansive moods that Angela was coming to recognize. She
thought he was like a big schoolboy, excited at a journey by train
to 'the big city'.

'This is getting to become a habit, buzzing off together to
London for the night,' he whispered. A few months earlier, they
had gone up to deal with an exhumation for the War Office at
the military hospital on Millbank.

'We're becoming creatures of habit,' she responded. 'Just like
last time, I'm going to haunt Bond Street this afternoon, while
you go to hit the library again at the Royal Society of Medicine!'

He grinned at her. 'But we can't go to see *The Mousetrap* this
evening, because we did that last time.'

'No, but you can treat me to a meal at a decent restaurant,' she countered. 'Then we'd better go back to the hotel and swot up our reports ready for tomorrow.'

Richard groaned. 'I've been through them so often, I could recite them by heart! But you're right, we have to do our best for poor Millie. We only get one shot at this.'

A few minutes later, the train plunged into the Severn Tunnel, the longest in Britain, and he felt Angela shudder.

'I hate tunnels,' she murmured. 'I always feel as if I'm being buried alive.'

He felt a sudden urge to hold her hand until they emerged into daylight again, but the presence of other passengers inhibited him. Before they reached Swindon, he suggested coffee in the dining car, partly to be able to talk without being overheard. As they sat facing each other across a table, they discussed recent cases and the personalities in their little world of the Wye Valley.

'Moira seems dead set on this law thing,' observed Angela. 'I don't know how we'll manage without her, but I'm glad she's found something to aim for. She's too young to just moulder away as a lonely widow.'

'I'm making enquiries at the universities in Cardiff and Bristol, to see what's on offer for someone like her,' he replied. 'She got good results years ago with her School Certificate and says she has her double-matric, so there shouldn't be any problem in qualifying for admission. Getting some financial help would be the thing – there must be bursaries and scholarships for mature students.'

Angela smiled. 'We're like a couple of earnest parents, trying to do the best for our children!' she exclaimed. 'You'll be getting Sian to do a doctorate soon!'

'Not just yet, though she's damned good at chemistry. In fact, I'm hoping to get us some work from that private clinic in Newport. They often want blood sugars, ureas, glucose tolerance tests and other clinical stuff. Sian could do those standing on her head, if we get the kit for her.'

Again she smiled at his enthusiasm. 'Who's left for you to help up the ladder, Richard? Perhaps you could send Jimmy on an Advanced Driving Course – or perhaps over to Burgundy to learn viniculture!'

'More likely he'd want to go to Evesham to learn how to grow bigger strawberries!' said her partner ruefully. 'Talking of viniculture, are we all set to go down to Chateau Dumas next week?'

Angela set down her GWR coffee cup and nodded. 'All I need to take are some syringes, needles and oxalate tubes. A sample each from father, mother and the alleged son.'

'Just as well you don't need one from Victor Dumas. He'd probably chuck your syringe over the nearest hedge!'

'It's such a shame that this has caused such a rift in the family,' she said sadly. 'Madame told me that the presumed son from Canada is adamant that he doesn't want any part of the inheritance. He says he has a good job and his foster parents in Montreal have told him that he will be their heir.'

Richard sighed at what seemed an intractable problem.

'Obviously Victor doesn't believe that. It has to be said that some confidence tricksters are very clever at covering all the angles.'

Angela poured more coffee for them from the pot on the tray, as their conversation drifted to other things.

'Priscilla looked very happy with her new job,' she observed. 'I'll bet she has half the red-blooded men in the university chasing her by now.'

'Only half? Everyone from the Vice-Chancellor down will be setting their caps at her.'

Priscilla Chambers had called in at Garth House the previous week, on her way back to Aberystwyth from spending Christmas with her parents in Oxford. Breezing in from her MG roadster, she was her usual lively, flirtatious self as she hugged and kissed everyone and handed out belated Christmas presents. She reported that she was getting on famously with Eva Boross and that they had already started on the excavation of the ancient monastery up in the hills.

'I'm glad she's happy there,' said Richard. 'I must have a drive up to Aberystwyth one day and see how she's getting on,' he added mischievously.

Angela eyed him suspiciously. 'Down boy!' she said sternly. 'Priscilla would eat you alive. Talking of Aberystwyth, have you heard if there's been any progress on the bog investigation?'

He shook his head. 'Not since before Christmas. I must give DI Thomas a ring when we get back. That's the trouble with being a pathologist, you do your bit at the post-mortem, then everything goes quiet until the trial. And if they don't charge anyone, then often that's the last you ever hear of it.'

Angela agreed. 'Same with many of our science cases. I used to learn more from the *Daily Telegraph* than I did from the police.'

'Not like it is in detective novels and films! If you believed those, you'd think that it was the doctors who solved all the cases, not the coppers who do all the leg work.'

The train slowed for Swindon and they went back to the compartment to reclaim their seats. Angela turned to her *Vogue* magazine, anticipating seeing the real thing that afternoon in the famous shops of the West End. Richard knew how keen she was on fashion and wondered again how she managed to dress so elegantly on her salary, especially since she had left the security of the public service for the more uncertain rewards of private enterprise. He strongly suspected that her well-heeled family subsidized the contents of the expensive-looking carrier bags that she carried when she returned from her shopping expeditions.

When the train steamed into Paddington station, Richard carried their overnight cases into the Great Western Hotel through the entrance at the top of the platform and booked them in at the desk.

'Here were are again, ready for another night of unbridled passion!' he said facetiously as they went up in the lift.

His partner regarded him coolly, used to his flights of fancy. 'Sure, Richard! You can have your unbridled passion in Room 321 and I'll have mine in Room 334.'

Next morning, they caught the Circle Line from Paddington to the Temple and walked up Arundel Street to the Strand. The huge Victorian-Gothic extravaganza of the Royal Courts of Justice loomed in front of them and they plunged under the great entrance arch into the cold magnificence of the main hall, more like a cathedral than a court of law. It was Richard's first visit, as he had never worked in London, but Angela had been there

several times during her years at the Met Lab, though her usual
stamping ground had been in the criminal courts of the Old
Bailey.

She led him to the row of varnished notice boards in the centre,
where the Order Papers for the day were pinned up.

'Better see which court we're in,' she advised. 'There are over
a thousand rooms in this place!'

A search of the Order Papers told them that the Court of
Criminal Appeal was hearing the case of Millicent Agnes Wilson
in Court Six and after following the signs, they climbed a twisting
stone stairway to a gallery that ran around the great hall at first-
floor level.

Though the ground floor was milling with people, up here it
was quiet, almost sepulchral. Everything seemed to be either
gloomy grey stone or dark oak. The entrances to the courts were
panelled doors leading into small vestibules, with an inner door
opening into the court proper.

'Here's Number Six, but no one seems to be about,' said
Richard. 'It's ten to ten, so we're in plenty of time.'

'Let's have a look inside,' suggested Angela, looking very
smart and businesslike in a slim charcoal-grey suit over a white
blouse. They went into the cramped vestibule and looked through
a window in the inner door. The three Appeal judges were not
yet on their high bench, but a group of bewigged barristers, dark-
suited solicitors and black-gowned ushers were standing around
the front of the court.

'There's Douglas Bailey and Penelope Forbes,' observed
Richard, pointing at the Bristol solicitor and the junior counsel.
They moved into the back of the court and very soon Bailey saw
them and came hurrying across to greet them.

'Good to see you both. We're going to be running a little late,
I'm afraid, a lot of legal wrangling to be endured.' He looked
worried and slightly abstracted as he spoke.

'Are there problems?' asked Richard.

'Some procedural issues about admissibility of evidence. I
hope we can get it sorted out, but I suggest you pop down to the
refreshment room for half an hour, to save waiting too long in
this mausoleum.'

Angela knew the way and they went back down the stairs and

out through a passage at the back of the main hall, following signs to a rather spartan cafe in the bowels of the building. Richard brought a couple of cups of indifferent coffee from the counter and they sat at a Formica-covered table to spend thirty minutes in these uninspiring surroundings at the heart of the British judicial system.

'Bailey didn't seem all that optimistic, did he?' said Angela, pushing aside her half-empty cup with a moue of distaste. 'I wonder what the problem can be?'

Richard was uncharacteristically cynical. 'Probably the lawyers spinning it out to increase their fees. They get paid piecework, so the longer it lasts, the more "refreshers" they get.'

When the half hour was up, they made their way back up to the court, to find an usher waiting for them.

'Mr Bailey asks if you would mind waiting outside here, please. Their lordships are sitting now, hearing legal arguments.'

He directed them to a bench outside the court, on the cloistered corridor that looked down at the floor of the great hall below. Like all the woodwork, the seat looked as if it had been there since the place was built eighty years earlier.

They waited patiently for an hour, Richard eventually getting restive, as the hard oak was becoming unkind to his backside. Both of them were free from any stage fright at appearing before Lords of Appeal, as they had been too long in the business of giving expert evidence to be at all nervous, but the delay was proving irksome.

'What the hell's going on?' said Richard, as he stood to walk up and down the corridor, partly to bring back the circulation into his thighs. On the second circuit, his question was answered, as Douglas Bailey and Penelope Forbes came out of the court-room to speak to them. Both looked despondent, though the woman looked angry as well.

'Big problem, I'm afraid,' growled Bailey. 'It looks as if we've brought you up to London for nothing!'

Richard stared at him in surprise. 'You mean you're not going to call us? Has there been an adjournment?'

Miss Forbes shook her head. 'More than that, I'm sorry to say. Their Lordships, in their wisdom, have decided that they will not hear your evidence. Not today, not ever, unless we manage to get another Appeal sometime in the future!'

Angela was indignant, in her usual dignified way.

'But that's outrageous! This Appeal was Millie's only hope. Why on earth have they refused to listen to us?'

Before the barrister could reply, the court door swung open and a very angry Paul Marchmont strode out. He was red in the face and his hair was dishevelled as he tore off his wig. Advancing on them, he began apologizing profusely.

'I'm so sorry, doctors! Both for you and poor Millicent Wilson! Those silly old fools in there should be retired, before they do any more legal damage!'

Though Marchmont was known as a bit of a rebel, this was strong language even for him.

'So what's happened?' asked Richard, perturbed that all his hard work seemed to have been in vain.

'The three wise monkeys in there declared that this was an Appeal, not a retrial. Their argument, from which I could not budge them, was that your opinions could have been given at the original trial and is therefore not new evidence.'

'But we were not involved at the trial,' protested Angela. 'We'd never even heard of Millie Wilson then.'

The QC threw up his hands in disgust. 'I know, but this has happened before. The judges take such a narrow view of things and stick like glue to the rules. I tried to preach the "natural justice" sermon to them, but they were not impressed. Obviously, they had made up their minds not to hear you before we'd even started.'

'I still don't understand why our evidence was not good enough for them,' persisted Angela stubbornly.

Marchmont waved his arms about in denial.

'My dear lady, it was first class! Their blinkered argument was that as you are not putting forward any new discoveries made since last year, the same evidence could have been offered at the trial, either by you or by some other competent forensic experts. I could not deny to their lordships that all you have so diligently put forward in your excellent reports was available knowledge last year. The judges said that the fact that it was not so offered was the fault of the defence team and that was not a factor that concerned them.'

Richard was becoming as exasperated as the senior counsel.

'So Millie will have to spend God knows how many years in prison because of some technicality seized upon by three elderly judges? Is there nothing that can be done for her?'

Marchmont mopped his brow with a flowing white handkerchief before settling his wig back on his head.

'After their lordships have lunched, I'll try to nit-pick a few points in the trial proceedings, but I know it will be futile. The success rate in criminal Appeals is abysmally low, as the judges' mafia stick together and the Lords of Appeal fall over backwards not to find any fault with the way their brothers in the lower courts conduct their business.'

With more profuse apologies and commiserations – and a reassurance that all expert witness fees and expenses would be met – the lawyers left them to make their way out of the vast building. Richard was still seething with indignation at having done all that work in vain, but Angela was more concerned with their inability to have helped Millicent Wilson.

'The poor woman will be devastated,' she said, as they walked out into the Strand. 'I don't envy Douglas Bailey for having to break the news to her.'

In the open air, away from the inimical atmosphere of the courts, Richard's mercurial temperament took an upswing.

'Come on, let's go and have a nice lunch somewhere, then get to Paddington and head back to civilization in Wales.'

Next morning at coffee in the staff room, they had to relate every detail of their abortive trip to Sian and Moira, who were equally incensed by the outcome.

'They say the law's an ass and now I quite believe them,' said their fiery technician, her socialist hackles rising. 'All those old judges, with their Eton and Oxford backgrounds, should be sacked and some younger ones appointed, who know what ordinary life is really like.'

Moira was more thoughtful about the debacle and got Richard to explain what had gone wrong. He repeated what the Queen's Counsel had said to them.

'What did he mean by "natural justice"?' she asked, her growing interest in the law evident once again.

'I'm not all that clear, but I think the general thrust is that, notwithstanding all the conventional rules of legal procedure, if a situation seems a flagrant disregard of common sense and fair play, then the rules should be circumvented . . . but you'll be able to tell me more about it in a year or two's time, when you're a legal expert yourself!'

Their forensic debate was interrupted by the phone ringing in the office and Moira went off to answer it. She came back to tell Richard that the police in Aberystwyth wanted to speak to him and when he picked up the receiver, he found it was Meirion Thomas on the other end. They spoke for about ten minutes and when Richard went back to his cold cup of coffee, he had more news to tell his colleagues.

'It sounds as if our Body in the Bog case has been wrapped up as far as it can go,' he announced.

The others clamoured for the details, all having had a stake in the unusual case. Angela had done the original serology on the tissue from the borehole, Sian had prepared histology sections of the skin and the bone disease, while Moira had typed all the reports.

'So who was he? And have they got the chap who killed him?' demanded Sian.

Richard retold the chain of events which Meirion had described to him.

'Some antique dealer recalled seeing a man with a Batman tattoo years ago. They traced his van back to Cardiganshire and found old blood stains in the back, of the same group as our corpse. The van belonged to a former Czech soldier, who was in a gang in Birmingham, then got moved to Borth to act as a fence for stolen goods and a lookout for sheep rustling.'

'Extraordinary story!' said Angela. 'You wouldn't believe it if you read it in a novel. They did pretty well to get a blood group from a van after a decade.'

'You haven't told us yet who he was!' persisted Sian.

'Some American seaman called Josh Andersen, who decided he didn't want to be torpedoed in 1942 and ran off to become a gangster in the Midlands. It seems that he started pinching money from the gang boss, who had him rubbed out, as they say in Chicago.'

He went on to relate what DI Thomas had told him, about the Czech's confession that he had been lumbered with a headless corpse for disposal.

'A pretty tall story, that!' observed Moira. 'Have they charged him with the murder?'

'Apparently not, though they're holding him as an accessory for the time being. No doubt the Director of Public Prosecutions will have to sort it out. Meirion thinks that probably either the gang leader, Mickey Doyle, or one of his henchmen actually did the deed. But Doyle legged it to Spain several years ago and they can't get him out.'

'So why cut his head off?' queried Sian with a little shudder of horror, even though she had known about it for weeks.

'Retribution for trying to fleece his boss, apparently. This Doyle villain seemed to have taken grave exception to this Josh skimming part of the profits from his protection rackets, brothels and casinos, so he had him killed and then exhibited his head on festive occasions as a warning to the rest of his gang.'

They kicked the topic around for a time, squeezing every last bit of information from Richard, who only knew what Meirion had told him.

'We must tell Priscilla about this, unless it's already all over the local papers down in Cardiganshire,' said Angela. 'She was in on it from the very beginning. In fact, she owes her new university post to this beheaded gangster, as otherwise she would never have met Doctor Boross!'

'Well, it certainly beats going down the Labour Exchange as a means of looking for a job!' giggled Sian.

It was one of those cold, fine days that occur in winter, with a thin blue sky looking down on frosted fields, as Angela and Richard drove to Cardiff on their way to the vineyard in St Mary Church. They had decided to make a day of it, as it was the first time that Angela had been to the city, declared the capital of Wales only a few months before. After an early lunch in the Angel Hotel, the place where Louis Dumas had met his alleged son, Richard walked her around the centre of the city, which he knew well from six years there as a medical student. She dutifully admired the huge castle and the superb buildings of the civic centre, although secretly she would have preferred spending the time in the three large department stores.

Then a forty-minute drive through the Vale of Glamorgan brought them to 'Chateau Dumas', as her partner insisted on calling it, where a rather apprehensive Louis and Emily received them courteously. They ushered them into the sitting room, where a tall young man rose to greet them. Black-haired and serious of face, the two doctors saw nothing of either of his presumed parents in his features – but Richard recalled that the younger son Victor also bore no particular resemblance to them. The father introduced him as Pierre Fouret and the soft-spoken Canadian replied in an accent which was more French than North American.

'I understand that we all have to undergo this ordeal of the needle!' he said, in a tone intended to lighten the rather tense atmosphere. Angela, who was rather taken by this good-looking man, went along with his ploy.

'Just a small prick in the arm, Monsieur Fouret. I guarantee that you'll survive!'

The bloodletting was performed swiftly and discreetly in Louis's study across the hall, Angela's experienced hands taking the three samples into her labelled tubes with the minimum of drama or disturbance. When she had repacked her bag and washed her hands, they went back to the sitting room for the inevitable tea and biscuits. They made rather strained small talk for a while, keeping off the subject of the Dumas family problems. Pierre told them of his life as a tractor salesman and the travelling it entailed.

'I'm off back to Quebec next week and will probably be in the States and Mexico for a few months,' he explained. 'I doubt I'll be sent back to Europe until the autumn.'

Richard wondered if this was a coded message that he would not be hanging around the family, seeking to ingratiate himself with them. The time soon came for them to leave and as they rose to go, Richard learned that Louis intended driving Pierre back to Cardiff to catch the train for London.

Richard and Angela made their way to the Humber, parked on the gravel area outside, as the Dumas clan said their goodbyes. Angela got into the front seat and as Richard was putting her case in the boot, he saw another car turning into the driveway from the road outside. It was a new yellow Triumph TR2, a two-seater sports car with the hood down, in spite of the winter weather. It drew up nearby and Victor Dumas got out, muffled in a heavy car coat and a scarf. He looked rather surprised to see Richard, but greeted him affably.

'Hello, doctor! I didn't expect to see you back here in this cold weather. I'm afraid the vines are all fast asleep for the next few months.'

Feeling rather uncomfortable, Richard saw no alternative but to say why he was there.

'Just called in to take some blood samples. We were just leaving, actually.'

Victor's face changed in an instant as he realized the implications. His smile vanished and his face reddened in anger.

'Is that bloody crook here?' he snarled. 'I'll not have him pestering my parents, they've suffered enough!'

As if on cue, the trio from the house appeared at the front door and stopped dead as soon as they saw Victor outside. As he marched angrily towards them, his father stepped forward and attempted to act as peacemaker.

'Victor, come and meet Pierre Fouret. He's just come to have a blood sample taken . . .'

He got no further, as Victor began ranting at the older man, who stood impassively under a barrage of invective and abuse, the thrust of which was that he was a scheming charlatan, out to make trouble and wheedle his way into his parents' affections.

Emily began to weep, Louis tried ineffectually to restrain his younger son and Richard wished the ground would open up under him, so that he could avoid witnessing this highly embarrassing family feud. He was glad that Angela was already in the car, hunkering down and pretending that she was unaware of what was going on.

The row escalated rapidly, as Victor closed with Pierre and tried to drag him away from his mother and father. Although the visitor had kept silent until now, he resisted Victor's physical force and told him to behave himself.

This further inflamed the aggressor, who began shouting at

him to go and continued to pull at his arm. Pierre shook him off, his self-control obviously weakening under the provocation. The climax came when Victor swung a punch at the other man, catching him on the shoulder. Pierre pushed him away, in a last attempt to distance himself, but this made things worse, as Victor followed up with a heavy blow in the stomach, which made Pierre grunt with pain. This was too much for his self-restraint and he landed a fist squarely on Victor's nose, which immediately began to bleed profusely. He staggered back and almost fell into Richard's arms, as the pathologist had decided that he had better try to dampen down the rumpus.

His first reaction was to pull out his handkerchief and offer it to Victor, who automatically clapped it to his nose, then thrust it back as he pulled out his own.

'I'm going and I'll not be back while that impostor is here,' he screamed emotionally, though it was somewhat muffled as he staunched the dribble from his bruised nose. Without another word, he almost ran to his car and sped away in a shower of gravel.

Angela was about to get out of the Humber, her better nature overcoming her reluctance to becoming embroiled in a family fracas. She thought she had better see if there was any female comfort she could offer the distressed Emily Dumas, but Richard, after a quick word with her husband, came back to the car and slipped into the driving seat.

'Louis says it would be best if we left them to cope with their embarrassment alone,' he explained and with some half-hearted waves from the group at the door, they left the unhappy house with a rather guilty sense of relief.

It took Angela almost the whole of the next day to put the samples through a wide battery of grouping tests and Sian and Moira had left by the time she went into Richard's room with a sheaf of papers in her hand. He looked up from his microscope, where he was going through some slides prepared by Sian that day.

'Have you worked your magic to a satisfactory conclusion, Doctor Bray?' he asked, being in one of his frequent whimsical moods.

Angela sat on a stool alongside him and waved the forms at him. 'I don't suppose you want all the details, as I know you have never grasped the beautiful logic of genetics.'

He grinned back at her. 'It's a blind spot in my otherwise powerful intellect! Could never fathom all these blood groups with fancy names – Rhesus, MNS, Lutheran and all the rest of them. Just give me the answer, lady!'

She dropped the papers on the desk in front of him.

'Right, if that's what you want. Firstly, Pierre Fouret or Maurice, or whatever you want to call him, is certainly not eliminated as being the biological offspring of Emily and Louis Dumas. In fact, in terms of probability, there's about an eighty-five per cent likelihood that he *is* their son, given the congruity of various subgroups.'

Richard gave a thin whistle. 'Well, well! I wonder what Victor will say when he learns that? Point out that there's still a fifteen per cent chance that Maurice is not his older brother?'

He stopped, as he saw that Angela was looking at him with an odd expression on her handsome face.

'Remember that handkerchief you gave him yesterday, when Victor had the punch on the nose? Well, I took it from the dirty-clothes basket this morning and ran a few simple ABO tests on the bloodstains.'

He stared at her, wide-eyed. 'You're not going to tell me what I think you're going to tell me, are you?'

She nodded slowly. 'I am indeed, Richard! There's no reason why Victor's mother can't be Emily Dumas – but Louis Dumas certainly isn't his father!'

Richard reached out and laid a hand on her reports as he spoke. 'Louis hinted that their marriage had a rough patch when they came back to Paris from Indo-China. Are we going to tell them?'

Angela looked at him sternly. 'No way! We were hired to determine whether Maurice was their son, not Victor.'

She slid the top report from under his fingers and carefully ripped it into a dozen pieces and then dropped them into the waste-paper basket.

'That's the best place for surprises like that, Doctor Pryor!'

*   *   *

It was another month before the next big surprise came their way, this time a much more welcome one.

Moira brought in the day's mail when they were sitting in the staff room for their elevenses and amongst the few envelopes for Richard was one with a Bristol postmark. Embossed on the back flap was the familiar name of a solicitor's firm.

'Let's hope this is a cheque for our fees and expenses,' he said hopefully. 'Though it usually takes months, even after umpteen reminders.'

He opened it and as he studied the few typed paragraphs on the single sheet of headed paper, his eyebrows seemed to climb up his forehead.

'Good God! I can hardly believe it!'

'So it's not a cheque, unless they've given us a couple of thousand,' said Angela drily.

'No, but it's from Douglas Bailey. Just a preliminary note to let us know that someone else has confessed to killing Arthur Shaw – and that it's expected that Millie Wilson will be released in the near future!'

The three women were agog with surprised excitement, as they had all been outraged by the rejection of Millie's Appeal in January. Even the usually reticent Angela demanded more details.

'How did that come about? Bailey must surely say who did it?'

'He says it was one of the other lodgers in that house, a lay-about called Roscoe Toms, who was one of those in the poker game that night.'

'Not the man who found the body next morning, was it?' asked Sian excitedly. 'In detective stories, it's usually the finder who did it!'

Richard shook his head and told them the rest of what the solicitor had written.

'At least this fellow Toms won't hang . . . because he's already dead! That's how it came to light a few days ago. He was in a drunken fight in some other back-street poker game in St Paul's and got his neck slashed in a knife fight. He bled to death at the scene, but made a dying declaration in the presence of a local doctor and a police officer, in which he confessed to killing Arthur Shaw. It happened at two o'clock in the morning during

a row over an accusation of cheating in the poker game, in which
Roscoe lost a lot of money to Shaw.'

'Will that be enough to exonerate Millie Wilson?' asked Moira.
'What's this "dying declaration" business?'

'I'm a bit hazy myself,' admitted Richard. 'It's a rare event,
but as far as I recall, a person must be dying and know that he
has no hope of survival, when it's assumed that he would have
no motive for not telling the truth. In those circumstances, any
statement he makes in the presence of more than one witness is
admissible in evidence.'

'At least that's more than ours was at the High Court!' remarked
Angela, rather bitterly.

Moira nodded sagely. 'And it gives a new twist to the meaning
of "natural justice" that we were talking about last month!'